ENDLING
THE LAST

KATHERINE APPLEGATE

illustrated by
MAX KOSTENKO

HARPER
An Imprint of HarperCollinsPublishers

for Michael

In nature nothing exists alone.
—Rachel Carson, *Silent Spring*, 1962

endling

noun ~ end•ling ~ \ˈen(d)-ling\

1. the last living individual in a species,
    or, occasionally, a subspecies.
2. the official public ceremony at which
    a species is declared extinct; a eumony.
3. (informal) someone undertaking a
    doomed or quixotic quest.

    —*Imperial Lexica Officio of Nedarra*, 3rd edition

CONTENTS

PART FIVE: THE BEGINNING ENDS

PART ONE
THE END BEGINS

1.
Endling

Long before I heard the word, I was used to being last.

I was the runt, the youngest and by-far-and-away smallest of my seven siblings, which meant I was the last to drink, the last to eat, the last to be protected.

As the lowest-ranking member of our dwindling pack, I accepted my place without resentment—much resentment, anyway.

It was, perhaps, only fair. My failings were many, or so I was often told.

I was too young to be clever, too small to be helpful.

My feet were large and clumsy. They tangled when I ran.

My coat was untidy, my manners dreadful. I once ate an entire leg of anteleer before my rightful turn.

I was curious to a fault. I wandered too far and wondered too often.

I was, in short, a disappointment at my only task in life, which was to do my best, like all dairnes, to stay quietly alive.

Those days, you'd have been as likely to pet a unicorn as you would to sight a dairne.

Our packelder, Dalyntor, white muzzled and frail, liked to speak of a time when our ancestors roamed in great bands, hundreds of dairnes at a time, across the Nedarran plains. At night they would form into family groups, gathering around to prepare wild grasses and berries, or perhaps cook the stray badger or cotchet.

But all that was long ago. Now there were just a few of us left in our part of the world, a single band of four families cowering together, meek as mouselings.

Hiding from humans, those most unpredictable of predators.

Hiding from the sun itself.

Some said there were more dairnes far away, living in mountain caves or on distant islands. Some said those sightings were the result of misguided hope. Dairnes were often mistaken for dogs. We share many physical similarities.

Dogs, however, lack opposable thumbs. They can't walk upright. They aren't able to glide from tree to tree. They can't speak to humans.

And dogs aren't—forgive me—the sharpest claws in the hunt, if you catch my meaning.

In any case, whether there were more of us or not, Dalyntor feared we would all be gone soon, slaughtered for our warm and silky fur.

Like the Carlisian seal, hunted by humans to extinction.

Or the red marlot, devastated by disease.

Or the blue-tufted ziguin, wiped out when its territory was destroyed in the Long-Ago War.

It seemed there were many ways to leave the world forever.

We didn't want to believe our days were numbered. But here is what we did know: once we'd been many, and now we were few.

My parents feared I would be the first among us to die when trouble came, and trouble, they knew, was fast approaching.

I was small. And sometimes disappointing.

But I knew I could be brave as well. I was not afraid to be the first to die.

I just did not want to be the last to live.

I did not want to be the endling.

2.
A Visit from Some Butterbats

The end began not so long ago, the day some butterbats came to visit.

It was early afternoon when I first heard them. I tiptoed past my sleeping family, nestled together like one great animal.

Dairnes are not night creatures by nature, but we no longer ventured out until the sun was long gone. We feared the giant cats called felivets, who hunted at night. But we feared poachers and the soldiers of the Murdano, Nedarra's ruler, even more.

Still, I was restless. And I was sure I'd heard something just outside the door: the air, moving beneath wings both delicate and powerful.

My sister Lirya yawned and opened one eye. "I'm so hungry I could eat you, Byx," she murmured.

"She's too scrawny to eat," said my oldest brother, Avar.

I ignored their teasing. I was used to ignoring my siblings.

It took some effort, squeezing through the door of our latest temporary home. An abandoned mirabear hive, it resembled a huge wasp nest that had fallen to earth. It was shaped like a honeycomb, with holes the size of large boulders, and glistened in the light like raw honey, though it was rock-hard to the touch. My father said the hive was made of volcanic ash, sulfur, and sand, mixed with sap from a bulla tree.

Dairnes used to fashion circle camps on the plains, or weave tree nests when we moved through forests. We didn't do that anymore.

There were many things we didn't do anymore. Or so Dalyntor, our teacher, the holder of our history, told us. He hinted at much more, but there were parts of the dairne story too harsh for our young ears.

Tree nests were too easy to spot, too vulnerable to arrows. Instead we moved from place to place, sheltering in caves or deep gullies, or within bramble patches in the heart of the forest. We left no evidence of our passing, no hint of nests or camps. We slept at the bases of cliffs, on remote beaches, in the deserted homes of other creatures. Our little band once spent the night in a large abandoned hunter's lodge.

That was the closest I had ever come to humans, one of the six great governing species. Those six—humans, dairnes, felivets, natites, terramants, and raptidons—had once been considered the most powerful in our land. But now all of them—even the humans—were controlled by the despotic Murdano.

I'd only encountered two of the other great governing species. I'd scented felivets, huge, graceful felines, gliding through blackest night. (No one ever hears them.) And I'd seen raptidons, lords of the air, carving arcs through the clouds.

Never, though, had I glimpsed a natite.

Never (thankfully) a terramant swarm.

And never a human.

Still, I knew more than a few things about humans. Dalyntor had taught us pups about them, drawing stick figures on a dried playa leaf. From him, I learned that humans have two eyes, a nose, and a mouth filled with blunt teeth. I learned they stand taller than we dairnes, but not by too much. I learned a great deal about their habits, their clothing, their villages and cities, their culture, their weapons, their languages, how they measure time and distance.

And I learned, most importantly, that humans were never to be trusted, and always to be feared.

I emerged from the mirabear hive into slanting sunlight.

The sound grew nearer, and then I saw them above the hive.

Butterbats!

There were four of them, easily three tails wide and

almost as long, with shimmery wings that wove rainbows out of the tree-filtered light. They must have thought there were still mirabears there, butterbats being great lovers of honey—and great thieves besides.

Despite the stiff breeze, they had no trouble hovering silently overhead like huge hummingbirds.

"Byx." The voice was soft, part concern, part scold. I turned to see that my mother had joined me. She looked weary, her dark gold fur mussed, her tail listless.

"Butterbats, Maia!" I whispered.

She followed my gaze. "So beautiful. They're heading north, I expect. It's migration time for them."

"I wish I could go, too."

"I know it's hard sometimes, this life." She stroked my back. "Especially for you little ones."

"I'm not little."

My mother nudged me with her nose. "Not so little anymore. True enough."

I sighed, leaning into her. She was as warm and safe as a patch of sun.

"I'm bored, Maia. I want to have fun. I want to chase my tail. I want to learn new things. I want to go on adventures and be brave."

"No need to rush toward bravery," she said softly. "No rush at all."

"The big ones call me runt. And whelp," I moaned. "They

say I ask too many questions." I was rather enjoying feeling so sorry for myself. "I hate being me."

"Byx," my mother said, "don't ever say that. There's only one you in the whole wide world. And I love that you ask so many questions. That's how we learn." She paused. "I'll tell you something. Something none of the other pups know yet."

My ears flicked to alert.

"The adults had a meeting last night. We'll be leaving here at sundown. Heading north, just like the butterbats. Myxo will be leading us. She said we've searched in the southlands long enough."

Myxo was our pathfinder. She had the keenest nose and the best instincts of anyone in our pack, and she'd traveled far and wide looking for more dairnes. Still, though we'd heard rumors of dairne sightings, nothing ever came of them. Our pack was down to twenty-nine members.

"This is a big move," my mother said. "A sort of migration of our own. We're going to search for the First Colony."

"But Dalyntor taught us they're long gone." I remembered our lessons about the First Colony, the original group of dairnes who migrated to Nedarra long ago. We'd had to memorize a poem—an extremely long poem—about them.

I love learning more than anyone in my family. But even I have to admit it may have been the most boring poem ever spoken:

Sing, poet, of the Ancients who dared forth—
Brave dairnes, o'er mountains treacherous and cruel,
Who crossed the frigid waters of the north
To Dairneholme, living isle and floating jewel.

That's all I recall. If Dalyntor hadn't let us draw maps while he recited it, I would have fallen fast asleep. Most of the other pups did.

"Maia?" I asked. "Do you really think there might still be a colony in the north?"

My mother looked across the meadow to the dark, wind-fretted forest, but didn't answer. "It's not impossible," she said at last.

Dairnes do not lie. There would be no point, since we can always detect an untruth, not just from our own kind, but from anyone.

No other species has this ability. Dalyntor often called it "our burdensome gift," although I didn't understand what he meant by that.

Nonetheless, although dairnes don't lie, we do sometimes . . . hope.

"But you don't think so?" I pressed, although I could already tell her answer.

"No, my love." It was almost a whisper. "But perhaps I'm wrong."

"I'm sure you're wrong. I'll bet we'll find hundreds of

dairnes. Thousands, even!" I stopped myself. "It's not wrong to hope, is it?"

"It's never wrong to hope, Byx," said my mother. "Unless the truth says otherwise." She gave me another nose nudge. "Now, it's back to bed for you. We have a long night's walk ahead of us."

The butterbats still circled, dipping and twirling just beyond reach. "A few more minutes, Maia," I pleaded. "They're so pretty."

"Not too long," she said, "and no exploring." She turned, then hesitated. "I love you, my pup. Don't ever forget that."

"I love you, too, Maia."

A long time passed before the butterbats moved on. Maybe they were amazed to have happened upon some dairnes. Or maybe they were simply enjoying the waves of warm air rising from the sun-touched hive.

As I turned back toward the entrance, something strange, something I couldn't quite place, caught my attention.

Not a sound, exactly, or a scent.

More like a hunch.

I took a few steps toward the small meadow separating me from a dark line of trees. Beyond it stretched the sea.

I consulted the scents on the whipping wind. The air was heavy with stories.

Was that treefox I smelled? Brindalet? It was hard to pin things down in the zigzag wind.

The forest called to me, silent but compelling, willing me to approach. Golden ribbons of light threaded through the trees. I'd never been there in daylight, only in the dead of night.

No, I told myself. We were forbidden to leave the pack, especially during the day, and most especially without permission.

And I didn't leave—not much, anyway.

I'd ventured to a stream fizzing with green bubbles. I'd sought the company of a friendly zebra squirrel and her babies. Yesterday I'd visited a cluster of star flowers, scented like sage and sea. It was a lovely spot for tail chasing.

I never took big risks. Never went far. But how could I possibly learn about the world if I never got to see it?

I knew I shouldn't go. But before we moved on, before we trekked to the next dark place, wouldn't it be wonderful to view the sea, just once, in daylight? I had only ever seen it by starlight.

My mother was back in our nest. I checked the freshening breeze: no danger.

Only a few minutes to cross the meadow, dropping onto all fours to run. Only a few minutes more to pass through that intimidating but enticing wall of trees.

Just a moment, I told myself. Just a glimpse of the sun, dancing on water.

A moment or two, and then I'd return, having never been missed.

3.
The Boat

I emerged from the towering wood onto a winding pathway. The trees kept their distance from the cliff's edge, as if they were leery of heights.

The grass was dry and warm, almost brittle. It was nothing like the feel of night grass, cool and damp with dew.

I came upon the remains of an ancient building, squat and crumbled. A watchtower, probably. Dalyntor had taught us a bit about human dwellings. Some were remarkable, he said. And some were remarkably ugly.

I clambered over great, rough-hewn stones that formed a crude stairway. At the top I stood in an ivy-laced gap that was no doubt once used by archers.

And there it was: the sea.

It was nothing like I'd imagined.

This was not a placid, rippling lake. Not a busy, musical

stream. The sea reached forever, as humbling and endless as the sky. An army of waves marched toward the shore, crashing violently in plumes of white spray. Black rocks veined with silver, the ones I'd heard called "Sharks' Teeth," pierced the water's edge like glistening swords.

The rush and rumble of the surf was deafening. I felt as if I were drowning in smells, rich and mysterious.

The breeze stiffened. My ears lay flat and my eyes stung. I looked to the sky and saw an advancing wall of iron-gray clouds. A storm was coming.

To my right a cliff curved in a great arc, nothing but jagged stone besieged by relentless waves. To my left the arc ended in a jutting finger of rock. At the very edge of that sloping peninsula stood a gnarled, leafless tree.

Only then did I spot the rowboat and its lone occupant.

It wasn't much to look at, more toy than boat, bobbing on the gray-green swells. Each surge brought it nearer to the cliffs. If it hit—when it hit—it would be smashed to kindling instantly.

I had to squint to be sure there was a creature in the boat. I wished I could smell the animal, scent being so much more precise than sight, at least for us. But when I tried to unbraid the air, all I smelled was the complicated sea.

Nonetheless, there was something down there in that rowboat. Something small and brown, pointlessly attempting to paddle.

Was that . . . ? I was almost certain: it was a wobbyk!

"What can a wobbyk possibly be doing in a rowboat?" I asked of no one.

The noise of pounding surf was huge, but I thought I might have heard a faint but desperate cry for help.

Which made sense. Because, though I couldn't quite make out the occupant of the tiny craft, one thing was clear: whether wobbyk or some other creature, whoever was in that boat was doomed.

4.
A Plea for Help

As I watched, a menacing claw of water lifted the boat high. It hurled the tiny craft and its tinier occupant toward the looming cliff.

I held my breath. I didn't want to watch. I didn't want to know. Death was seconds away.

To my shock, the same sea that had propelled the boat forward showed temporary mercy, drawing the rowboat back and away.

But it wasn't far enough. The respite would be brief. Another surge or two, three at most, and the wobbyk—I was convinced that was what he must be—would die.

Once, when I was very young, my mother made us a dinner of wobbyk. We'd been living on grass and grubs for far too long, and it was the first meat we'd had in ages. If we hadn't been so hungry, I doubt it would have tasted as good as it did, but even now the memory makes my mouth water.

Still, despite the fact that wobbyk can make an unsatisfying but healthy addition to a dull diet, I wasn't thinking about eating him. I didn't wish his death. (Truth be told, I was a feeble and softhearted hunter. In fact, I'd never actually killed anything, except a few bugs.) Instead I was amazed to find that part of my brain was already busily considering a rescue, analyzing angles, rates of descent, and the probable weight of the little creature.

Even as I was calculating, the wobbyk looked up at me, desperate, his mouth open and moving.

I heard a faint "Help!" Or maybe I only imagined the sound, but there was no imagination needed to see the fear, the frantically waving paws.

"I can't," I said, and my words flew back at me like wind-blown leaves.

I could use my glissaires, the thin extensions of our coats that we use for brief glides. Maybe, with incredibly lucky timing, I could actually manage to snatch the wobbyk.

But short of a miracle, I'd never be able to carry him.

Not far, anyway. Just a few yards. Just enough to . . .

The ocean sucked back, uncovering a narrow strip of sand in a cleft between rocks.

No, the timing would be impossible.

The wobbyk looked at me, speaking unheard words. He was begging for life.

My father had a saying: "To rush is not necessarily to

arrive." He said it to me often. He meant: think first.

And so I did.

On the one hand, I would probably die.

On the other hand, what a great story to tell around the fire. How impressed my siblings would be!

On the one foot—but I stopped myself there.

I'd been so absorbed in the wobbyk's peril that it took me a moment to register the too-sweet smell of domesticated dogs, followed by the unmistakable stench of horses.

A third smell hit me, new and unfamiliar.

Unfamiliar, but not unknowable.

Only one species traveled with horses and dogs as company.

A drumbeat of hooves vibrated the pads of my feet. I turned toward the trees and saw startled birds flap skyward.

How could I have missed such obvious scents? The damp forest, the frantic wind, the distraction of the drowning wobbyk?

I heard a warning call, the piercing howl we use that signals danger.

Strange: it hadn't come from a dairne. The pitch was wrong. Was that a human sound?

The dense trees ripped open like a clawed hide. Horses emerged behind me. And atop those horses were what could only be humans.

The men were imposing, their limbs thicker than I'd expected, their shouts more terrifying.

Could they be the Murdano's soldiers?

I flashed on the rhyme Dalyntor had taught us: "If you encounter silver and red, run away, dairne, or end up dead!"

The clothing these humans wore was motley, a mix of dun and gray. Their weapons were mismatched. Two of their horses carried, instead of humans, roped stacks of furs and hides.

Poachers.

The same voice, the one that had signaled danger, was screaming, "No! No! Don't kill it!"

The leader of the poachers, a great bow in his left hand, rode a towering black-and-white horse. Both man and beast stared at me with deadly intent.

With his right hand, the man plucked an arrow from his quiver. He fitted it to the string in less time than an eye can blink.

"No!" I cried.

My heart banged madly in my chest, all rhythm lost.

I watched in horror as the man's muscles strained and the bowstring drew back.

His eyes saw nothing but me.

I saw nothing but the glittering arrowhead. The fingers that released. The string that snapped.

And then I leapt.

5.
Rescue at Sea

Dairnes cannot fly.

We can glide, but we can't defy gravity. We can only soften it, turning plummeting falls into slow arcs.

I spread my forelegs, exposing my glissaires. With all four inches of my deadly back claws digging into crumbling stone, I kicked myself away, thrusting toward the boiling clouds.

Arrows sliced through the air like deadly rain.

I caught the wind.

The knife-sharp tip of a Shark's Tooth grazed my tail, just as the blustery wind filled and lifted me.

Panting horses pranced and reared at the cliff's rim. I saw furious human faces glaring down at me. Hard, experienced eyes planned trajectories.

An arrow shot past, faster than a diving raptidon. It flew so near that I could see the color of the feathers, the design painted on the shaft, the trident head. And the thin filament that would allow me to be hauled back.

A poacher's arrow.

I let go the wind from my glissaires, gathering speed, and risked a midair cutback.

Far below me and almost as far ahead, the wobbyk stood in his boat, waving, mouth open, eyes wide.

The boat was rising on the biggest wave yet. I banked left, aiming at this moving target.

I felt the swift passage of time and distance as the boat smashed into a pillar of black rock, shattering the wood and splintering it.

The wobbyk screamed. This time I had no trouble hearing him.

He leapt upward. Not a great leap—wobbyks are stout little creatures—but enough.

Maybe.

I was gliding faster than I had ever done before. Between us an arrow shot past. I dodged beneath the filament as the wobbyk began to fall away.

I spilled more air and surged like lightning.

The wobbyk reached desperately.

"Here!" he cried.

I snatched one paw.

The effect of his weight was like hitting a wall. Dairnes

cannot carry anything heavy in a glide.

I somersaulted through the air. I wobbled and plummeted. But momentum carried us forward as the sea retreated and there, there it was: the narrow, V-shaped patch of sand.

We plowed in a tangle through bubbling surf that grabbed at us both, tugging at our feet as though willing us to fall and be carried away into the depths.

But one foot somehow found a fragile grip on wet sand. Another foot, and to my amazement, I realized that I still had hold of the wobbyk's paw, and he had hold of me.

I staggered and we fell into the surf. I sucked salt water into my lungs and coughed.

I wondered if I was going to die.

I wondered if my parents would be mad at me if I died.

The waves were quickly returning, gathering strength to crush us against the cliff face. The first fat drops of rain fell.

"Up!" I gasped. "Climb!"

Black rock lay before us, rock that in a second would be underwater, but we were all frantic claws, scrabbling, fighting for every handhold, slipping, banging elbows and knees.

I pushed the wobbyk up and away.

The wave crashed around me. I was helpless against its power. It lifted me, holding me as I paddled futilely, all sense of direction lost.

This was it.

This was how my life would end.

Foam covered me. Water filled my mouth and forced its way down my throat.

But then I felt it.

Something grabbing the fur at the back of my neck.

It was a tiny paw, a weak grip, and yet it was enough to buy me a moment more.

In the extra second I'd been given, I found a handhold and then a foothold. I windmilled hands and feet, panicked, indifferent to bruises and cuts, and my head came up and out of the water.

Air. Yes. Air.

I climbed. Just ahead of me the wobbyk climbed.

"Look out!" he yelled, and an arrow clattered against the rock, so close it parted the fur near my ear.

Seconds more, and all at once we were over the top of the rocky spur, falling down the far side where no arrow could touch us.

The poachers couldn't reach us there, not without running their horses down the greensward and across a deep-cut channel.

A burst of lightning lit the sky. The black clouds ruptured, pelting us with icy rain.

I looked at the wobbyk. The wobbyk looked at me.

We breathed.

6.
And You Are a . . . ?

"Greetings," said the wobbyk. "You're so very kind to rescue me." Wobbyks are known for being remarkably polite.

I was not feeling polite.

I was soaked, cold, trembling. And feeling far from safe.

I shook my head. I tried to focus.

The cliff. The poachers. The arrows.

My rattled brain replayed the details of my desperate dive. I had the feeling I would relive that scene many times in dreams, the kind that wake you up at night, gasping and sweating.

The downpour drenched us while lightning carved the clouds. Thunderclaps drowned out the sea's roar.

I blinked away rain and stared at the wobbyk. He was small, perhaps a third of my size, and comical looking, especially in his waterlogged state. His silver-blue fur was bedraggled, as were his three tails. Huge white oval ears extended from his head like giant wings.

Everything else about him was round: round head; round, protruding stomach; round eyes, big and shiny as river plums. Even his paws—white, like his ears and muzzle—were round as lily pads. The lower half of his face reminded me of a fox, with its black nose, long whiskers, and upturned mouth that looked perpetually amused. He wore a leather belt low on his sizable belly. Attached to it was a small drawstring pouch.

"We have to hide," the wobbyk said. "They may still come after us."

With a sigh, I forced my body, leaden with the dulling effects of fear, upright. The wobbyk was correct. We had to keep moving.

We picked our way down the rocks onto a stretch of sandy beach.

"Walk in the surf," I suggested. "It will cover our tracks." We dairnes are experts at concealment.

"I wonder if I might . . . if I might inquire as to whether you have a plan?"

"My plan is to avoid arrows!"

The wobbyk fell silent, head drooping. I felt a bit guilty, so I added, "Let's make for the shale ahead. Hopefully, our tracks won't show quite as much there. We'll climb where the cliff has collapsed and make our way through the forest. I have to get back to my family."

"I don't see anyone following us."

"And I don't smell them," I replied, panting. "But this rain masks sounds and smells as well. We need to get out of here as quickly as we can."

"My name is Tobble," said the wobbyk. "I am most grateful to you. And I don't wish to be a burden."

"Too late," I said, only half joking.

I reminded myself that the wobbyk hadn't brought the poachers.

On the other hand, he certainly had tried to row a boat into a cliff.

"How, by all the Ancients, did you end up stuck in a rowboat?" I asked.

"I was taken prisoner by a pirate ship."

I blinked. "Did you say—"

"Pirates," the wobbyk confirmed.

"And how does a wobbyk end up with pirates?"

"The usual way."

"The usual way?" I asked. "How can there possibly be a usual way to be captured by pirates?"

"If you're fishing for sticklers and have a full coracle, well, pirates are certain to want your cargo," Tobble said. He gave a little shrug. "Even pirates like grilled stickler."

"Do they?"

"Indeed! My brothers managed to leap off the coracle, but I was tangled in the net and they left me." He didn't seem upset by this fact but, seeing my disapproving frown, added, "I'm the youngest. My brothers often overlook me."

There we had something in common.

Tobble studied me. He tilted his head so far to one side, it nearly touched his shoulder.

"Would it be impolite if I were to inquire as to what kind of animal you are? You look like a dog, but you walk upright and you can speak—"

"Dog?" I repeated. "Are you joking?"

"So what are you, then?"

"Hungry, for one thing. Cold, for another. And wet."

"I, too, am hungry. I am also a wobbyk."

"And I am a dairne. Of course." I said it with all the pride I could muster.

Tobble warbled a high-pitched laugh. Even wobbyk laughs are comical. "Yes, and I'm a four-headed wood sprite." He narrowed his eyes. "Wolf family? Perhaps. But your fur is golden, much finer than a wolf's coat. Hmm. You can glide, like a flying squirrel. You have a pouch, like a marsupial. You have hands with thumbs, but doglike paws for feet. You stand erect, and you're a female."

"Thank you for stating the obvious."

"There's almost a human-ish quality to your demeanor."
Tobble circled me as we walked. "On the other hand, I just
watched humans try to kill you." Another head tilt. "Still and
all, humans are well known for killing each other."

"I'm a dairne," I repeated firmly. "And you're a wobbyk.
And for the record, dairnes eat wobbyks."

Tobble snorted. "There are no dairnes," he said, as certainly as if he'd just stated that water is wet. Which was
certainly proving to be true.

"And yet here I stand before you, wet and cold and hungry. I'll admit there aren't as many of us as there used to be.
But I can assure you that I know what I am."

We scrambled up the fallen cliff face and plunged at last
into the shadow of the trees. The rain still fell, but the canopy
of branches overhead kept most of it from hitting us.

"I just don't understand," Tobble continued. "Dairnes
are . . . no more." His voice was low, as if he were telling me
a scary bedtime tale. "My father said so. My grandfather. My
great-grandfather. You're, if you'll excuse the word—I realize it's a bit harsh—you're extinct."

I stopped moving and stood as tall as I could manage. At
full height, I towered over the little wobbyk. "Now I'm certain I'm going to eat you."

"You saved my life. You can't eat me."

"Setting aside the fact that I don't exist and so cannot be

held to any rule, why is that?" My own whisper was too loud, and I reminded myself to be quiet.

"It's just not done. It's impolite." Tobble twisted his head around, raised one of his tails, and licked it. "So who was that trying to kill you?"

"Poachers," I said. "You're changing the subject."

"And now I shall thank you for stating the obvious." Tobble smiled. "Poachers don't bother wobbyks much."

"Probably because you taste like turtle."

"I don't know whether to be insulted or relieved."

"They kill us for our fur," I said.

"May I?" Tobble asked, pointing to my arm. When I shrugged, he timidly patted my shoulder. "Even damp," he marveled, "you are remarkably soft."

I shrugged. "My father says the whole world is trying to kill dairnes these days."

A branch snapped, and Tobble grabbed my arm.

We froze in place.

I studied the air with my nose. Tobble's left ear swiveled like the head of a skittish owl.

"There!" He pointed. "They're waiting for us!"

7.
The Poachers Return

I motioned for the wobbyk to stay low—unnecessary, given that a wobbyk standing on tiptoes is still shorter than a dairne creeping on all fours. Leading the way, tree trunk to tree trunk, I calculated each step for silence.

The scents of human and horse and dog grew stronger. I strained my ears but heard nothing but my thudding heart.

It was the dogs I feared. The nose of a dog is almost as talented as a dairne's. But the breeze was my friend, blowing them to me and concealing us. One human was nearer, I was sure of it. The others were farther back with the horses.

With movements so slow and cautious that I doubted any predator, human or otherwise, could detect them, I pushed aside the brambles of a billerberry bush.

And there he was.

He stood alone near a fallen log in a small clearing, intense concentration on his face. Slender and tall, he was dressed in simple peasant clothes: a faded brown shirt beneath a leather jerkin, fastened with a belt, woolen trousers, and tall buff leather boots.

I knew almost nothing about human emotions, and yet I sensed, somehow, that this one was anxious.

No, more than that: he was angry.

"Did ya ever catch sight of it again, guide?" It was not the slender boy but a yell from deeper in the forest.

"No, master," the boy called back. "Drownt in the sea, most likely."

I heard the faint sound of horses stamping their hooves impatiently. Nearby I heard two sets of feet—human, I thought—plodding through the underbrush.

Two bearded men came into view on either side of the boy. One was short and heavyset. The other, tall and gaunt, I recognized as the leader of the poachers. They were dressed in cast-off bits of armor over leather jerkins. Each had a sword, a bow, and two knives.

"What was it, d'ya think?" asked the leader.

"Thought it was a wolf, or a dog, maybe," said the other. "But the way it practically flew right off that cliff? I'm thinkin' it had to be a dairne."

"Never seen a dairne in my life. Never met a soul who's seen one." The leader leaned against a thick pine tree, arms crossed. "Boy, what d'ya think it was?"

"I'm not sure," the guide answered. "S'pose we'll never know."

"They say dairne fur's the softest and warmest in the world. One pelt'd feed us all for a year, and then some," said the short man.

"True," said the guide, "but I daresay a dairne would fetch far more alive, rare as they are."

"Cursed creatures." The short man spit. "My grandfather saw two back when he was a boy. Claimed their noses were bewitched. They can smell a fart a hundred furlongs off."

The leader grunted a laugh. "Here's hopin' where there's one dairne, there's more."

"If we do catch sight of one," said the boy, "please don't kill it." He paused when the leader sent him a dark look. "I just mean to say it'll be more coin in our pockets if we can capture it."

"Worth plenty dead, and quicker by half," the leader grumbled. "Speakin' o' which, I ever hear you scream, 'Don't kill it!' in the middle of a hunt again, and it'll be your pelt we're takin' to market."

The boy looked at the ground. "Yes, master."

"Where to, then, boy," asked the leader, "seein' as you're so clever?"

The guide turned, then stood still as stone, staring into the trees.

He was looking in our direction. Despite the thick cover of the billerberry bush, I sensed that he saw us.

The men fell silent.

The guide closed his eyes.

"He's catchin' the trackin' spell again," the first man said.

"Then shut your gob and let him at it."

The guide's eyes opened. In spite of the distance between us, I could see that they were deep brown, heavy lidded and thoughtful.

"Head north," he called to the men. "I'll grab my mount and catch up with you."

The older men moved away. The boy waited in silence, taking in the scene. Then he, too, departed.

But before he disappeared into the trees, he stopped and glanced back toward us, and I thought, though I could not be sure, that he was smiling.

8.
Three Tails, Three Saves

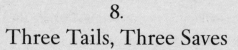

As soon as the danger had passed, my stomach began to whine, as if it had been waiting to complain until things were safe.

Tobble startled. "What was that?"

"My stomach. I'm hungry."

"My stomach growls when it's hungry."

"Ours whine." I stood carefully, nosing the air for any sign that the poachers hadn't actually left. "That guide," I said. "I feel certain he saw us."

"But why wouldn't he have said something?"

"I don't know." I shook my head. "It makes no sense."

I realized at that moment that I was utterly exhausted. The mad leap off the cliff, the impossible glide, the salt water followed by rain, the cold, the fear: I just wanted to be home, safe in the huddle of my sleeping family.

I'd been curious enough for one day.

I looked at Tobble and wondered what to do with him. I didn't know much about hunting. But I had the feeling you weren't supposed to converse with your prey.

Tobble seemed to sense what I was thinking. "You do realize you cannot eat me until I return the favor of saving your life?"

Despite myself I smiled. "You're going to save my life?"

"What I lack in stature I make up for in spirit." Tobble dusted wet dirt off his rear end. "Besides, it's Wobbyk Code. You saved my life; I must save yours three times."

"Why thrice?"

"Because that's the rule."

"But why is that the rule?"

"Because I have three tails."

I frowned. "But that doesn't make any sense."

"I don't make the rules. But I do obey them."

A noise like thunder rumbled again in the distance. We both flinched, worried the noise might now signal returning hooves rather than angry sky.

"There's no need to thank me," I said. Especially, I added silently, since under different circumstances I might well be feasting on you for dinner.

"So. Where to?" asked Tobble.

"You're not coming with me. My pack has been living on worms and bark for weeks. They'll eat you in a flash."

"That's a risk I'll simply have to take."

"You may not come," I said firmly, surprising myself with the voice my parents so often used on me.

"And yet I shall."

I decided to try logic. "You'll slow me down. And you'll make too much noise."

"If you think I'll make noise on the ground, then let me ride on your back. I'm too big for your pouch." Tobble jutted out his fuzzy chin. "Three times," he said. "Wobbyk Code. You couldn't get rid of me if you tried."

"I could if I ate you," I muttered, trying to sound intimidating.

Before I could say another word, Tobble climbed up onto my back. "I do hope you don't mind," he said.

"That there's a furry meal hugging my neck?" I asked. "As it happens, I do mind."

"It seems I've neglected to ask your name," Tobble said, ignoring me.

I sighed. Loudly and with feeling. "It's Byx."

"Byx," he repeated. "A fine name indeed for a fine dairne." He leaned close to my ear and whispered, "If that's really what you are."

I twisted my head and sent him a grimace. "Just a jest," he said with a wide grin. "Don't mind me."

"That may prove difficult."

Circling back meant a longer return trip, but I wanted

to be very sure I didn't accidentally lead the poachers to the mirabear hive.

The sky was covered with clouds and the sunset wasn't far off. I went east, then north, then at last turned in a straight line toward my temporary home and my permanent family.

Tobble didn't weigh much, but the question of what I was going to do with him once I got to the hive definitely weighed on my mind. At least he'd provide a distraction from the bigger question of why I'd strayed so far.

In any case, even hungry dairnes are civilized. If I claimed Tobble was a friend, I doubted anyone in the pack would try to eat him. They would, however, want to know why I'd befriended a potential meal.

I tried one more time. "You truly should hop off and be on your way," I told Tobble.

"I understand your concern." He ducked his head as I raced through stinging brambles. "But I can fend for myself."

"With what?" I half hoped he had some unrevealed power.

"With my derring-do," Tobble said confidently. "Let me just say this: You do not want to see me mad. I am a terrible sight to behold."

"I'll remember that," I said, trying not to smile.

"So where are we headed? Your home?"

"Yes. No. We don't really have homes," I said. "We move from place to place. Never too long in one spot."

"I thought you nested in trees. That's what I always heard."

"We used to. Not anymore. My parents taught us how to make nests, though. It takes a lot of practice. We weave silk from orb webs, bog reeds, and willow branches, and line the nests with moss and thistledown."

"I'm impressed. Of course, it probably helps that you dairnes have thumbs."

"They're quite useful." I wiggled them in the air.

"Show-off," said Tobble. "I'll bet you can't do this."

I turned my head to see his huge ears spinning like tiny cyclones, twisting and untwisting.

"Intriguing," I said. "What purpose does that serve?"

"None whatsoever," Tobble said with a grin.

After a few more minutes I stopped, checking for anything new. I had an odd sense that something wasn't right, although the wind brought me no useful news. I smelled pine sap and mold. Willowweed and ginger flowers. I heard a crimson owl fussing with her nest in the crook of a spruce.

"Do you hear anything?" I asked.

"Nope," Tobble said. "And with my ears, I hear everything."

I concentrated again. Nothing. Nothing I could name, anyway. Of course, that feeling often hit me when I'd made an unwise choice. Only afterward did the risk of what I'd done fully register.

My explorations had, for the most part, been careful. Timid, even. But today I'd gone too far. I was not looking forward to explaining myself to my parents. Still, I wanted to get home as quickly as I could. I'd made a big mistake, a very big one. I wanted to avoid any more.

"We live underground," Tobble volunteered, perhaps trying to distract me from my worries. "In amazing tunnels. They go on for leagues. I have my very own room. It's gigantic. And luxurious."

"That's nice," I said as I started walking again, even faster than before.

"I share it with my brothers Blaxton, Roopwart, and Piddlecombe."

"Hmm."

"And McGuppers, Jellyhorn, and Bribbles." Tobble paused. "So it's not exactly only my room."

Again I stopped. Something was wrong. Something in the air.

My fur stood on end. My nose tingled.

I shivered, even though I was no longer cold.

I'd been dawdling, indulging my own weariness.

"Hold on," I said to Tobble.

I dropped to all fours and took off at a gallop.

9.
Fear

I raced through the trees, then across a stretch of exposed rock dotted with tiny purple flowers. Twice I stumbled, but Tobble hung on, his little arms tight around my neck.

"Keep a sharp lookout," I said, panting.

"I shall, Byx," Tobble replied with worrying seriousness, and we both fell silent.

The clouds were breaking up overhead, driven inland by the wind. The sky, revealed in patches, had taken on an angry glow as day eased into night.

I was heading back to the mirabear hive from a different angle, but it didn't matter. I needed no signposts. I moved on instinct, nose set for home, home, home.

I leapt over a small stream and stopped cold.

"What is it?" Tobble asked.

I didn't move. I froze the way my parents had taught me and took everything in. To rush is not necessarily to arrive.

Ahead of me, I caught the scent of humans. The guide, perhaps? The horses, the dogs, the rest were farther away.

A two-minute run at full pace, home awaited.

"Something's wrong," I said, shaking my head as if arguing with myself.

"What is it?"

"Shhh." I listened, and so did Tobble.

They weren't there yet, the noises I was searching for. Wasn't I near enough to hear the movements of my fellow dairnes? They'd be packing up. They'd be looking for me. Were the trees so thick they muffled sound?

We were about to set out on a huge journey. Preparations should have been underway. Food had to be wrapped in poonan leaves, tools had to be put away, the few mementos we carried had to be slipped into pouches.

What I heard was not a sound. It was an absence of sound. A void.

I tried to pin down a fleeting scent. It was almost nothing, almost impossible for me to make out. The wind didn't serve me well, but from the dark recesses of my mind, an ancient emotion grew.

Fear.

I sat on my haunches and Tobble slid off.

"I have to go," I said, and by the time Tobble began to answer, I was already on my way.

I ran, tripping over a fallen branch, slipping on leaves.

I wove. I darted. I plowed through the undergrowth, heedless, eyes half closed to avoid the whipping branches.

Again I stopped.

Lost. I was lost.

Frantically I panted, hating my short legs and weak lungs that never, ever allowed me the pleasure of being the first or the fastest.

The treacherous breeze shifted and it hit me.

A smell so thick and horrible that it crawled down my throat like lava.

I knew before I knew.

"No," I whispered.

The world was silent, except for Tobble, far behind but gamely trying to catch up.

I saw a hill that I recognized because of the huge, lonely pine that stood atop it. The camp was just over the hill.

I panted and gasped, climbing up and up, and there at the summit where the mass of earth no longer stifled sound, the silence was gone.

I heard.

Howls and screams.

Agony.

Pain beyond words.

Terror and despair.

I ran.

10.
The Unthinkable

It took forever. And yet it came too quickly, the moment when I was sure.

Careening through the trees, I saw the humans in silver and red with their arrows and their broadswords, their drooling dogs and panting horses.

They were mayhem. They were blood. They were darkness.

Not poachers. These men were something else. They didn't wear motley clothing, they didn't wield mismatched weapons. They wore identical red-and-silver tunics, revealing arms covered in chain mail. Their heads were protected by conical steel helmets cut with a narrow slit for their eyes. Their boots glittered with spurs. Some men had swords. Others clutched spears.

These were not poachers. These were the Murdano's soldiers.

The mirabear hive, thirty feet high and twice as long, was golden and slick from the rain. Fires raged inside. Black smoke billowed from every opening.

One of the soldiers leapt off his horse and poked at a mound of fur with his spear.

It was Dalyntor, the elder of our pack. White muzzled, but wise in the ways of humans.

Not wise enough.

And then I saw them.

All of them.

My father.

My mother.

My siblings.

They were piled on the ground like discarded hides, blood pouring, white and pearly, soaking the leaves, eyes glassy and open, mouths open. Torn and stabbed.

They lay in a mound, as if they'd been too late to scatter, my parents on top, protecting as always.

I ran.

I ran to maim, to kill, to exact revenge, growling from some primitive place inside me that I didn't know existed.

I was almost in the open when something struck me hard in the side. It yanked me onto my back, legs tangled.

I stared in disbelief at the trident arrowhead buried in my right side. The filament attached to it, nearly invisible but capable of restraining a charging vulf stag, was taut.

I tried to pull out the arrow, but the points were barbed. It wasn't a killing arrow. It was an arrow meant for capture.

I grabbed the filament and tried to break it with my teeth. I raged and kicked.

From behind a tree I heard a voice. "Be still, you fool!"

I would not be still. I would not be stopped. I would go to my mother, my father. I would go to my brothers and sisters, my pack, my—

I heard a rush of feet, twisted too late, and felt a blow on the back of my neck.

But I felt it for only a second, maybe two, before I was lost in swirling darkness.

PART TWO
CAPTIVES

11.
The Guide

In my mind I was moving, but I could not move.

I could see.

I could smell.

I could hear.

But I could not move. I was restrained, held in place.

I was hanging, stomach down, over a saddleless horse. I rocked forward and back as the beast navigated a stony path. Somehow I didn't slip off. Was I tied to him, as well as bound hand and foot?

My face bounced against the horse's side. The stink of him—sweat and dung and weariness—was suffocating.

I was a carcass, dangling like a dead mouse in the jaws of a woodcat.

What was happening? My thoughts came slow and thick as mud.

My head lolled and snapped with each jerky step. When I strained to raise my head, I saw pine and bulla tree branches low to the ground, their tangy needles scratching the horse's legs.

I realized with a shock that we were in sunlight. Evening and night had come and gone. Had I been unconscious that long?

I saw hard-packed dirt and sharp-edged rocks.

I saw dappled gold and black horsehair rippling over ribs.

I saw a pair of legs, cloth-covered, feet bound in leather, striding surely, just ahead. A boy. I remembered him, at least I thought I did.

The boy. The poachers' guide.

Memories assaulted me. Poachers and arrows. Water and terror. A strange little wobbyk.

And something else . . . something terrible. So terrible my mind shut down.

The guide murmured softly and the horse halted.

With his hand on my shoulder, the guide steadied me. He lifted me up a little in order to see my face.

High above me, light stabbed through the thick overhang of branches. I felt it on my back. I saw the short noon shadows it cast.

I twisted my throbbing head and saw the rope holding me in place, the fat knot. I turned my head the other way and saw the horse's ears twitching. His mane was a tangle of shimmering gold and black.

The guide put a waterskin to my mouth. Just a bit to wet my lips, but I couldn't swallow well at that angle. Gently he wiped away the drops slipping down my cheek. Cupping his hand, he poured water into it, and I lapped like a dog. I was desperately thirsty.

"If you're awake, we need to get that arrowhead out of your side," he said.

He spoke the Common Tongue, the speech of traders and travelers. It's a mixture of words and phrases from a dozen different languages. Dalyntor had taught us pups how to speak it fluently, though among pack members, we spoke only Dairnish.

"The poison has worn off, and I suppose the numbing effect as well."

He was right. I felt the barbed tines, sharply cold, and a dull ache. The impact had bruised me as well as penetrated my flesh.

The guide jerked his head right, left. He was taking in the threats, listening intently. Sniffing the wind with his feeble human nose.

He lifted me, grunting at my weight, and set me down against a mossy hillock in the shade of a generous elm. I dared to look down at my side. The arrow's shaft had been cut away, leaving only a few inches. Blood, once glistening pearl, was now crusting brown.

I looked at the guide, trying to search his eyes, to understand. I racked my fuzzy memory for all I knew of humans, all I had heard in poems, in lessons, from my—

From my—

It came at me like a boulder down a mountain, and I could not flee the knowledge.

My mother. My father. My brothers and sisters.

I remembered the rest.

The burning mirabear hive.

The soldiers and their spears.

I remembered it all.

I closed my eyes and heard the screams. I smelled brackish blood, steel and iron, sword and armor.

I saw a spear poking at the dead bodies, the pitiful dead piles of fur.

A terrible rage grew within me.

I wanted to hurt someone. I wanted to hurt this boy.

I wanted to tear his flesh apart with my teeth. I wanted him to bleed like my family had bled.

"I won't lie to you," he said. "This will hurt."

Good. Let it hurt, I thought. Let me feel actual, physical pain.

The guide gathered dry twigs and a handful of dead

grass. He drew out his tinderbox and struck flint to iron. The sparks touched the grass and smoke curled.

"I couldn't start a fire at night," he explained.

His voice was strange. It was two voices. One was a gruff baritone, but beneath that, as if concealed, was a second, softer voice. "We won't make much smoke, and the angle of the sun will blind anyone pursuing us."

He drew a knife.

I drew a sharp breath.

But he didn't stab me. He held the knife blade over the fire. "The weir women say a hot knife heals better," he said.

I didn't care. I didn't want to heal. I wanted to kill, or to die, and the two things were one in my mind.

All dead. All of them.

All of them.

"I have to make three small cuts," the guide explained.

I heard his words, but they were just empty noise.

My family. My pack. All dead.

The blade burned as it pierced my skin, and I couldn't help flinching. Luckily, the guide's hand was swift and sure.

The pain went deep, but I did not scream.

I would never be weak for this human.

The second cut was worse. I had to grit my teeth until I feared they would crack.

The third cut was easier to endure. I was adjusting to the pain.

It was nothing compared to the pain inside me.

"I have to wiggle the arrow a bit," said the guide, "to get it out."

He did, and it hurt, but he was able to remove the arrow quickly. He cut the arrowhead from the broken shaft, wiped off my blood, and dropped the sharp point into a pouch on the side of his quiver.

I made an inventory of his weapons.

The bow and arrows.

The rusted sword that was too big for him and awkward when he knelt.

The knife in his boot.

The guide opened a leather pouch on his belt and drew out a crushed green leaf. He placed it over the wound in my side.

"Hard to keep in place on fur, but it will help the healing," he said. He tied it in place with a long rag wound around my chest. "I was aiming for your leg, but you moved at the last minute," he added, as if by way of apology.

"I wish you'd hit my heart dead-on," I muttered, surprised to find myself capable of forming words. "At least I'd be with the others, where I belong."

The guide gazed at me. They were the first words I'd

spoken to him, and he seemed to be debating how to answer.

"I'm glad you survived," he said at last.

I looked away. "I am not."

With a sigh, the guide kicked the fire apart, scuffing dirt over it. "We need to move on," he said.

Although he didn't free my hands, tied uncomfortably behind my back, the guide undid the rope binding my back feet. He lifted me again, still tied, and with a heave that was at the limits of his strength set me astride the horse. I was sitting upright, no longer baggage.

With liquid grace, he leapt up behind me and reached around for the reins, and we were off at a quick trot.

We emerged from shadow into light. I didn't recognize our location. This was not the forest or the meadow or the sea. We were in a dry place of low scrub and exposed rocks.

The boy kept his horse to the rocks as much as possible, making it harder to track hoofprints.

I told myself to see everything, that every detail would be useful for escape.

I tried to focus on the path ahead.

But it was no use.

No matter where I looked, all I saw were the piled bodies and sightless stares of everyone I had ever loved.

12.
Whispers

We moved on. Slowly our surroundings changed. The terrain grew rockier and more treacherous. The stand of pines that had been on our right thinned and finally ended. Every step, for both horse and guide, seemed to be a struggle.

The guide appeared tired. Yet he pushed on, urging the horse around outcroppings of glittering rock jutting so near that both the guide and I had to shift to avoid being scraped.

I studied the wind for something familiar, something knowable, and found nothing. It whispered and moaned but told me nothing of where I was or where I was going.

The wound on my side ached and burned. The crude bandage around my chest wouldn't let me draw a full breath.

We crossed a chuckling stream, and I realized how thirsty I still was.

I heard the whispering wind, the stream, and perhaps—could it be?—something more.

My name on the breeze.

"Byx."

I waited, and there it was again.

"Byx!"

I strained to listen but heard nothing else. Was it some echo of my mother's voice? Did she still call to me from the land of the dead? But all I could hear was the clatter of the horse's hooves on rock and the guide's breathing.

You're not thinking clearly, I told myself. Hearing what isn't there.

And yet again it came.

"Byx!"

I was hearing, perhaps, what I wanted to hear: someone, somewhere, searching for me. Someone who knew I was still alive.

The wind whispered its eerie music, and another memory came unbidden. My parents had been talking softly, just a few days earlier. They were sitting in the far corner of our makeshift home inside the mirabear hive, whispering about us. About my siblings and me.

They thought we were asleep.

We weren't.

When it comes to the subject of sleeping pups, parents are strangely skilled at fooling themselves.

"If trouble comes," my mother said, her voice hushed.

"When trouble comes," my father corrected.

"When trouble comes," she continued, "I worry for them all. But especially I fear for Byx."

I heard my name and startled. Still, I kept my eyes shut and my breathing slow and even. No one feigns sleep better than I.

"Why Byx, love?" my father asked.

"She's so young. So small." My mother's voice trembled. "I had a dream, a terrible dream. They came for us. I dreamed she was the first to die."

"The first to die." My father was silent for a long while.

I remembered lying motionless, silent, scarcely breathing, waiting for more.

"I, too, had a dream," my father said at last, sighing. "Worse in some ways. I dreamed"—his voice caught—"I dreamed she was the last to live."

"No," my mother said, and I could hear that she was softly sobbing. "Don't even think such a thing."

"They say humans have a word for it. Endling."

My mother laughed bitterly. "They would have a word for it, wouldn't they?"

My brother Reaphis, sleeping near the bottom of our tangled pile, nudged me with his foot. "Don't worry, Byx," he said. "They won't waste arrows on a runt like you. You're not worth the trouble of eating."

"They don't kill us to eat us," my oldest sister hissed. She was the smartest among us, perhaps because she was the best eavesdropper. "They kill us for our fur. That's what Dalyntor says."

We'd all heard that rumor many times before. Not that it made it any less painful to hear.

"Are you asleep over there?" my mother called.

We knew well enough not to answer. My parents grew quiet, and so did we.

"Byxer?" my brother Jax murmured hours later. He couldn't sleep either, it seemed.

"Yes?" I said softly.

"Don't worry. Whatever happens, I'll protect you."

Jax was a year older. He was sweet and silly, and had one violet eye and one green one. He was my favorite, and I was his.

"I'll protect you, too," I said.

If I'd said that to any of my other siblings, they would have scoffed. Not Jax.

He reached for my hand.

When I woke up hours later, he was still holding on tightly.

13.
The Cave

We came to a stop. The guide said something to the horse, a short, terse-sounding word in a language I didn't understand. The horse shifted his weight.

A mossy, wet-stone smell filled the air, and the wind moaned like an old animal struggling to breathe.

The guide spoke again to the horse, this time in the Common Tongue. "Stay here, Vallino."

Vallino did as he was bidden, standing still and dropping his graceful head to snuffle for the few bits of grass peeking out between the rocks.

I tugged at the knots holding my hands, but it was pointless. My captor was clever with ropes.

Moments later the guide returned and, with some effort, yanked me off Vallino. My feet hit the ground with a soft thud. Gently the guide directed me forward around the bluff. I smelled damp air wafting from the entrance to a cave.

I tried to jerk free, but it was a useless gesture. I stumbled into the cave, and as we rounded a bend, the light from the entrance was nearly extinguished. I struggled to make out shapes in the featureless dark.

"This is far enough," the guide said, again using the Common Tongue.

He settled me down onto my rear, not a comfortable position for a dairne. "Wait here," he said, as if I had a choice. "I'm getting Vallino."

The clip-clop of hooves echoed against the walls. The horse was skittish, wary in the enclosed space. I understood how he felt. It was so dark it was almost like being blind. I could barely make out the guide's form until he was right next to me.

Carefully he peeled away the bandage and the medicinal leaf. "That's good," he said. "The bleeding has stopped."

That voice. Once, when I was just a pup, I heard men's voices from a distance. We'd strayed too close to a village, close enough to hear the shouts and grunts as the men pursued us.

Yesterday, again, I heard voices like theirs: guttural, deep in the chest, booming.

But this boy's voice was different. There was hidden music in it, like a lark's call from a faraway tree.

He retrieved his water pouch and a blanket off the horse's back. "Vallino won't mind," he said, but the horse's angry snort said otherwise.

I caught a flash of white teeth and wondered if the guide might actually have smiled, but I couldn't be sure.

He draped the blanket over me, tucking it around my shoulders and feet. "Caves are chilly," he said. Raising the waterskin, he directed a stream of cool water into my greedy mouth.

I would have liked to throw the blanket aside—I was already well acquainted with the odor of horse—but I needed the warmth. I was shivering like a cornered chipmunk.

As night fell in the world outside, the cave came alight with a soft glow of moonsnails. They dotted the ceiling and walls, barely moving, but moving nonetheless. Their translucent shells slowly pulsed with light, changing color from pale pink to deep orange like tiny, traveling sunsets.

The guide returned to Vallino, fumbling around in a leather bag. He pulled out a canvas feedbag with straps and tied it over Vallino's nose, then brushed the horse's coat. After picking brambles from Vallino's gold-streaked mane, the boy raised each hoof in turn and carefully pried out stones and dried mud with his knife.

Only when Vallino had been cared for did the guide sit across from me. He had a small slab of dried meat and tore off a piece to share. I would have refused, wanted to refuse, but if I was to escape, I had to stay strong. He ripped the hard brown meat into smaller bits and fed me like a pup.

"I wish I could make a fire," he said, almost apologetically, "but in this location the Murdano's men may notice smoke if it escapes the cave."

The guide studied me, and I studied back.

He had likely never seen a dairne. I wished I had never seen a human.

His furless skin was a soft brown. The only significant hair he possessed grew in black waves, tied back with a leather cord into a stubby tail. His dark eyes were not unlike my own, though it was hard to be precise in the strange light. He had no muzzle, only a strangely flat mouth. Full lips alternately covered and revealed useless teeth that could never take down prey.

"So," he said. "You're a dairne."

"And you're a human boy," I spit back.

A wide smile formed. "Well, I'm glad that I can fool you, too."

"Fool me?"

"Indeed." Suddenly the gruffness that had always sounded false to my ears was gone. His voice was higher in register—serious, but not grim.

It hit me with the clarity of a lightning bolt.

"You're female!"

"Correct," said the guide, in that same amused-but-serious voice. "I'd have thought the fabled dairne sense of smell would have exposed me by now. But then, I suppose after weeks hunting in the wilds, I'm dirty enough to smell like the foulest man."

"I'm sorry." I blurted the words automatically. I'd been raised to be respectful, never to call any creature by the wrong name. "I've had little experience with humans." Then, recovering my anger, I added, "And I wish I'd had still less."

"I've had no real experience with dairnes," the guide replied. "You're the first I've been near."

"Then it wasn't you who sent out the dairne warning call near the cliff?"

"So you heard it?" The guide looked pleased. "Yes, that was me. I've learned what I could about your kind over the years. One of the poachers taught me that call." She tilted her head. "How did I do?"

"The pitch was all wrong."

"Perhaps you'll teach me how one of these days."

"So that you can capture more dairnes?" My throat tightened. "If there are any more of us."

He—no, she—looked down. "I'm sorry about your . . . about the others."

I felt words inside me bubbling to the surface like bile, but I didn't speak. I could not say the word "family." I could not say "brother" or "sister." "Father" or "mother."

The pain of it would have choked me.

Instead I focused on sense memory. I recalled the smells of the poachers and the Murdano's soldiers and compared them to the scent of this girl. I picked out the differences and tucked them away. Never again would I confuse male and female humans.

"Do you have a name?" the girl asked.

"Do you?"

"My name is Kharassande, though everyone calls me Khara, which can be a name for either boy or girl. But I've been called 'boy.' Or 'guide.' Or 'you there.'"

"Are humans so stupid they don't know that you're female?"

"Humans see what they expect to see. I dress as a boy, speak as a boy. So they see a boy."

"But why?" I asked, my natural curiosity getting the better of me for a moment.

"Why am I disguised as a boy?" Khara tore me another chunk of the meat and pushed it into my mouth. "Girls aren't allowed to hunt. Girls aren't allowed to do many things. Most things."

It was a strange notion, but then, I knew so little of humans. It was the truth, of that much I was certain.

There is no point in lying to a dairne. We will always feel the falseness. And while dairnes may exaggerate or tell tall tales, may joke or be playful with words, we do not lie the way other species do.

Sometimes this is a good thing. Sometimes it's not.

"And you?" Khara asked casually.

"I am female," I said. "I have no reason not to be."

She nodded. "Lucky."

"I'm not feeling lucky."

"I suppose not."

Khara stared at me. So much about her human face was unfamiliar, and yet her gaze was every bit as intelligent and searching as any dairne's.

"If we were to run into the wrong sort of person," Khara said carefully, "being female might get me hurt." She paused. "Even killed."

Instantly I understood what she was doing. She was telling me that she'd entrusted me with dangerous information.

I did not trust her. I would never trust her.

But I no longer feared her.

I looked into her eyes. I said, "My name is Byx."

14.
An Unexpected Visitor

In the middle of the night, my eyes flew open. At least, I assumed it was the middle of the night. It was hard to gauge time in the depths of a cave.

Two strange sounds competed for my attention.

The first sound was odd breathing coming from Khara. On each inhalation she made a sustained snorting noise, not unlike a bog toad.

I assumed all humans did this when they slept.

The second sound seemed to be a rat scrabbling over the stony cave floor. But my nose immediately corrected that impression. It wasn't rat or mouse.

It was wobbyk.

My heart leapt.

I strained to listen. Scrabble, scrabble, pause. Scrabble, pause.

And there he was.

Tobble.

He flashed a grin. In the faint light from the moonsnails, his black eyes glimmered. I shook my head, silencing him before he could speak. We could not afford to waken Khara.

I rolled onto my side to show Tobble the rope that still bound my wrists. His nimble little paws, along with his teeth, went to work. My hands tingled with their newfound freedom.

I patted Tobble in thanks. He seemed pleased, for he produced a purring sound, a softer, more melodious version of Khara's heavy breathing.

We crept inch by inch, Tobble in the lead. Vallino heard us, of course. He was a clever beast, and herd animals have sharply developed senses. He could have exposed us with a single nicker or a loud snort, but he stayed silent.

I suspected Vallino did not enjoy carrying my weight along with Khara's. He was probably happy to see me leave.

We soon emerged beneath a star-strewn sky and moved away from the cave as quickly as we could while still remaining silent.

"Many thanks," I whispered. "So that was you I heard calling my name on the trail?"

"Yes. I wanted to give you hope."

"I thought I was imagining things."

"Your wound," Tobble said, pointing to my side. "Are you well enough to travel?"

"I'm fine."

Tobble jutted his chin toward the cave. "Did the human girl plan to kill you?"

"You knew she was a girl?"

"Of course," said Tobble. "You didn't?"

"No," I admitted. There are times when dairne honesty can be a disadvantage.

"So do you think she wanted to kill you?"

"Why do you ask?"

"Because I need to know whether or not I saved your life."

"Ah. Well, you certainly rescued me," I said. "And I'm deeply grateful. But whether she meant to kill me, I can't be sure. I don't know what she was planning."

The wobbyk made a disgruntled sound. "In that case, I suppose I can't count it as an actual lifesaving."

"Of course you can."

Tobble shook his head. "It's Code, Byx. You cannot argue with Wobbyk Code."

I sensed it was best not to debate. "So," I said, changing the subject, "where do you think we are?"

"Well, as best I can tell, we are at the end of a ridge, between the Forest of Null and the Therian Marshes."

"The Forest of Null?" Every dairne pup had heard of the

Forest of Null. It was featured in many bedtime stories. Not the happy sort of bedtime story. The type of story involving fell beasts, monsters, and carnivorous plants.

Tobble nodded solemnly. Even a solemn wobbyk looks a bit silly.

"I've never been to the marshes," I said.

"Nor have I," said Tobble.

I tried to recall my geography lessons. "And what lies beyond them, do you think?"

Tobble tapped his chin. "The plains. The capital. Rivers. Mountains. Some other stuff. And then a whole different country, Dreyland."

"That sounds about right," I said. "Geography was never my best subject."

"Well, I can tell you this: we certainly don't want to get too close to the border."

"As if we could ever get that far!" I replied. "But why do you say that?"

"Rumor has it that the Murdano is planning to invade Dreyland soon."

"How do you know?" I asked.

"We wobbyks are seafaring folk." Tobble grinned proudly. "We know a great deal about a few things, and a few things about a great deal."

"Then perhaps you could help me decide where to go."

"That," said Tobble, "I shall leave up to you."

How to make a decision? If only, I thought desperately, my parents were here to guide me. Myxo, Dalyntor, any of my siblings: they would all have better instincts than I. What did I know? I was the runt. The least important member of our pack.

I knew nothing.

No, that wasn't entirely true. I knew that the important thing at that moment was to get as far away from Khara as possible.

I looked at Tobble's trusting, expectant face. "Marshes it is, then," I said, trying to sound decisive.

Tobble pointed to the north. We set off at a pace limited by his stubby legs. I realized with a guilty start that Tobble must have been running all day and much of the night to keep up with Vallino.

To rescue me.

"You must be exhausted. Would you like me to carry you?"

"I wouldn't hear of it! You've been injured," Tobble said. "In any case, the wobbyk metabolism is a marvel to behold. I once ran for six days straight without sleep or sustenance."

My dairne instincts told me I was hearing more than a little exaggeration. But I said nothing. In any case, I could hardly rush ahead and abandon him. He'd taken risks for me.

I would not let myself forget that fact.

The dank odor of the marsh wafted our way before we arrived at the first grayish, spongy mound of drooping grass. It smelled of rot and decay, too sweet in the upper registers of scent. It smelled of living things slowly dying.

But as we pushed on, as I dragged my feet out of sucking mud, I smiled to myself. Khara might follow this way, but Vallino would not.

"We should walk for a bit longer, then turn southwest," I said.

"Back to—to where we started?"

The question brought me up short. Was the burned and blood-spattered mirabear hive my destination?

Why? To return to dead bodies? What would I do when I got there?

I hesitated. "I could speak a ritual for the dead," I finally suggested.

Tobble accepted my answer, but it didn't satisfy me.

Did I truly have no destination?

The realization flooded me with despair. I was in the middle of a stinking marsh with nowhere to go.

I had no family. I had no home. The only reason to head back was because I had no better destination.

I belonged nowhere. To no one.

For as long as I could remember, I'd been part of

something bigger than myself.

Part of a family.

Part of a pack.

Part of a species.

What was I now?

You're still a dairne, I told myself. You're alone today. But that doesn't mean you'll be alone forever.

Myxo had planned to lead our pack north. She must have believed more dairnes could be found.

If she could hope, then I could, too.

I remembered, with a sudden pang, my mother's words the last time we were together: It's never wrong to hope, Byx.

Of course, she'd also said: Unless the truth says otherwise.

"Byx?" Tobble asked. "Are you all right?"

I gave a small nod. I might have been the only dairne in all the southlands. In all Nedarra. In all the world, perhaps.

I didn't know the truth, couldn't guess what lay ahead. Not yet.

But perhaps I wasn't entirely alone. Not with this little wobbyk by my side.

We trudged on. It became harder to advance. The gloomy landscape was dotted with wide, shallow pools and soggy mounds of earth. Each step forward meant yanking a foot from sucking mud so determined to hold us in place that it almost seemed alive.

The moon hung low in the sky like a yellow claw. Ahead of us, skeletal trees glimmered in the moonlight. They were leafless, with huge knots of exposed roots digging into the mud like thousands of gnarled fingers.

"Those are marsh demontrees," Tobble said. "Perhaps we could rest there?"

"How scenic," I said. "Perhaps tomorrow we can camp in a graveyard."

We settled onto a nearly dry spot atop a mat of roots. I began scraping muck from my feet with a stick. Tobble groomed himself for a moment, muttered something incomprehensible, and instantly fell fast asleep.

It was probably for the best. I could stay awake to keep watch.

I yawned, shook myself, yawned again.

Stay awake, I told myself. You can sleep later. Stay awake.

Another yawn.

Stay . . .

15.
Attack of the Serpents

I woke at dawn as something slithered over me.

"Ahhh!" I screamed, but I was pinned beneath something heavy, something heavy and moving.

Something heavy, moving, and alive.

"Snakes!" I cried, and Tobble yelped, "Snakes!"

A black serpent's head darted before me, its forked tongue tasting the night air. Tasting the smell of . . . me.

I struggled, but with each movement the enormous snake coiled around me, tightening its hold. Its skin, black with green and yellow stripes, gleamed in the pale light.

"Let me go!" I yelled at the snake's head, which was even larger than my own.

The snake was not impressed.

I kicked and hit nothing but air. I tried to free my arms, but the strength of the huge serpent was infinitely greater than anything I could muster. It was slow-moving but relentless, shifting, tightening, surrounding me with more and more of its incredible length.

I was helpless. Don't panic, I told myself. Don't panic. Don't panic.

But the more I tried to calm myself, the more I shivered with terror.

I looked up and saw that some of the branches above me were moving. There were more serpents.

Dozens. Perhaps even hundreds.

"I'll save you, Byx!" Tobble cried.

He leapt to my defense, digging his teeth into the serpent that had pinned me, but suddenly the little wobbyk was snatched away, as if someone had him on a string. One of the snakes above had dropped a nooselike coil around Tobble's chest.

"Help!" I shrieked, though I knew I wouldn't be heard.

The serpent's skin was as cold as a corpse.

"Oh, dear me!" Tobble yelped. "This is most unpleasant."

"Help!" I cried again. "Somebody help us, please!"

"Are you sure you want help?"

I knew that voice, that soft, sardonic tone.

I knew it. And, desperate as I was, I welcomed it with all my heart.

A coil covered half my face, thick as the trunk of a young tree, leaving me with only one useful eye and a muffled mouth.

"Yes!" I managed to say. The snake tightened its grip, and I felt the air squeezed from my lungs.

"Do you swear by all you hold sacred not to escape me again?"

I was not in a position to bargain. "Yes! Yes! Save us!"

"Well," Khara said calmly, "if you insist."

The metallic ring of a sword being drawn met my ears, and what a sweet sound it was.

Khara raised her blade as my one eye stared in astonishment.

Her sword had been rusty and ancient, with a bent hand guard and a simple, leather-wrapped grip. But now, impossibly, the hilt was encrusted with jewels, and the blade glowed like forged iron fresh from the fire.

Khara brought it down hard on the snake's tail.

I heard the clang of a cleaver on meat.

The snake hissed, turning its beady yellow eyes toward Khara. Still it wouldn't release me.

My head swelled with blood. My limbs were numb. The world vibrated as the vision in my one free eye narrowed.

"I have no fight with serpent folk," Khara warned, "but I will take your head next!"

I saw movement above her. I wanted to shout a warning, but I had no breath left. All I could do was moan.

A massive snake dropped from a branch directly above Khara.

She sliced it into halves midair, and the two pieces thudded to the ground. They writhed for a moment, then went still.

The snakes were done toying with us.

They were everywhere at once, slithering toward us, all but indistinguishable from the tangle of exposed tree roots.

They spiraled down branches by the hundreds. They lunged out of the water.

For a split second, Khara took it all in.

And then she went to work.

She twirled through the air. She leapt. She pirouetted, her shimmering sword leaving trails of golden light like a shooting star.

I felt hot sprays of serpent blood like fitful rain. But the great serpent who held me, the largest of all, did not relent. It raised its head high and opened its hideous mouth, revealing the deadly curve of two huge black fangs.

Please, I thought, if I must die, let it be swift.

With lightning speed the serpent dived at me. The top of my head wedged in its rank mouth, fangs just grazing my ears. My skull was too large to swallow, but the serpent meant to make it impossible for Khara to kill it without also killing me.

The slime, the putrid breath, the fangs beaded with venom: it was as if my head were trapped in some hideous, reeking helmet.

I gagged. The foul stench was more than I could bear.

And yet I had no choice but to bear it. I could not move, not even a hairbreadth.

I caught a glimpse of Khara's sword inscribing a graceful arc. It swung horizontally.

Directly at my head.

The blade struck flesh.

Fortunately, it wasn't mine.

The serpent went slack.

Khara had cut through the snake's head, all the way through until the last fraction of an inch, the blade stopping within a finger's width of slicing into my own face.

A collective hiss went through all the other snakes, like a wordless argument quickly concluded.

Tobble, released at last, dropped from above and landed with a muddy gloop near Khara's boots. The snakes left in slow, sinuous retreat.

With the serpent's grip loosened at last, I pulled myself partially free of its carcass. But its horrible mouth was still firmly attached to the top of my head. Try as I might, I didn't have the strength to remove it.

"I could use some help over here," I said, but Khara seemed more interested in Tobble.

"Who are you?" she demanded, kneeling beside the trembling wobbyk.

"Me?" Tobble squeaked. "I'm here to rescue Byx."

"You're a little late," Khara said. "Do you have a name?"

"I'm no one," Tobble replied in a small voice.

Khara stood. "Then we shall call you breakfast."

"No! He's a—a friend," I cried.

"Hmm," Khara said. "Then I suppose we shall feast on serpent instead."

16.
Breakfast Is Served

We headed back to the cave, bedraggled and chastened. No one spoke.

Khara didn't bother to tie us up. She seemed to know we wouldn't be attempting another escape anytime soon.

Vallino snorted in annoyance when we arrived. It was a good thing Khara had made the decision to leave the horse behind and track us on foot. He would have been mired in mud in no time.

Risking a small fire, Khara grilled chunks of serpent on a stick. It felt a bit odd, eating something that just tried to eat me. But that didn't change the mouth-watering flavor.

We ate in silence until Khara asked why Tobble hadn't touched his food.

"Wobbyks don't eat meat," he explained, although I noticed he was eyeing the charred serpent with a certain fascination.

"What do you like to eat?" Khara asked. "Maybe I can find something."

"I'm fine, thank you very much." Even under the circumstances, Tobble couldn't seem to stifle his natural wobbyk politeness.

"We've a long way to go." Khara poked at the fire with a stick. "You're certain you don't want to eat something?"

"Absolutely," said Tobble, just as his stomach let loose with a growl so ferocious, it would have made a felivet proud.

"Your stomach says otherwise." Khara licked her fingers and smiled. "You're plant eaters, right?"

"Plants and bugs. Bark, in a pinch."

"I'll see what I can find." Khara leapt to her feet.

"Please don't bother." Tobble crossed his arms over his chest. "I can't accept food from you. You're our captor."

"Tobble," I urged in a low voice, "eat while you can. We'll need our strength for—"

"Not for another escape, you won't." Khara wagged a finger at us. "I'll be right outside the entrance, so don't get any ideas."

We watched her leave. "I don't have any ideas," Tobble said. "Do you, Byx?"

I rubbed a sore spot on my nose. One of the serpent's fangs had grazed it. "No," I admitted, feeling weary and defeated. "Not any good ones, anyway."

When she returned minutes later, Khara's leather pouch was stuffed with grass and leaves. She opened her right hand to reveal a squirming ball of orange centipedes.

I'd eaten my share of bugs, but these looked far too much like miniature serpents for my taste. Still, Tobble's eyes lit up.

"You need to eat, Tobble," I said with an encouraging nod.

With a peevish sigh, he thrust out his paw. Khara dropped the slimy mass of centipedes into it. Tobble shoved the whole writhing bundle into his mouth and munched loudly.

Khara laughed. It was the first time I'd heard the sound, and it reminded me of a brief and wordless song. I was surprised at how pleasant I found it, in spite of our circumstances.

"I'd rather eat badger dung than centipedes," she said.

"Have you ever tried one?" Tobble asked, his mouth still full, manners momentarily forgotten.

Khara nodded. "Awful. They're dull as dirt."

"Not as dull as wobbyk meat," I added. Instantly I regretted my words when I saw Tobble's expression.

"It's rather hard to enjoy a meal," he said, "when your companions are discussing how you taste."

On the cave floor next to Tobble, Khara piled the grass and leaves she'd collected. "So I've gone from captor to companion?"

Tobble didn't answer. His mouth was already full of dorya leaves.

Khara sat cross-legged close to the fire. She stared at Tobble and me as if she were solving a puzzle. "You two make a strange pair indeed. What was it that brought you together?"

I resisted responding. Khara had no right to know anything about us. Still, I had many questions myself. If I answered hers, she might return the favor. And what I gleaned might aid me in the days ahead.

"I rescued Tobble from a sinking boat," I said. "And he seems to think he must return the favor three times."

"Wobbyk Code," Tobble explained, green leaf juice dribbling down his chin.

"Ahh," said Khara. "And how old are you, Tobble?"

"Forty-two." Tobble wiped his mouth with the back of his hand. "I'm the baby of our family."

"At forty-two?" Khara exclaimed. She narrowed her eyes. "Wait. How long do wobbyks live?"

"A very long time. I'm perhaps"—Tobble stopped to taste a fresh leaf—"perhaps eight in human years."

"And you, Byx?" Khara asked.

"I'm eleven."

"And dairnes live about as long as humans, as I understand it."

"They could," I said darkly, "if it weren't for humans."

Khara nodded. "Sadly, that is true."

"How old are you?" Tobble asked.

"Fourteen. Old enough to marry, and then some." Khara made a sour face. "Or so they tell me."

"I answered your questions," I said. "Now you must answer mine."

Khara half smiled, half nodded. "Fine."

"Why are you a poacher? Why kill for money?"

"A girl needs to survive. Or a boy. Or in my case, a little of both. As it happens, I don't have many options these days." Khara stared past me. "I used to," she added with a shrug. "In any case, I've always had a gift for tracking."

Tobble licked his palm. "It's wrong to kill living things."

"Tell that to the centipedes in your belly," Khara said, rolling her eyes.

"They're not . . ." Tobble hesitated. "It's not the same with bugs."

"I suspect the bugs would beg to differ."

Tobble opened his mouth to respond, but instead decided to stuff a wad of grass into it.

"How long did you work for them?" I asked. "Those poachers?"

"A few months, mostly as a guide. Before that, I worked for another group of them. And before that, another. I take work where I can, when I can. I rather like to eat."

"Won't they be mad that you ran off?" asked Tobble.

"For a bit, no doubt. That's why I'm lying low, keeping to the back trails." Khara waved a hand. "Although, truth be told, that crew of simpletons couldn't find me without me there to guide them."

"Two more questions," I said.

Khara kicked at an ember. It sent up a few halfhearted sparks. "Have at it."

"Your sword. It changed while you were fighting the serpents."

"Yes," Khara said with a sly smile. "That is a story for another day."

"Answer me this, at least," I said. "Where are you taking us?"

Khara pursed her lips. She seemed to be debating whether or not to answer me. "I suppose," she said, "you have a right to know. Whether you like it or not, I'll tell you the truth."

"And whether you like it or not," I said, "I'll know if you are lying."

"Ah, yes. I've heard those stories. Is it true what they say? That dairnes don't lie?" Khara asked, crossing her arms over her chest.

"We don't. It's not in our nature."

"Does that mean you can tell when I'm lying?" Tobble asked a bit nervously.

I merely smiled.

Tobble gulped. "Oh my. How can you know a lie for sure?"

I had to think for a moment. "I haven't had a lot of practice. Adult dairnes don't lie to each other. Pups try sometimes, until they realize there's no point. Once, my brother Jax—"

I stopped myself midsentence. Just saying the name out loud made me reel. I didn't want to talk about my family.

I didn't want to venture anywhere near that icy black chasm of pain.

"But what does it feel like, hearing a lie?" Tobble pressed, too busy eating, apparently, to notice my discomfort.

Khara was watching me closely, clearly intrigued.

I took a steadying breath and forced an answer. "It feels like . . . Have you ever heard a mockingbird mimic a seajay, or maybe a Dawson's hawk? It's an almost perfect imitation, but not quite. There's something missing, and you hear the wrongness of it. You feel it in your belly." I looked right at Khara. "The false note you sounded when you tried to make the dairne warning call? That's what it's like when I hear a lie."

"My," said Tobble, eyes wide. "I'm not sure I would enjoy having that power."

"In any case, Byx, what I have to say to you will be the truth," Khara said.

I leaned forward, ready to listen. "I'll be the judge of that."

17.
Khara's Plan

"We're going to Cora di Schola."

I exchanged a look with Tobble. No, he didn't know what that meant, either.

"And that is . . . ?" I asked.

"It's an island city. Its real name is the Isle of Ursina. But everyone calls it 'Cora di Schola.' It means 'Heart of the Scholars.'"

"Why do they call it that?" Tobble asked.

"It's shaped roughly like a human heart. And it's home to scholars and students. The Imperial Academy of Alchemy, Astronomy, Theurgy, and Science is housed there."

I had to digest each word separately.

"Alchemy," I'd learned from Dalyntor, was the art of blending substances to create new substances, like medicines. "Astronomy," I thought, had something to do with stars. "Theurgy" was the study of spells and incantations.

And "Science"? I was not quite certain what that was, but it sounded impressive.

"Imperial" sounded impressive, too, until I remembered—

"Imperial?" I cried. "As in the Murdano?"

"His Imperial Highness, the Murdano of Nedarra, Defender of Truth, Guardian of the Righteous, Peacemaker of the People, and so on and so on and so forth," Khara said, waving her hand.

"But—but it was the Murdano's soldiers who—"

"You'll see very few soldiers on the isle," Khara said. "Soldiers aren't welcome there. It's a place of learning."

"But still, it's called the Imperial—"

"He's the Murdano. Everything is his, I suppose. He remade the calendar. He rewrote the dictionary. He has power over everything in Nedarra, including the great governing species." Under her breath she added, "At least that's what he thinks."

"But why are you taking us there?" I pressed. I was mindful of my promise not to attempt escape again. I was even more mindful of what had happened when I'd tried. But I wasn't about to march to my own death, if that was what Khara had planned.

"We have to go," Khara said. "We have no other options."

"I don't like this," I said. "I've never been to a human city. It sounds too risky."

"I don't like it either," said Tobble.

Khara held up her palms. "You have no choice."

"I won't go," I declared.

"You realize I could have let the poachers kill you like the Murdano's men—" Khara fell silent, avoiding my eyes.

I felt daggers in my heart. My imagination conjured pictures—pictures that turned sadness to slow-burning anger.

"I shouldn't have said that," Khara said, and I sensed that she was sincere. She rubbed her eyes. "I'm tired, and not speaking as carefully as I should. Forgive me."

I gave a little nod but said nothing. There was nothing to say.

Minutes passed. The only sound was Tobble's enthusiastic chewing.

I didn't want to speak. But far too many questions were boiling in my brain. I needed answers.

"So," I finally said, keeping my voice even, "your plan is to hand me over to the Murdano?"

"Hah!" Khara gave a dark laugh. "I'm not exactly on friendly terms with the Murdano or his men. No, I'm taking you to a man I know, a famous scholar. A wise man. His name is Ferrucci the Gharri."

"What's a 'Gharri'?" Tobble asked.

"A title of honor. It's bestowed only on the greatest scholars. They're men who know all there is to know about the stars, or the shape of the world, or animals, or history.

Ferrucci is a good and honest man." Khara shrugged. "I've brought him unusual finds in the past."

"'Finds'?" I repeated.

"Rare animals or plants. Ferrucci studies ways to protect them. My plan is to take you to him and seek his advice. He'll know what to do with a dairne."

"And why are you bothering to do this?" Tobble asked. "What do you get out of it?"

"I'm trying to help Byx," Khara said evenly. "But if Ferrucci sees fit to reward me for my efforts, I won't argue."

"So that's your plan, Khara? You're going to sell Byx?" Tobble leapt to his feet, whiskers quivering. "Byx is my friend, and I do hope you understand that I will not let any harm come to her."

"I told you," said Khara. "This is the best I can do."

"It's only fair to warn you," said Tobble. "You do not want to see an angry wobbyk. We are fearsome to behold. I in particular am known for my fierce temper."

"Thank you, Tobble," I said. "But—"

"Back home they called me Tobble the Terrible."

Khara stared at the ground. She might or might not have been smiling.

"So sell me it is?" I said. "To the highest bidder?"

"You think I have choices." Khara's voice was a whisper. "When I have none. I have no other way to help Byx. And if helping Byx helps me, so be it. I need the money for my family."

I looked at her sharply. It was the first Khara had ever mentioned her family.

"Why not sell your sword?" Tobble asked.

Khara pulled the sword a few inches out of its scabbard. "This rusty thing?"

"It wasn't rusty when you were dicing up serpents," Tobble pointed out.

Khara leaned toward us, her gaze intent. "This sword," she said slowly, "has been in my family for generations, and I am the first woman ever entrusted with it." She shoved the sword back into its worn leather scabbard. "It will stay safe while in my care, even if that means my death."

Tobble held up his paws. "Fine. If you value a rusty blade over the life of my friend Byx, so be it."

"It's not that simple, Tobble," Khara said. "It never is. Dairnes are rare in this part of the world for a reason. They've been hunted to near extinction for their fur—"

"It is amazingly soft," Tobble interjected.

"But there's something else at work here, something I don't understand." Khara chewed on a nail, lost in thought. "What the Murdano's soldiers did at the mirabear hive"— she looked at me, then looked away—"didn't make any sense. They were killing for killing's sake. And I don't know why.

What I do know is that Ferrucci, at least, will value Byx as a living creature. He's a scientist, not a killer. This is Byx's best chance to stay alive. You have to trust me."

"From trust to dust," I muttered.

Khara cocked her head. "What did you say?"

"It's a dairne saying. It means if you trust a human too completely, you'll end up as nothing but dust."

"And yet you have no choice."

We fell into a cold and uneasy silence. Khara was the first to speak, and when she did, her voice was muted.

"Byx," she said, and then she added, turning, "and Tobble, you, too"—she inhaled deeply—"you love your families, yes?"

"Loved," I muttered, "might be the more appropriate verb."

Khara gave a small, terse nod. "Well, I love my family, too. And it is my job to help them weather hard times. No matter what the cost."

She locked her eyes on mine. I saw dark, deep pools of sadness. Whether it was my own gaze, reflected in hers, I could not say.

"My family is in dire straits," Khara said. Her voice cracked. It was a vulnerable sound, something I hadn't heard from her until now. A giving in, like winter ice on a pond tested too soon.

"My relatives are often hungry," she continued. "Ill. Sometimes even desperate. When I can, I send them the few extra coins I've managed to collect from my work as a guide. Finding Byx means I have a chance to truly help them, for the first time in my life. And it means helping Byx, too." She shrugged. "At least, that's my hope."

"Your hope?" Tobble demanded.

"Ferrucci is a good man, Tobble. Yes, he will probably pay me for bringing him one of the last of the dairnes. But he will also protect Byx." Khara rubbed her eyes. "If a safe haven exists for her, Ferrucci is the one man who can find it."

Khara reached toward Tobble and touched his shoulder, a gesture of penance, it seemed to me. "I can't do that for Byx, Tobble," she whispered. "And neither can you."

"I can try," Tobble said. "Which is more than you are doing."

Khara exhaled, long and slow. We avoided each other's eyes.

"I have a different question for you," I finally said to Khara. "When we get to the island, what will this Gharri person do with Tobble?"

"Oh, no one has much use for wobbyks," Khara said with an apologetic nod to Tobble. "They're mezzitti."

Tobble snorted.

"What's 'mezzitti'?" I asked. It was a word I didn't recall from my lessons.

Khara looked incredulous, clearly surprised by my ignorance. "Well, of course, there are six governing species: humans, raptidons, felivets, terramants, natites, and dairnes. That's according to the Antic Scrolls of the First Coimari. They are the species that can speak—"

"I speak," Tobble interrupted.

"—can speak," Khara continued, "can make tools, can learn and pass along learning, and are capable of theurgy."

"Unfair," Tobble grumbled. "What use is theurgy, anyway? Silly spells. Magical potions. Ridiculous visions."

"I wouldn't know," Khara said. "The law decrees you must be fifteen to begin training in theurgy."

"Dairnes don't practice theurgy much," I said. "Dalyntor calls—called—it a 'lost art.'"

"Women aren't allowed to study it," Khara said. "Not anymore, anyway."

"Anymore?" I repeated.

"Before this Murdano took power, some women were allowed to learn theurgy. My mother used to know a bit."

"So what are mezzitti?" I asked again.

"Mezzitti can't perform even the weakest theurgy.

"Mezzitti are species like wobbyks, starlons, and gorellis," Khara continued. "They can communicate with humans and use tools, but they lack the ability to do magic."

Tobble sighed loudly. "Totally unfair."

"The six great governing species may not prey on one

another, according to the Scrolls. At least that is the decree. Whether it is actually adhered to is another story. Especially when it comes to my own species."

"Meanwhile, feel free to eat me," said Tobble.

"Below mezzitti come all the species that cannot communicate with humans, use tools, or do magic," Khara said.

"Inferritti," said Tobble.

"Yes." Khara nodded. "Chimps, whales, crows, crickets, and on and on and on."

She stood, hands on hips. "Well, that's enough for now. We should rest. I hate to waste a day, but you two are in no shape to travel."

"I have more questions," I said. "Many more."

"I'm sure you do," said Khara. She looked at me with a strange mix of frustration and sympathy. "Get some sleep. We've a long way to go. We'll leave tomorrow morning before dawn."

"Rest," I muttered. As if that were possible after all I'd just heard. And yet when I looked over at Tobble, he was once again fast asleep.

I wondered if the ability to sleep anywhere, under any circumstances, was a wobbyk gift.

Khara draped him with a blanket and handed me one as well.

"I wish I could do more for you," she said quietly. "I really do."

She wasn't lying, that much I could tell. But it was cold comfort indeed.

Perhaps there is another way, I told myself. A way to avoid Ferrucci, to escape with Tobble, to find more dairnes, to . . .

I fell asleep, my mind whirring with plans, none of which seemed any better than the fate about to befall me.

18.
A Crumpled Map

I dozed fretfully off and on throughout the day. We had serpent again for dinner, and Tobble munched on leaves and bugs, but there were no more questions asked or answered. Khara seemed preoccupied. She spent much of the day near the cave entrance, pacing back and forth.

That night, I tried to force myself to sleep. But every time I closed my eyes, I thought of the horrors I'd witnessed. The deaths of my packmates. The hideous serpents. Who knew what more lay ahead?

It seemed like only moments ago I'd been safe in my mother's embrace, watching butterbats flutter overhead.

"Byx?" Tobble whispered late that evening. "Are you asleep?"

"No."

Tobble crawled closer, trailing his blanket. "Are you scared?"

"Yes," I said, because it was not in my nature to lie. And because I wanted someone else to know the truth.

"I'm not," Tobble said, his voice wavering just a bit. He gave me a sidelong glance. "Could you tell that's a lie?"

"Let's just say I'm beginning to see that there are many kinds of lies," I said gently. "You were very brave today, Tobble. You bit that giant serpent. What on earth were you thinking?"

He smiled, and his huge ears wiggled. "I wasn't."

"I'm grateful you tried to save me."

"Trying doesn't count."

"It does as far as I'm concerned."

Tobble rolled onto his stomach, chin cupped in his paw. "You're the one who's brave, Byx. I couldn't believe it when you leapt off that cliff."

"I couldn't either." I smiled in spite of myself. "To be honest, I had a little encouragement. In the form of people trying to kill me."

"What's it like to fly?" Tobble asked.

"I wish I could fly," I said. "But dairnes can only glide." I stretched my arms to reveal my glissaires. "Still, it's pretty wonderful."

"I fly in my dreams sometimes," Tobble said. "I'm usually gigantic, too. With big, sharp teeth. And I'm always brave."

I reached over and patted the little wobbyk's shoulder. His fur, though muddy in spots, was long and soft, the lovely silver-blue of a new moon. "You've been plenty brave, Tobble.

I think you should try to go home. Where is home, anyway, for you?"

Tobble's chin trembled, and for a moment I feared he was going to cry. "Bossyp. On the northwest coast. Far from here."

"They must be worried sick about you."

"I suppose. Although my parents tend to lose track of us." Tobble smiled wistfully. "It's perfectly understandable. Last time we counted, I had one hundred and twenty-seven brothers and sisters."

"One hundred and—"

"Wobbyks have eight litters a year. And most of us stay put. We don't move out. We just build more tunnels." He shook his head. "You should see us when we have a stibillary."

Khara, who was dozing by the fire, made one of her bog toad noises. Tobble and I shared a smile.

"What's a stibillary?" I asked.

"A ceremony, I guess you'd call it. We have them when we're forty-three, but only if we've achieved an act of bravery by then. It's to signify that we're grown up. There's a big celebration, and of course the official tail braiding."

"You mean your three tails?"

"You may not braid them into one tail until your stibillary. And you may not attend the stibillary until you have done something to prove your bravery."

I tucked my blanket under my chin. "Well, you've done that, and then some."

Tobble rolled onto his back, and we both stared at the moonsnails pulsing with pale light across the ceiling.

"You must miss everyone," I said.

"I do. But I know they'll be there waiting for me when I return." As soon as he said the words, Tobble gasped. "Oh, Byx. I'm so sorry."

"It's not your fault, Tobble," I said. I tried to hide my pain behind a forced smile, but I knew he could see my trembling lower lip.

I would never have that again. A family to wait for me. A family to miss me.

"For now," I said at last, "my only home is here. With you. But Tobble, whatever Khara's plans for me, this isn't your fight."

"Oh, but it is. Three saves, Byx. Wobbyk—"

"Code. Yes, I know. But still."

"There are some things I've been meaning to give you, Byx." Tobble sat up and reached inside the leather pouch he always carried. He pulled out several bunches of grass and weeds before he found what he was looking for. "Here. I'd forgotten about them until I opened my pouch at breakfast."

He removed a pawful of items and placed them on the floor. "I found these when I followed you. They were on the ground near the mirabear hive. I don't know why I picked them up. I thought you might want something, perhaps, from . . . there."

I stared at the objects. Bits and shards of my old life.

A broken pink-striped seashell. A little toy pup made of woven reeds. A small, flat rock with words carved into it. A frayed playa leaf.

One by one, I slipped the items into my pouch. I reached for the playa leaf. It was torn and singed at the edges, but even in the wan light of the moonsnails, I knew what it was.

"My map! My map of the First Colony." My fingers trembled as I held the leaf close, smudged and torn.

"You mean it belongs to you?" Tobble asked.

I could barely read my own writing, and not just because of my tears. Dairnes have a simple alphabet, and we all learn it as pups. But because we were always moving from place to place, we had little use for writing, and even less practice doing it. My handwriting was almost illegible.

Tobble rearranged his blanket and curled up just inches from me. "What is it?" he asked.

"A map based on an ancient poem. It's where the first dairnes are supposed to have landed." I pointed to a spot on a small island. "That's Dairneholme. My pack was headed there when . . ."

"To find more dairnes?"

"That's what they were hoping, anyway."

Slowly I began to recite the poem. When I got to "a living isle and floating jewel," I glanced over at Tobble. His eyes were closed, his breathing even. I assumed he was fast asleep again, but he surprised me by reaching out his paw.

I grabbed it and held tight. It was almost round, with rough black pads and small but impressively sharp claws. I was surprised at how light it was, and how warm.

I couldn't help but remember the night Jax and I had held hands and promised to keep each other safe.

And I couldn't help but think about how we'd failed.

"I should have been there," I murmured. "I should have died with all of them."

"Don't say that, Byx." Tobble squeezed my hand.

"I wish I could have saved them," I said, clutching the map to my chest. "But I can't even save myself."

"Don't worry, Byx," said Tobble. "We'll save each other."

When Khara woke us up a few hours later, I was still holding Tobble's paw.

19.
Dairne Meets Dog

Shortly before dawn, Khara, Tobble, and I headed out to fill waterskins at a nearby stream. The day's journey would be long, Khara warned us, and we couldn't count on finding water when we might need it.

My mind buzzed like a hive brimming with bees: questions, escape plans, possibilities, impossibilities. And yet nothing made sense. Nothing seemed realistic. Was I just going to acquiesce to Khara's plans for me?

What would Jax do? I asked myself. Myxo? My brave father? My intrepid mother? What would Dalyntor do in the face of this fate?

You are the runt, I told myself bitterly. A disappointment at your only task in life, which is to do your best, like all dairnes, to stay quietly alive.

It was my own fault I'd been captured. My own fault I didn't die bravely with my pack.

There was no valor in being the last to survive. Only humiliation and gut-wrenching guilt.

We left Vallino and our meager belongings in the cave. The approach to the stream was too rocky for him to navigate easily.

We drank freely from the cool water and filled Khara's waterskins to bursting. The sun, flushed as a ripe peach, peered over the horizon as we returned. We were almost to the cave when I caught a stray scent on the air and stopped short.

"What is it?" Khara asked. Instantly she retrieved the knife in her boot with her left hand. Her right hand hovered over the hilt of her sword, which once again appeared to be nothing but a rusty relic.

"Someone's there," I said under my breath. "Human. Male human." I would not be making that mistake again.

I sniffed again. "And a dog. Also male."

Khara motioned for us to follow behind her. Stealthily we crept forward, hugging the rocky wall.

When we came to a large boulder surrounded by stickle-grass, she paused.

"You two," she whispered, her voice barely audible. "Hide in the brush as best you can. Byx, if by chance you're seen, not a word from you. And get down on all fours. Don't let anyone see your pouch. Or your fingers. Or—" She sighed. "Just don't get seen, all right?"

Her tone was urgent, and there was no time to question the plan. I knew what she was saying: if anyone discovered me, I should act like a dog, not a dairne.

Tobble and I moved behind the boulder. It wasn't much of a hiding place, and the barbed stickers on the grass pulled at our fur. Still, we crouched out of sight as best we could.

Khara continued down the path, her footsteps soundless. She was just about to round a curve when something big, foul, and evil-smelling bounded into her, knocking her flat on the ground.

Khara lay motionless.

"She's unconscious," Tobble whispered.

We leapt from the bushes, all promises forgotten. We were halfway to Khara before I realized I was about to save the very person holding me captive.

Just at that moment, with a gasping intake of air, Khara came to. She blinked, saw the wiggling beast on top of her, and raised her knife, preparing to thrust it deep into the creature's side. But before she could move, it revealed a dripping pink tongue and promptly licked her nose.

Only one animal could be that moronic.

A dog.

"Stop!" a low voice yelled. "He's harmless!"

Around the bend hurtled a young man, a half-eaten pear in one hand and Vallino's reins in the other. The big horse followed behind.

With a great heave, Khara threw off the slobbering dog and jumped to her feet. The dog romped over to the young man.

"Thief!" Khara cried, using her unnaturally low voice, pointing at Vallino with the knife in her outstretched hand.

"Well, yes, as a matter of fact," the young man said calmly. "Is he yours?" he asked, nodding at the horse.

"Well, yes, as a matter of fact," Khara replied, perfectly mimicking his tone. In one flourish, she speared the pear with the tip of her knife and held it to his throat. "Explain yourself now, or you'll find this pear in your stomach. And it won't be because you ate it."

The young man seemed unfazed. "I was heading up the path when my dog scented your horse. He went into the cave and I followed. I thought perhaps the horse's owner had died."

"Died."

"Fallen off a cliff, for example. Or been consumed by a felivet. Why else would anyone leave such a fine mount behind?"

Khara rolled her eyes. "To forage, perhaps. To find water. To—"

"Relieve oneself? I suppose that's—"

"I was going to say," Khara interrupted sternly, "to gather grass for the horse." She pulled the knife away a few inches and removed the pear. Vallino watched hopefully.

"And speaking of dogs." The young man jerked his head

in my direction. "Yours is quite talented. Doesn't he get tired, walking on his back feet all day like a trained bear? Tell me: Can he juggle, too?"

Khara turned to see Tobble and me standing in the path. "I told you to—" she snapped, then caught herself.

Tobble and I looked at each other helplessly. Was it too late for me to play dog? I dropped to all fours and made fists of my hands. Then I opened my mouth and let my tongue loll out, pretending to pant. I even wagged my tail.

The real dog, lanky and brown and unkempt, bounded over to me. If he could tell I wasn't a dog, he showed no sign. His tail waved so frantically I thought it might break off and sail into the sky.

With absolute determination, the beast began to sniff me. My head, my feet, my back, my tail, my . . . everything. It was humiliating, but I knew better than to say anything.

When I could stand it no more, I let out a low, hopefully persuasive, growl.

The dog looked at me with wounded eyes.

"Dog!" the young man yelled, and the hound ran over to him, licking the man's hand in an appalling display.

"You named your dog 'Dog'?" Khara asked.

"Suits him perfectly, don't you think?"

"I can only assume that you answer to 'Thief.'"

"True enough, but you may call me Renzo. And you and your friends?"

"I'm Tobble," the wobbyk offered. "And this is—"

"None of your business," Khara finished for him.

Khara held out the half-eaten fruit to Vallino, who took the pear between his teeth, not willing to part with it. But even as she did so, her eyes never strayed from the young man.

He was taller than she was, with gold hair and intelligent, dark blue eyes. He carried three knives with him that I could see—one in each black boot, and one at his waist. I judged him to be a bit older than Khara, but since he was only the second human I'd ever been this close to, it was merely a guess.

"I'm going to let you live, Renzo," Khara said, keeping her voice deep, "but only because I'm too weary to kill anyone else this week."

"Most obliged." He raised a brow and pointed toward the cave. "You know, it seems we've yet to enjoy breakfast, Dog and I."

"Pity," said Khara. "It seems you won't be enjoying it with us."

"A pity indeed," Renzo said, not sounding altogether surprised. "Then before we take our leave, I must inquire: Might you be willing to sell your sword? It's not much to look at, but I lost mine in a wager, and I rather find myself in need. All kinds of scoundrels and blackguards in these parts. One can't be too careful."

"My sword is not for sale."

"I'll give you far more than it's worth," Renzo said, stroking Dog's head.

"I gave you my answer."

Renzo sighed. "Your dog, then. How much for him?"

I tried not to look alarmed. Khara was my captor, but I doubted Renzo would mean an improvement in my circumstances.

"He's not for sale, either."

"Shame. Dog here could use a companion on our journey."

"Mine's not much of a dog," Khara said, glancing my way with a smirk. "Disobedient in the extreme."

I busied myself chewing on my tail.

Renzo retrieved a walking stick and a leather bag on a long strap. He slung the bag over his shoulder, doffed his cap, then looked at Khara, his brow furrowed, as a slow smile dawned on his face.

"Fare thee well then, my good"—he paused for just a split second—"sir. I'm headed north. And you?"

Khara merely stared, her hands on her hips.

"Be wary, should you be traveling that way, too," Renzo said. "The Murdano's spies are everywhere. He's planning an invasion of Dreyland, some say."

"We won't be going that far," said Khara.

"So we are headed the same way. Perhaps our paths will cross again."

"They won't," said Khara, "if you plan to keep on living."

As Renzo passed by, his mangy dog paused to touch noses with me. He smelled of skunk carcass, of squirrel droppings, of all manner of things I didn't want to dwell upon.

"Off we go, Dog," called Renzo. "They don't want to play with the likes of us."

We watched them saunter away until they were out of sight.

"He seemed harmless enough," Tobble said.

"Can't say the same about his dog," I muttered, standing upright and flexing my fingers.

Khara slipped her knife back into her boot and grabbed Vallino's reins. "Man or dog, until we get where we're going," she said, glancing down the path one more time, "assume everyone—and I mean everyone—wants to do you harm."

20.
Questions

We headed off after a quick breakfast.

I walked beside Khara, my head just at the level of her feet, which were hanging over Vallino's side. Tobble, who seemed to have boundless energy, often ran ahead. He quickly learned not to walk directly in back of Vallino. Horses occasionally deposit "gifts" behind them.

We kept moving all morning. Khara led us to the northwest to avoid the Therian Marshes. "It's a slow route," she admitted. "But at least we'll avoid the mud."

"And the serpents!" Tobble added.

Around noon, we stopped near a sweet stream and ate some dried snake and thin-sliced onions Tobble had foraged. I borrowed Khara's knife, lashed it to a straight stick, and showed off my dairne skill at fishing. It took a while, but I gaffed two fish, a small trout, and a slightly larger purple twigfish.

It wasn't much of a showing. Any of my siblings would have done a better job by far.

As we moved on, I sensed that Khara's fear was lessening, even as a new nervousness was growing. She still checked the trail behind us, and from time to time she asked me if I smelled anything unusual. But it seemed her thoughts and hopes were directed forward now.

At night we made camp in a low depression within a glen. Tobble and I gathered twigs and branches, and Khara started a fire. We dined on cooked fish (for Khara and me), whirligig beetles (for Tobble), and berries (for all of us).

After we ate, I lay on my back and watched the stars stake out homes in the endless sky. I felt strangely at ease, lulled into a comforting place without questions. For long minutes, I didn't dwell on my past or fret about my future. I didn't ask if I would ever again look into the eyes of another dairne.

I just listened to the steady pulse of cricket song, throbbing like the earth's own heartbeat.

Khara and Tobble seemed calmer, too. They sat near the flames, gazing at the fire's hypnotic dance. I wondered what they were thinking, and at last, curiosity got the better of me, although I hated to interrupt the calm.

"You no longer seem worried about the poachers," I said to Khara.

Khara raised her eyebrows in surprise. "What makes you say that?"

"Dairne intuition?"

"Well, you're right, as it happens. Poachers are outlaws everywhere within the kingdom. But as a practical matter, they're only in real danger when they approach settled lands."

"So we're getting close to our destination?"

Khara pointed vaguely to the east. "The United Villages of Dolgrate are a few leagues that way." She twisted and pointed to the northwest. "The Free Traders City-State is a few leagues in that direction. We still have to keep an eye out for the Murdano's men, but soldiers aren't stealthy. We'll hear them if they're near."

"You know this area well, then?" I asked.

"Well enough."

I hesitated to ask my next question, given my own experience. Still, there was so much to know about this girl. "Do you have any . . . family nearby?"

Khara looked at me, her face expressionless. "In a manner of speaking."

"How about friends?"

"I don't have any friends."

Tobble's eyes went wide. "But everyone has friends!"

"I didn't," I said. "Not really. I mean, my siblings were my friends, I suppose."

"Friends are a luxury we can't always afford," Khara said without emotion.

I wanted to press further, but I was coming to understand that Khara was frugal with words. She spoke when she wished to and otherwise remained silent. No prodding on my part would get her to say anything she was not ready to say.

We were a bad match, as captive and captor went. I wanted to ask a thousand questions. She rarely wanted to answer even one.

I love that you ask so many questions, my mother had said to me. That's how we learn.

But sometimes questions have no answers. And even when there are answers, they may not be what we want to hear.

The gentle wind shifted, laden with familiar scents of honey and lavender: smells from my past, from my life before pain.

I closed my eyes to keep the tears from coming, as homesickness washed over me like a cold and biting wave.

We traveled for two more days. When Tobble or I grew footsore, Khara put us up on Vallino's back to ride for a while. In exchange, we gathered tender beeflowers that grew alongside the path and fed them to the horse.

Sometimes he would nuzzle us in thanks, or let out a satisfied nicker. He seemed to be especially fond of Tobble.

"I wonder what Vallino thinks about all day," Tobble said while riding atop the big horse on the second evening of our journey.

"He has two thoughts, I'm guessing," I said. "One is 'I'm hungry.'"

"And the other?" asked Khara.

"'I'm not hungry.'"

"You're just saying that because he's not one of the six governing species," Tobble objected. "That doesn't mean he's not pondering great philosophical questions."

As if in answer, Vallino lifted his tail to leave a particularly odorous "gift" on the path.

"Never mind," said Tobble, and Khara and I both laughed.

At the point where the trail became a road, Khara said, "Well, I suppose it's time for me to become a boy once again."

"Why?" Tobble asked.

"We'll soon be encountering fellow travelers. And it's easier to accomplish just about anything as a male," Khara explained as she tied back her hair.

"That's not fair," Tobble said. "It shouldn't matter whether you're a male or a female."

"No," Khara agreed. "But it's been my experience that life is rarely fair." She looked me up and down. "We have to disguise you as well, Byx."

"Because I'm a dairne."

"Yes. You're a rarity. And rare things draw unwanted attention."

I shifted uncomfortably. "How will I disguise myself?" I asked.

But of course I knew the answer.

Khara grinned. "If you walk on all fours, avoid speaking, and occasionally wag your tail—"

I sighed loudly. "I know I have to do this. But let me make clear: I am not a dog."

"Yes, I know," Khara said. "If you were a dog, I wouldn't be debating this with you."

"I've never liked dogs," Tobble volunteered. "They love to chase wobbyks. Also eat us."

"Here's the thing," I said. "'Dog' used to be an insult to dairnes. I don't mean that we despise dogs. We love them—"

"Try being treed by a hungry hound and then tell me how you feel about dogs," Tobble interjected.

"But in stories from the old days," I continued, "in the time when humans and dairnes lived side by side, one of the insults hurled at us was that we were 'nothing but dogs.'"

"Sorry, Byx," said Khara. "It's for your own good."

"I know." With a mighty sigh, I dropped to all fours. "Arf," I said without conviction.

"Who knew," Khara said, giving my head a perfunctory pat, "that it was possible to bark with such bitterness?"

21.
Civilization

Walking like a dog was comfortable enough for my bones and muscles, but the palms of my hands aren't tough, like the pads of my feet. As much as possible, I avoided the cobblestones of the Murdano's road and walked in the grass bordering it. Always I kept my fingers close together, and I never exposed my stomach, so that my pouch would not be revealed. My glissaires are only visible when I spread my arms for gliding, so they weren't an issue.

Apparently, passersby were convinced. Once, when a group of knights trotted past us, one actually leaned down from his massive battle horse to scratch the back of my neck with his gloved hand and call me a "good girl."

Tobble and Khara laughed under their breath, but I was not amused.

Still, I had to admit that humans generally treated dogs

well. More than once the people we passed tossed me morsels of food, which I forced myself to lap up without using my hands. Several children skipped over to pat my head and scratch my back.

The truth is, I found those interactions strangely pleasurable. Pleasurable but undignified.

"Your dog is so soft!" a young girl carrying a wooden bucket exclaimed. "Much softer than our dog."

"She just had a bath," Khara said, quickly herding us along. Later, we stopped by a small pond, and she spread a thin layer of mud all over my coat. "Dairne fur is much softer than dog fur," she explained. "That won't be as noticeable when the mud dries."

I sniffed at my muddy tail. "Let me know if you think of any other way I can humiliate myself."

Khara stepped back to admire her handiwork. "I'll be sure to."

The more we walked, the more people we encountered, both coming and going. Some had wagons pulled by horses. Some carried bags over their shoulders. Some walked purposefully. Others meandered, chatting amiably. I saw far more men than women, and just a handful of children.

Once we saw an old man, elegantly dressed, stop mid-stride just ahead of us. I'd noticed him limping, favoring one foot, for some time. He yanked off his boot and tossed it aside, cursing creatively.

As we neared, we could hear him muttering under his breath, an odd, unmusical string of syllables.

"Theurgy, no doubt," whispered Tobble.

Suddenly, in a puff of pink smoke, the old man's worn boot was replaced.

Unfortunately, it was replaced with a delicate pink lady's shoe.

Tobble rolled his eyes. "Told you magic is ridiculous."

Khara stifled a smile as we passed the old man, who was now cursing even more creatively. "It does sometimes seem like a dubious distinction that the six governing species hold," she said. "Just because an old man can conjure a shoe, does that make him more fit for power than, say, a brave and resourceful wobbyk?"

Tobble smiled, clearly pleased at her words. "I wonder if theurgy could be used to help Byx find more dairnes?" he asked. "That would actually be useful."

"I doubt it," said Khara. "Theurgy has limited use, unless it's been studied for years by someone with natural talent."

About an hour later, I smelled the sea, a fact I whispered to Khara when no one was around to notice.

"We're getting close," she acknowledged.

"Will we find a boat to the island?" Tobble asked.

"We'll find the natites. The water is their rightful domain. They will take us, or not, as they choose."

"Have you ever seen a natite, Byx?" Tobble asked. He had a habit of forgetting that I was not allowed to speak.

Either that, or he enjoyed tormenting me.

I gave my head a subtle shake to indicate "no."

"Well, there are many types of natites," Tobble explained as he waddled beside me. "Some are almost as vast as whales. Others are the size of men, but with special neck flaps for breathing underwater. And their skin is green."

After a moment, he added, "Also, some are dangerous."

And after another moment: "And of course they're quite slimy."

When Tobble fell quiet, Khara took up a song, which she sang in a gruff masculine voice that disguised her sweeter natural tones:

"In ancient times
When life was new,
The great ones met
At Urman's yew.
Beneath the tree,
Beside the sea,
They planned the world
For you and me."

She laughed shyly. "I'm no singer. There are many other verses to the story."

"Tell us," Tobble urged.

"Well, it's mostly myth, but Urman's yew still stands, the oldest of trees. The story goes that all species gathered there on high ground as a flood swallowed much of the land."

I had of course heard of the flood, but not of any magical tree.

"There the ancients decided on how to organize the world once the flood receded. They decreed there would be governing species, each with its own domain and its own rights."

I nodded. I had heard all this from Dalyntor. How much, I realized with sudden affection and longing, I'd learned from that wise old dairne!

"Still and all, no rights for wobbyks," Tobble muttered.

"The natites, water breathers, would rule all the waters that opened onto the sea. Rivers, but only for the first league of their estuary, along with the mouths of bays and inlets. The felivets were given the northern forests, where they still rule and where no one goes without their permission. They're free to hunt in other forests, but they have no power there."

Felivets, those mighty and terrifying felines. They'd haunted my dreams since early childhood.

"The terramants were given the earth below its crust, the deep mines and hidden underground rivers and lakes," Khara went on.

I shuddered. Terramants were insects the size of horses. Another reason for bad dreams.

"And then, of course, there are the raptidons. They rule the sky and the upper reaches of trees and mountains, where they make their nests."

"And humans?" Tobble asked, stepping aside to let a carriage pass.

"Humans were given the rest of the world."

Tobble jerked his head my way. "What about the dairnes?"

Khara sang:

"The dairnes so true,
So free of greed,
May come and go,
Take what they need."

I waited until we reached a shady corpo tree, laden with pale yellow flowers with a fragrance of wet grass, and sat down to rest. Leaning against the trunk, hidden from the road, I felt free to use my voice again.

"What does that mean, Khara," I asked, "'the dairne so true, so free of greed'?"

Khara tilted her head. "Have you been taught nothing of your own people?"

"We have our poems and tales and songs," I said. "But . . .

well, dairne poems are only about dairnes. At least the ones I learned."

"In ancient times dairnes were everywhere," Khara said. "Most lived with their own kind, but they were honored guests at all assemblies. The ability to separate truth from lies made dairnes valuable, especially where humans were concerned. Valuable and dangerous."

"Valuable and dangerous," I repeated, considering the words.

If I could tell the truth when others could not, if I was one of the few remaining dairnes—or even the very last, the endling—what would happen to me? Would I be exploited?

Or would I, somehow, be able to exploit my gift?

I shook my head. Was it really a gift, the ability to read the untidy hearts of humans?

Or was it a terrible curse?

Was that what Dalyntor had meant when he'd called truth telling a "burdensome gift"?

Perhaps I would find a way to to use my skill once we got to the isle. Perhaps Tobble and I could slip from Khara's grasp and make our way to . . . make our way to . . . where?

I realized, not for the first time, how exposed and rootless I was, without the guidance of my pack and my family.

In the world of dairnes, the pack is everything: root and branch, heart and soul.

Still, Myxo had pinned her hopes on the northern colony, and so had my pack.

I could start there.

It would provide me with a beginning, if not an ending.

With a little clutch at my heart, I recalled another of my father's sayings: "Only fools know both the beginning and the end of the story."

How I missed his calm and good-humored wisdom! So many times I'd rolled my eyes at his old-fashioned sayings, his proverbs and maxims. And yet I'd have given anything to have him there by my side.

It was strange, but the idea of escaping from Khara and striking out on my own filled me with dread. As long as I was with her, I felt relatively safe.

Well, perhaps not "safe."

But slightly less likely to be killed, at least.

It was an illusion, of course. Once she gave me to Ferrucci, who knew what my fate would be? Would he imprison me? Kill me? Put me on exhibition, like a two-headed freak?

And what would happen to poor Tobble, who had proven his loyalty more than once during our journey?

The closer we got to civilization, the more odd and disturbing, but also exciting, things became. Until now, my life had been nothing but a handful of packmembers and the natural world we'd inhabited. This world was different, full of tall humans and horses, of wagons and carts loaded with unusual objects and unfamiliar food, of shouts and noises.

And smells. Always more smells. Some I recognized. Some Khara would explain, if I gave her a questioning look. What a dizzying mix it was: feces, urine, roses, cloves, brackish water, dirt, lavender, mold, burning charcoal, smoked meat, marjoram, rotting fish, fresh bread, ale, mead.

My poor nose was exhausted by the possibilities.

We'd grown, if not friendly, at least accustomed to each other, the way your back adjusts to an uncomfortable nest. After a while you give up tossing and turning and accept your fate, whether it be sharp, dry straw or stony, chill ground. You sleep, not well, but enough. You awake, not rested, but resigned.

So it was with our little band. We grew comfortable in our silences. We stared each night at our meager fire, lost in weary thoughts of life before, and life beyond.

After two more days, we arrived at last, weary and hungry, at Velt, the easternmost port, a bustling place crowded with ramshackle wooden buildings, some as many as three stories high, that towered above us like rickety trees. Lining the road to Velt were tables stacked with clay pots full of olives and peppers, preserved geet, strings of rockroot and garlic arrayed in rows. Khara fended off a relentless stream of beggars and sellers offering rugs, pots, knives, roasted cotchets on sticks, hats, and insects trapped in amber. I wove between stalls and legs, oddly afraid to lose sight of Khara, while at the same time vaguely hoping an escape route might present itself.

Finally we approached the water's edge and found ourselves looking out at a swaying forest of masts. I recognized many types of boats from my lessons with Dalyntor: tiny pinnaces, skiffs and jolly boats, even bloated freighters.

Tobble hissed. "Pirate ship!" he said, pointing at a boat slightly smaller than the freighters. It had two raked masts and shining brass cannons arrayed down each side.

"Don't worry. We have no business with pirates," Khara assured him. "We're looking for a ferry to the isle."

I looked around and risked a whispered question. "If the natites rule the seas, why do they allow pirates?"

"That's a very good question," Khara said. "They allow fishing boats and freighters but will not allow the Murdano to build a navy. No one knows for certain why the natites do anything, but most people believe they tolerate the pirates in exchange for information about the world of the land. I doubt that's the only reason, though."

We found the ferry landing after a frustrating search. A boxy vessel was nestled up to the dock by way of a series of gangplanks. Humans and horses and carts moved along in an orderly system overseen by men wearing identical shifts of blue and green.

"Neither of you speak," warned Khara, who was sitting astride Vallino. "This may be . . . complicated."

We stood in line and shuffled slowly forward as people ahead of us climbed aboard. Finally it was Khara's turn to speak to one of the two liveried men acting as guards.

"We're going to the isle," she said.

"Oh, are you just?" the guard said, half belligerent, half amused. "A boy, a horse, a dog, and a wobbyk. And what is your purpose in visiting the isle?"

"I have a valuable scientific specimen to show to the academicians."

"Is that right? What valuable specimen?"

"It's not for you," Khara said sharply. "I have orders to present it only to certain people. To certain high scholars."

This was a Khara I had not yet seen. She was commanding, even haughty.

Cautiously, the guard peered up at Khara. "Name?"

"Khara Melisandra."

"You're a Melisandra? What are you doing in Velt? You're southerners, you people."

"We're free farmers," Khara said. "My father's estate is twice the size of this filthy little town. And I've already told you why I am here."

I had no idea what a "Melisandra" was. I knew Khara was

lying, and I was astounded to realize that the man did not. Why wouldn't she tell the truth?

But I kept silent. Silent as a dog.

Not that I was resentful.

The guard shrugged. "I don't know you. You do not carry the natite pass, so you'll have to talk to them. Tie your horse up and go into that building. Tell them your story."

I sensed Khara's nervousness, but she obediently tied off Vallino. We stepped through a darkened doorway into a fine two-story building, not leaning, but straight, not shabby, but freshly painted in blue and green. Most of the building extended out over the water, supported on stilts.

We stood on a narrow platform. It was dark, with just a single guttering torch. The only light came from sun prismed through the water, bouncing curves of light around the walls.

Immediately before us were four taut ropes running from massive pulleys that hung from the ceiling. Two more humans in green and blue wore bored expressions. As soon as they saw us, they sighed and began hauling on rope ends that slowly turned the pulleys.

Like some great, sea-dwelling beast, a rusty steel cage rose from the water.

Tobble stared. Even Khara's eyes went wide.

Within that cage I saw a creature from a dream, a fantasy thing made of fish scales and shimmering green skin.

"That," said Tobble, "is a natite, Byx."

22.
The Ferry

The natite was smaller than a human, but larger than a dairne. Its head was shaped like a ship's bow, a bony ridge down the front separating two huge eyes the deep blue of the sky at day's end. Its mouth was a triangle, flattened a little at the top, its ears mere filigree placed high on the sides of its head. Below the ears were gills, three flaps of bloodred flesh that extended from the bottom of the ear down the neck.

I tried not to stare too long at its body. It was vaguely human in shape, thought it would never be mistaken for a human. Green flesh covered its powerful shoulders and chest, and two huge, writhing tentacles rose from the creature's shoulder blades.

The natite's body fused into a sort of fishtail covered in scales. The tail ended in horizontal flukes, but with a nasty surprise: rising between the flukes was a sort of spike perhaps a foot long, an ivory horn that was serrated along the bottom and glittering sharp at the point.

The natite sat, almost daintily, in a steel chair bolted into the cage. I noticed that the cage extended only on three sides, while the back was open. The cage was meant to protect the natite from—well, from us, I supposed.

The creature blinked slowly. A translucent membrane covered one eye, then retreated as another membrane lowered over the other eye.

"Eret wik thung woa chulas scrit?" it said.

One of the bored humans translated. "Why shall we grant passage over the sea, our home?"

"We wish to go the isle," Khara said. She repeated the lie she'd told earlier.

"Woa eret escapil nyet?"

This turned out to mean "Why have you no sea pass?"

"It was destroyed in a fire."

The natite considered this. Then, after translation, it said, "You must pay the blood tax."

Khara bristled and shook her head, but after three more rounds, the natite was unmoved.

"What's the blood tax?" Tobble said, echoing my thoughts.

"It looks as though you're about to see," Khara said grimly. She stepped to the very edge of the platform. The natite leaned in and one of the massive tentacles on its back whipped forward, seizing Khara's wrist.

The natite shifted closer, and with a sudden speed that caused me to emit a very undoglike yelp of surprise, it sank the green needle teeth at the end of its tentacle into her wrist.

Khara flinched at the pain.

The natite sucked on her wrist for several seconds. Then the tentacle released her and she drew back a wrist covered in slime, with two bloodred punctures.

"Du aster cun wallek," the natite said. Translation: "You are free to use the ferry." Its human servants began winching it back down into the water.

"They eat blood?" Tobble cried as we stepped back out into the sun, breathing sighs of relief.

"No," Khara said. "The natites sample blood. They can pin down elements in it that identify a particular person. Somehow, by means we don't understand, they can share this information instantly with every other natite in the world. Once they know who you are, if you cross the sea again, they will know you by some obscure natite sense, even long after your wound heals. It's like having your travel documents."

"Did it hurt?" Tobble winced at his own question.

"A little," Khara said. "But the pain is not the problem. The problem is that I am now known to the natites. Any time I wish to cross again, they'll recognize me and know where I am." In a low voice she added, "I do not wish to be known to anyone, let alone tracked for the rest of my days anytime I travel on water. In the past, I've always managed to get hold of a forged sea pass. Usually by way of a hefty bribe. In that case, you don't need to go through . . . all this. I just didn't want to risk attempting a bribe, not with you in tow, Byx."

We retrieved Vallino, who snorted suspiciously at the slight wound on Khara's wrist.

The ferry had two levels. The lower one, in a dark passage, held banks of weary-looking men at their oars. "Who are they?" Tobble asked in a whisper.

"Indentured servants," Khara answered, her brow knit in a frown. "Some prisoners, perhaps."

We moved on to the flat main deck. It was open to the air, which was calm and cool and almost as crowded as the streets of Velt had been.

After a while the human crew began casting off ropes, and a deep drumming began. The oars lowered into the water and swept in time to the beats.

I watched Velt recede as we pulled away, a shabby, wild, dirty place I felt no desire ever to see again. I was more concerned about what lay ahead, and I took advantage of my dog status to scamper up to the bow and look.

The sea was dotted with all manner of craft, some heading to the isle, some rowing between boats, some hoisting sails en route to the sea.

But as fascinating as all that was, it was Cora di Schola,

growing slowly closer, that captivated me. It was edged by a stone wall, ten feet high at least, punctuated by towers rising twice that height. Beyond the walls were pillared marble buildings with round windows, decorated with stone carved to resemble flames.

Above all that rose a ziggurat, a rectangular tower atop a circular base level, ringed by a walkway that rose in stairlike levels, higher and higher. The huge temple glowed red in the lowering sun.

Khara and Tobble joined me. Khara, following my gaze, nodded. Pretending to speak only to Tobble, she explained, "That's the Pillar of Truth. It's controlled by the scholars. Each level is devoted to one of the great governing species."

"Is there a level for the dairnes?" Tobble asked, as if reading my mind.

"There was the last time I was here," said Khara. "But it was mostly just a dusty library. No . . . staff."

No dairnes, is what she meant to say, I thought bitterly.

We ate what little we had and drank from the cistern amidships. When night came, we curled up together at the feet of Vallino. I tried to sleep, but each time I closed my eyes, a wave of despair overtook me. What should I do now? What could I do now?

On the one hand, I could try to escape again.

On the other hand, what would happen to Tobble?

On the one foot, I had nowhere to go, even if I did escape.

On the other foot, if I did nothing, I was leaving my fate to others.

I opened my eyes and saw stars, pinpricks in the blanket of night.

I had nowhere else to be. I had no family to pine for.

I was alone.

I had no idea where I was going, or why. I had no plan. I had no goal. I was baggage being escorted by Khara to an end I could not imagine. But part of me, a large part, I am ashamed to confess, did not care.

I remembered with perfect clarity my father's whispered words about me: I dreamed she was the last to live.

The last to live. The endling.

I pulled the wrinkled map from my pouch. Were there more of me—more dairnes—somewhere in the world? My pack had thought so—hoped so, at any rate.

But I had no pack anymore.

And even if I tried to find out if there were more dairnes in the world, did I really want to know the answer?

When next I closed my eyes, they stayed closed. I dreamed of my mother and my father, of my brothers and sisters.

But even in my dreams of them, I knew they were no more.

PART THREE
MY FUNERAL

23.
Cora di Schola

Although the trip took only a few hours, we weren't able to disembark until the next morning, the water was so crowded with vessels. It was a relief to stand, once again, on dry, unmoving land.

The port was shaped like a crescent moon, deep and wide, with stone piers jutting far out into the water. At every possible docking point, passenger boats, private yachts, and freighters were tied up two, even three, deep, so that people on the outermost berths had to walk across other boats to reach land. I'd had no idea there were this many ships and boats in all the world, let alone right here.

"This is far busier than the last time I visited the isle," Khara said, frowning. "Something's going on."

We pressed our way into the crush of humans and horses. Workers shuffled by, hefting big loads on their backs.

Expensively attired nobles rode on palanquins that jostled by the crowd. Horses and donkeys vied for space.

It had not occurred to me that the isle was also a town. Somehow I'd pictured nothing but libraries full of scrolls, where brilliant minds debated important matters. But of course even scholars needed to eat and sleep and buy clothing. And Cora di Schola wasn't just any town. It was a town filled to bursting with representatives of the great governing species.

We hadn't gone far before a pungent scent struck me with the force of a hammer. A felivet, and close, no less!

I turned and my blood froze. A huge, sleek, catlike creature, black with golden stripes, sauntered casually between two men who seemed entirely unafraid of it.

It was one thing to have scented felivets when I'd been with my pack. It was quite another to be within clawing—or chewing—distance of one.

Tobble and I dropped back in fear, but Khara urged us to keep pace. "There's no need to be afraid of the felivets here on the isle," she said. "All species are bound by treaty to avoid violence."

Indeed, as we made our slow progress I saw sidewalk cafés where humans sat in chairs while felivets lounged on wooden benches. Their fur varied wildly. I saw single colors like indigo, maroon, and black, along with striped, spotted, and patched coats. But they all shared the same terrifyingly muscular body shape, one that said: I could kill you with a single swipe of my great paw.

Raptidons were everywhere, too, often perched on T-shaped poles, tearing at animal flesh stuck on skewers. Those, at least, I'd glimpsed before, in my former life. Like felivets, they seemed to come in many variations, but all had massive wingspans, fearsome talons, and hooked beaks that made me shudder.

We even passed several pools for natites. They lounged in the water, their lower halves submerged, chatting amiably with felivet, raptidon, and human alike.

I saw no terramants, and to be perfectly honest, I was relieved. The sight of felivets lying within a single great leap of me was disturbing enough. Raptidons, creatures that could easily snatch puppies or badgers to their nests for a quick meal, preened far too close for my comfort. And I was still unsettled by my introduction to the natites. I didn't need any carnivorous insects to make me nervous. I was plenty uncomfortable already.

Vallino and Tobble didn't seem particularly thrilled, either. Both eyed the crowds warily, looking as anxious as I felt.

"Let's find a room and a stable for poor Vallino," Khara said. "I know a place."

We left the main street and entered a network of alleys so narrow that Khara had to dismount and lead Vallino through. The horse's flanks brushed both sides of the stone buildings looming above us.

We came at last to a large courtyard. On one side was a pretty, whitewashed inn bearing a sign that read *The Hanged Cow*. A painted illustration softened the name a bit: it showed a cow suspended by a rope around its middle.

"That's a tad grim," I whispered.

Khara laughed. She untied her bag of belongings from Vallino's back and held up an index finger. "Wait here," she instructed. "And don't talk to anyone. You'll find that most on the isle, no matter the species, speak the Common Tongue instead of Nedarran."

We watched as she slipped behind a stack of wooden boxes piled high at the far end of the courtyard. A few minutes later she emerged, not as Khara the boy, but as Khara the girl. She wore a long blue dress trimmed in white, and her hair hung loose, freshly combed.

"I see you're a female again," I said in a hushed voice. "Must I remain a dog?"

Khara nodded. "For now."

"Arf," I muttered.

"Why the change, Khara?" Tobble asked.

"The isle is more relaxed," she said. "A place of intellectual freedom where women are treated more equally. At least that's how it used to be."

Khara told Vallino to stay put, and she, Tobble and I entered through a low door. The inn had seemed quiet from the outside, but the interior was bustling, filled with crowded tables and boisterous customers. Two barmaids threaded through the crush of people, carrying pitchers of ale, mead, or cider. The proprietor, a large man with a hairless head, a round belly, and forearms covered in tattoos, rushed the length of the bar, taking orders, pouring, and cleaning.

Khara received some strange looks as she pushed her way to the bar, perhaps because there were very few women in the room. To me, that seemed far less disturbing than the ten-foot-long felivet lounging on a deep bench against the far wall. The sleek cat seemed to be absorbed in conversation with a grizzled old man.

I wondered what on earth they could possibly have to talk about.

"Eldon!" Khara called to the barman. When he didn't respond, she called again, more forcefully, "Eldon! Over here!"

The barman turned, registered the source, and grinned.

"Khara! It's been a long time." He lowered his voice. "You still . . . living the high life poaching?"

"Sadly, yes. Do you miss it?"

Eldon rolled his eyes. "Gets much wilder here than it does in the forest."

"I'm hoping you can help me, Eldon. I need a room for myself, my dog, and my pet wobbyk, and a stable for my horse."

Tobble bristled a bit at being described as a pet. I felt no pity: I was being described as a dog.

"A room?" Eldon was incredulous. "But there isn't a room for rent anywhere on the isle!"

Khara frowned. "What do you mean?"

"This eumony has the town swollen to three times its normal population."

"This . . . what?"

"Eumony. Isn't that why you're here?"

"Eldon, let's begin again. What is a 'eumony'?"

Eldon shrugged and made a face. "A new thing, cooked up by Araktik, the Murdano's Seer, and the Council of Scholars. It's a sort of funeral, though the mood so far is anything but sad, as you can see." He indicated the raucous room.

"A funeral?" Khara asked. "Who died?"

"It's not a who, it's a what. An entire species. It's been announced officially that the dairnes are extinct."

Khara blinked.

Tobble reached a trembling paw for me.

I yelped and covered it with a bark.

"It's a sort of funeral for the species, as I understand it," Eldon said. "Three days of drinking and carousing. And some solemn speeches, no doubt. But mostly—"

I heard no more.

I slipped through the crowd to the courtyard. I found a dark, ivy-laced corner and crouched there.

I could not seem to stop shivering.

I could not seem to stop sobbing.

I had arrived in this place just in time to witness drunken revels for the death of my species.

Until this moment, I'd feared that I was the last of my kind.

But I hadn't truly believed it.

Now I did.

I yanked my map from my pouch. I looked at it through tears.

I saw rivers and valleys, plains and mountains. I saw a moving island in a vast sea.

I saw a silly drawing by a silly pup, taught by a silly old dairne.

I saw the truth.

I was an endling.

24.
A Dairne Alone

I barely spoke after the morning's revelation, though Khara and Tobble tried, off and on all day, to talk to me.

We spent much of the day sitting in the courtyard, waiting to see if Eldon could find a place for us to stay. It was early evening before he finally secured the last stall in a filthy stable not far from the inn.

Once we were settled there, Eldon brought Khara blankets and a basket filled with leftovers from the kitchen: sausage, slices of bread, carrots, goat cheese, white olives, plika fruit, and a jug of water.

"Wish the accommodations were a mite better," he said, kicking at the dirty straw.

"I'm grateful for your help," she said. "We'll be fine."

Eldon leaned down to pat my muddy head. "Nice doggie," he said. "Needs a bath, I'd wager." He straightened. "You'll be staying for the eumony, then?"

Khara glanced at me. "No, I've business at the Academy tomorrow. Then we'll be off."

"Sorry again I can't do more for you, Khara."

"You've done plenty, Eldon. You have my thanks."

"You're most welcome," he said as he took his leave.

Khara spread out the food Eldon had procured. "Byx," she said, "you haven't eaten all day. Try to eat some meat, at least."

Tobble stroked my shoulder. "Please, my friend," he said. "You have to eat something."

"Why?" I asked. "Why should I eat, Tobble?"

"Because . . . because you have to stay strong."

"I'm the last dairne on earth. What point is there in staying strong? What point is there in living at all?"

"It seems to me," said Tobble gently, "that when you're the last of anything, you're especially important to the world."

"My father had a saying," I said. My voice was hoarse from crying. "Well, he had lots of sayings. But the one he repeated to me and my siblings from the moment of our births was this: 'A dairne alone is not a dairne.'"

Tobble tilted his head. "I'm not sure I understand."

"It means," Khara said, placing a slice of sausage and a piece of cheese beside me, "that Byx feels she doesn't have a place to belong in the world without the company of other dairnes."

"It means," I said, "that the pack is everything. And without it, I am nothing."

Khara handed Tobble the carrots. He passed one back to her. "For Vallino."

"Are you sure? Eldon found some hay for him, and a bit of barley."

"Rhime shhr," Tobble replied, his mouth already full of carrot.

Vallino accepted the carrot with a grateful nicker.

"Byx," Khara said, tearing off a piece of bread, "I don't have a 'pack' to speak of, myself."

"But you have family somewhere," I said. It was half statement, half question.

Khara didn't answer right away. "I . . . believe so."

"And you're clearly not the last human in the world."

"No, but—"

"Then you can't know what I'm feeling," I said flatly.

Khara chewed on her bread, gazing at me thoughtfully. I saw pity in her eyes, and perhaps even sadness.

"Here's one thing you might not have considered," she said at last. "This species funeral, this 'eumony,' as they call it, is a ceremony to acknowledge that dairnes are officially extinct, correct?"

I gave a terse nod.

"Well, forgive me if I'm mistaken, but I seem to be talking

to a real, live dairne at this very moment." Khara placed some olives next to Tobble. "Explain that."

Tobble slapped his forehead with a paw. "Khara's right, Byx. If they're wrong about you, they might be wrong about other dairnes. Maybe there's still hope."

"And maybe there isn't," I said.

"But you can't know for sure," Tobble insisted.

I tried, for a moment, to find the part of myself that had always been so hopeful and curious. Could I have lost that old Byx so quickly and completely?

Khara gulped water from Eldon's jug. "And here's another question," she said. "Why did the Murdano's soldiers kill an entire pack of dairnes, knowing that the species was about to be declared extinct? Why weren't they under orders to take you all alive?"

"They were on patrol, far from the capital. Perhaps they didn't know," Tobble said.

"Very little happens in Nedarra without the Murdano's say," Khara said. "Trust me on that."

I shrugged. "Does it matter? They did what they did. And now here I sit in a horse stall, in a town I never wanted to visit, pretending to be a dog, the captive of a girl who intends to sell me tomorrow to the highest bidder." I shot Khara an angry glare. "Think about it, Khara. When your friend the scholar sees that I'm a dairne, you'll be able to charge a high price indeed for me. For you, this eumony couldn't come at a better time, could it?"

Khara looked wounded. "If it weren't for me, Byx, you'd be dead right now."

"As I should be," I whispered. "As I should be."

25.
The Pillar of Truth

It was a long night. A very long night.

I woke, eyes crusted with sleep, and rinsed my head in Vallino's water bucket, to his great annoyance. Khara tore apart pieces of stale bread and shared them with us, but I was in no mood to eat.

"Let's get this over with," Khara said. Her voice was resigned. She stood and brushed stray bits of straw from her dress. "At least you'll be able to stop playing dog, Byx."

Tobble yanked at the hem of Khara's dress. "Please, Khara," he said, his big eyes shiny with tears, "isn't there some other way?"

Khara looked from Tobble to me and back again. "You must believe me. If I thought there was another way to protect Byx, I would do it."

"Even a way that didn't line your pockets?" I asked.

"Yes," she said. "Even then. But with the eumony coming, I can't protect you from the world, especially not now. And not even here on the isle. Neither can you, Tobble."

"I can try," Tobble said, crossing his arms.

"Ferrucci is our best hope. He is powerful. He is wise. And he understands the ways of the Murdano."

"Tobble," I said, "I'm grateful for your loyalty. But I think you should make your way home now. There's no telling what will happen to me after today. And you heard Khara: they'll have no use for a wobbyk here. Even the bravest of wobbyks."

Tobble shook his head. "By now, my friend, you must have realized I'm not that easy to get rid of."

That word—"friend"—made me smile, even as hot tears filled my eyes. I looked to Khara for help, but she merely shrugged.

"Wobbyk Code, Byx," she said. "Tobble has a mind of his own. There's nothing I can do."

We left Vallino in the stable. Eldon had assured us the horse would be safe, and with the swelling crowds on the streets, taking him with us would have been challenging indeed.

It was still early when we left for the tower, but already the town was more crowded than the previous day. Crowded and festive. It seemed the loss of my species was quite the cause for celebration.

We came at last to the base of the Pillar of Truth, which towered grandly above us. It was protected by a low stone wall, behind which hired men wearing the black-and-gold livery of the Academy stood guard, tall pikes at parade rest, brass helmets shiny in the morning sun.

A line of people waited to speak to the gatekeeper, a gnarled old man. He, too, was impressively arrayed in Academy livery, but armed with a staff rather than a spear. He made quick decisions, jerking his staff back to indicate that petitioners could enter, thrusting it forward to tell the hopeful to leave.

We stood in line silently. Khara refused to meet my eyes or talk to Tobble.

"Don't worry," Tobble whispered to me, stroking my head, but I could feel his paw trembling.

For my part, I felt strangely calm, resigned to my fate, whatever it might be. I'd seen my pack, my family, my life destroyed. What more could anyone do to me?

The three of us came at last to the gatekeeper, who glared at Khara.

"I am called Kharassande. I am known to Ferrucci the Gharri. I wish to speak with him on an important matter."

The gatekeeper said, "And what are these with you?"

"This wobbyk is called Tobble. He's my servant. And this is my dog, Byx."

The old man glanced at Tobble only briefly before settling his gaze on me. He stared at me for too long and I felt helpless to look away.

"A girl, a wobbyk, and a dog," he said, with a faint shake of his head.

He jerked back his stick and we moved through the gate along a paved walkway until we reached an arched entry as tall as a maple tree.

The whole lower level of the tower was a vast circular open space. Massive lights, filled with some glowing red substance, hung on thick chains from the distant roof. Stairwells curved along the concave walls. I saw dozens of humans, two tan-and-black felivets, and a vividly orange raptidon flying lazy circles above us.

The space also boasted a long slit trench lined with stone, a pool for natites from the watery level below.

I expected a long wait, standing awkwardly in the midst of echoing space, but a messenger, a uniformed student carrying a list, approached us almost immediately. He was thin and gangly, perhaps Khara's age, with a clever face.

"Your name?"

"Kharassande."

"Follow me."

I'd seldom had occasion to use stairs, and never on all fours. They were quite a challenge to master, and the only way to do it, I realized, was at a run.

This meant I arrived at the next level of the tower before the others. The next level: the home of the terramants.

It was black as a moonless night. The air stank of rot.

And then it got worse.

I saw a dim and sickly light glow in the darkness. The light was green, but a red tracery appeared, revealing the shape of a terramant.

It reminded me of a beetle, or perhaps a mantis. Far larger than either, far larger than I had imagined. Bigger than a dairne. Bigger than the humans I'd seen, though its size was mostly in length. It had a low, sleek body, wings folded like armor over its back, and six large hind legs, jointed and spiked like a spider's.

The terramant's head was triangular, with two bulbous eyes. Around its mouth, which opened and closed with mathematical consistency, were four additional limbs, small but strong arms that each ended in a sharp, curved blade. The blades were useful, I suspected, for slicing through roots and soft earth under the ground. They could also be used to catch and eat various animals—including, according to the scary stories my older siblings had often told, dairnes.

More green and red lights glowed, and I realized my eyes were simply adjusting to the dark, making out the shapes of dozens of the huge bugs.

Khara, Tobble, and the messenger caught up to me.

"Terramants," Khara said with a shudder, looking almost as uncomfortable as I felt.

Again, in order to climb stairs on four legs, I had to run ahead, but this time I was prepared. I knew that the next level would be almost as disturbing as the last.

I emerged at the top of the stairs into a high-ceilinged room dense with trees. They were true trees, but unnaturally shaped, with shimmering blue leaves. Their branches were more horizontal than vertical, and woven together at various points, creating rough platforms.

On many of these branches, distributed in small groups and chatting amiably, were felivets.

The messenger arrived with Khara and Tobble.

"The felivets are, of course, perfectly safe," the messenger said. "They are bound by the agreements and treaties that govern the isle. These are the most learned of felivets: brilliant artists, poets, and philosophers."

Learned they might be, I thought, but I saw more than one pair of glittering eyes trained on me as we climbed up to the next floor.

"Where is the dairne floor?" Tobble asked the messenger.

"Top floor. But of course it's unused now."

We continued on to the human level, located below the raptidons. Here a sort of building had been constructed within the tower, a tower within a tower. None of it touched the outer wall, creating a broad, paved pathway that circled all the way around.

The messenger led us to the inner tower, and we stopped before an imposing gold door. He lifted his hand to knock, but before he could do so, the door swung open, held by a dark-haired young man wearing the simple gold-and-black tunic and trousers that seemed to be the student uniform.

"Please come in," he said. "I am Luca, Ferrucci's student. Also his assistant."

Khara and Tobble stepped inside, but my limbs seemed to freeze in place.

Luca grinned at Khara. She met his gaze and returned the smile—shyly, it seemed to me. "Your dog?" Luca said.

She turned. "Byx," she said. "Come."

Whether she was addressing me as a dog or a dairne, it didn't matter.

I took a breath and crossed the threshold, knowing my life was about to change again, and that I had no control over the outcome.

26.
Ferrucci

The room we entered was like nothing I'd ever imagined. It was cavernous, with walls entirely covered in deep shelves. Stuffed onto every square inch of those shelves were scrolls and leather-bound volumes. Rolling wooden ladders put even the highest books within reach.

I'd seen a book once. It had belonged to Dalyntor and was his most prized possession. It was small and thin, hand sized—nothing like these heavy tomes—and made of bark and pressed leaves. His great-grandmother had made it for him, filling it with ancient poems she'd carefully transcribed. Like many dairnes before her, she'd used a raptidon's talon for a writing implement and clairberry nectar for ink.

The words in that book, small enough for Dalyntor to keep in his pouch, might fill just a page or two of the enormous volume lying open on the wooden desk in the center of the room.

How much knowledge was contained in all these books and scrolls? It seemed to me that every fact in the world must be here within reach. Was there a question that couldn't be answered? A problem that couldn't be solved?

For a moment, I forgot my circumstances, forgot, even, my companions. Still on all fours, I headed toward the nearest bookshelf, fascinated by the scents of ink and paper, dust and leather.

"Ferru!" Khara exclaimed, and I stopped in my tracks. I turned to see her embracing an old man in a long gold robe inscribed in black with writings, runes and glyphs. He had cloudy green eyes and pale, papery skin. His long white beard fell in stiff waves, like a frozen waterfall.

"It has been far too long, Khara," Ferrucci said. "Have you come to witness the eumony? It will be quite the event. The Murdano's Seer, Araktik, is coming to officiate!"

Khara dropped her hands and said, her voice suddenly serious, "Well, I may be disrupting that ceremony a bit." She jutted her chin in my direction. "As you can see."

"My eyesight is not what it used to be," Ferrucci said with a sigh. "What is it you're referring to, my dear?"

"Byx," Khara said, "come closer."

I walked over, slowly, deliberately, on all fours.

"Well, what have we here?" Ferrucci asked.

Khara drew a deep breath. "Ferrucci, meet Byx."

"Your dog? Well . . . good boy. Good doggie."

I stood up on my hind legs and said, "I am honored to meet you, but I am not a dog."

Ferrucci gaped at me, speechless.

Luca dashed over, grabbing his teacher by the arm, as if he might topple over at any moment.

"I don't . . . ," Ferrucci said, peering at me through his cloudy eyes. "It's not . . ."

"It is, Gharri," Luca said, his eyes wide. "It's a dairne." He reached out a hand to touch my shoulder, and I instantly recoiled. "The fur, the pouch, the erect stance." Luca leaned close to examine my right hand. "The fingers, almost human!" He pulled back, head tilted, a strange, knowing smile blooming. "Under the forearms, there! A hint of the glissaires. Less visible than I'd imagined."

Slowly Ferrucci shook his head from side to side. "No, no, no," he said. He shot a stunned look at Luca, then Khara. "No, this is not possible!"

"But . . ." Khara frowned. "But it is possible, as you can see. Dairnes are not extinct, at least not yet."

I felt like an insect, trapped beneath the intent gazes of both scholar and student. I stepped back a few paces, and Tobble stood resolutely beside me.

"I brought Byx here," Khara said, "because I felt certain you would know what to do with a dairne. She masqueraded as a dog during our journey. You can imagine how worried I was that she'd be recognized for what she is."

"Of course," said Luca. "Far too many in Nedarra would pay any price for the last dairne. You were wise to come to Gharri Ferrucci."

Ferrucci blinked several times, as if he were waking from a nightmare. "Luca," he said urgently. "Lock the door immediately."

"Yes, Gharri."

"The rest of you, come with me, quickly!" Ferrucci snapped. "And you," he said to me, "on all fours, now!"

He practically ran from the library—impressive for a man his age—and waved us into a side room, also stuffed with scrolls and books. We crowded in, Khara and Tobble and I sharing questioning looks.

"Luca!" Ferrucci shouted. "Get your lazy rear end in here!"

Luca joined us, a thin layer of perspiration on his brow. "The door is locked."

"Then lock this one as well," said Ferrucci impatiently.

"Ferru," said Khara, and I could hear her forcing calm into her tone, "why the panic? I thought the Academy would be the one place we could relax. Do you not trust your fellow scholars?"

"For every true scholar here, there are ten of the Murdano's men, pretending to be students," Luca said under his breath.

"My assistant speaks the truth," said Ferrucci. He twirled

an arthritic finger through his beard, lost in thought. "The Academy is not . . . what it used to be."

"Then if it's not safe here, we must get Byx to a location where she can be sheltered," said Khara. "Perhaps in the north country. You must know any number of people who could provide a safe place."

Ferrucci waved an indifferent hand at Khara. "There's no safe place for an endling dairne."

"But you have to help Byx!" Tobble cried.

"Quiet, rodent, or I'll have you for lunch," Ferrucci said. He turned to face Luca. "Luca, take this dog—and yes, it is a dog, whatever you may hear—to the cells."

"Wait." Khara's eyes went wide. "What?"

"Cells?" Tobble squeaked.

"Never fear," Ferrucci said. "You will be rewarded, Khara. Handsomely rewarded."

"But why must Byx to be taken to the dungeon?" Khara demanded.

Dungeon. The word alone was terrifying.

I'd never seen one, but I knew, from Dalyntor's lessons, its purpose. Panic swept through me, hot, then cold. I could not seem to find enough air.

"I've committed no crime," I cried.

Ferrucci ignored us. "Luca, note this well: this conversation never took place."

"Yes, Gharri," said Luca. He unlocked a second door at the back of the little room. "Byx, come with me."

"I don't understand," Khara said, desperation creeping into her voice. "Please, Ferru, explain."

The old man patted her hand. "Trust me, my dear. I'm doing what's best. This is the only way."

"Byx," Luca said again. "Please follow me."

"I'm going too!" said Tobble.

"Impossible," said Ferrucci. "You'll stay here. With Khara."

"Patience, Tobble," Khara said. She exhaled slowly, sizing up the situation. "Byx, we have no choice but to trust Ferru."

From trust to dust.

I looked from Khara to Tobble and back again.

Would this be the last time I saw them?

I hugged Tobble briefly. "Be strong," I said, although my own voice was trembling.

"No, Byx—" he whimpered.

To Khara, I said nothing. What was there to say?

She gave me a bleak smile.

Ferrucci beckoned Luca close and whispered something in his ear. I caught some of the words, but unfortunately, they were in an unfamiliar language, probably Nedarran.

Once again on all fours, I followed Luca down a dank hallway. Behind me, the sound of Tobble's sobs and Khara's questions echoed softly against the black walls.

27.
Imprisoned

Reluctantly, I followed Luca around a circular interior stairwell that led downward, lit by wall-mounted torches.

A braver dairne, I thought, might try to escape. But I saw no path: no doors, no windows, no corridors. And nothing that could be used as a weapon.

In any case, there was no point. I might, perhaps, evade Luca for a moment, but only for a moment. I didn't know this place. Indeed, I knew very little about the nature of human buildings at all.

I tried to picture the vast tower in my mind. Would the dungeon be belowground?

At one point Luca paused and turned to me. "I'd tell you not to be afraid. That you're safe. But if what I've learned of dairne abilities is true, you'd know I was lying."

I didn't respond, although I was seething at his calm, almost smug tone.

Luca continued walking. I stayed on all fours, walking beside him. "My focus of study here at the Academy is dessag fauna," he said.

Again, I said nothing. But that didn't seem to dissuade Luca from continuing.

"It's a new term in the *Imperial Lexica Officio*, the Nedarran dictionary approved by the Murdano," he said, rolling his eyes. "Every edition, it seems there are new words to learn. Like 'eumony,' a funeral for a species. Or 'endling,' the last member of a species." He gave a wry laugh. "We humans are good at naming our mistakes."

We paused at a small landing, then continued down the winding stairs. The circle they traced had grown larger, spiraling like a sea shell.

Think, I told myself. Look for an opportunity, then take it.

At the same moment, I recalled my father's words: to rush is not necessarily to arrive. A moment might come for action. But for now, I would have to bide my time.

Luca was still babbling. "Dessag fauna," he continued, "are species that are in danger of becoming extinct. There are designated levels of threat, based on resources available, number of members left alive, that sort of thing. The Carlisian seal, for example. They were considered Level Three until last year. Then, like that"—Luca snapped his fingers— "they were moved to Level Five. Officially extinct."

As was too often the case, my curiosity got the better of me. "Do they have these . . . eumonies . . . for every species that's lost?"

"Small ones. More informal. Nothing like the one planned for the dairnes."

"What an honor," I said bitterly.

"Dairnes are one of the great governing species. That level of extinction has never happened before." Luca laughed. "And seeing you by my side, it's clear it still hasn't."

We reached a grim stone chamber, vaguely circular, with six massive iron doors around the perimeter. I smelled rot and mold and heard sounds behind three of the huge doors: sniffling, muttering, sluggish movements.

"Master jailer!" Luca called.

A strange creature appeared from the shadows. He was human—at least I thought he was—but more muscular by far than any human I'd yet encountered. Broad in shoulder and chest, his legs thick and lightly furred. He wore clothing, but it was a mere leather skirt. The rest of him was bare but for dark drawings that I'd gathered from Khara were called "tattoos." Tattoos of human faces.

"What do you want, boy?" the jailer said. He had a higher voice than I expected from such a terrifyingly bulky man.

"My master, Gharri Ferrucci, directs that this dog be locked up."

"Lock up a dog?" the jailer demanded. "But dogs ain't for locking up in no dungeon. Dogs need to run free!"

"If you value your own life, master jailer, you will lock up this dog and speak nothing of what you may see or hear."

With a quick nod the jailer complied, wielding a fat ring of iron keys.

Luca followed me into a chamber with no window, no light, and vile, vermin-ridden straw on the floor. "Close the door," he instructed the jailer. "I'll summon you when I'm ready to depart."

"All right, then." The jailer slammed the iron-barred door shut with such force that I shuddered.

Luca leaned close once the jailer was out of earshot and asked, "Do you recall when Gharri Ferrucci whispered something to me before you and I departed?"

I nodded. "I heard but couldn't understand. I don't speak Nedarran, just the Common Tongue."

"That was deliberate," said Luca. "He didn't want you to understand."

"But why?"

"Because," said Luca, "he ordered me to have you killed. Killed, and then burned, so there's no evidence you ever existed."

Killed. Burned. The words stung like fresh wounds.

My throat was so tight I could barely swallow. I looked Luca in the eyes. Was it pity I saw there? I couldn't be sure.

But I was certain of one thing.

Luca was telling the truth.

"The jailer's not a bad sort, really," Luca continued, "but he will do it if I tell him to."

"I don't understand," I said, my trembling voice betraying me. "What I have done wrong?"

"Done? You've done nothing. But you exist, and that is a crisis."

The jailer walked past, and I waited till he was gone. "But why?" I asked. "Shouldn't the existence of a dairne—even just one dairne—be a good thing?"

Luca looked away, groaning. When he looked at me again, this time I knew it was pity in his eyes. "Oh, poor dairne, you really don't understand humans, do you? Araktik, the Murdano's Seer, is coming. That's a huge honor for the isle. The only reason she's coming is because Gharri Ferrucci certified to the Chief Scholar that the dairnes are, indeed, gone."

"I still don't—"

"The Chief Scholar then told the Murdano that the dairnes are extinct. How do you suppose they would enjoy being humiliated? Do you think Araktik—who's had hundreds of people drowned, impaled, or burned at the stake—will like having her time wasted? Being made to look a fool?"

I had no answer. I could only stare at Luca in disbelief.

But slowly it dawned on me that Luca must be taking a great risk saying these things, things his master, Ferrucci, clearly did not want me to know.

"Why are you telling me this?" I asked. "Do you intend to help me?"

"Don't be so sure I'm helping you," he replied. He rubbed his chin, staring at the iron bars that marked the boundary between freedom and imprisonment. "I am a scholar, first and foremost, Byx. I've watched species disappear. Do you know what's in the cellar of this monument to knowledge?"

I shook my head. I doubted I wanted to know.

"The stuffed remains of dozens of endlings. Endlings, just like you. Mounted, labeled, gathering dust. Dragged out once a year for a natural history class." Luca cleared his throat. I wondered if he might cry. "I am a scholar above all, Byx. My loyalty is not to you. My loyalty is to science. You may be an endling. But you will not die because of me."

That was true. In parts, at least. But I sensed it was not the whole truth.

Luca strode to the iron gate. "Jailer! Let me out."

The door opened for him and closed again.

A rat skittered over my tail. I listened to Luca's footsteps fade away.

I wondered if Tobble knew how to find me. Could he even try?

He might. Sweet, silly Tobble. Just the thought of him made my heart ache.

And what of Khara? Was she already long gone, her pockets heavy with coins?

I curled up in a corner, my back to the wall, and covered myself as best I could with the rank straw.

It was going to be a long night.

But then, I was getting used to those.

28

The Felivet

I had finally dozed off when I woke to a nearby voice.

"Oh . . . doggie?"

The sound was not human. I was sure of that. What it was I didn't know, but it was too hoarse, too low, too oozing with sardonic menace.

I sniffed the air.

"Doggie?"

A felivet! In the cell next to mine.

"Oh, doggie," it said in a chilling, singsong voice.

"Y-y-yes?"

"Ah, it is a talking doggie," said the felivet.

"I'm not a dog. I'm a dairne," I said, too fearful to sound as defiant as I'd hoped.

"A dairne, are you? Have you come to witness the funeral of your species?" I knew nothing of felivets, aside from the usual horrifying stories of how quickly they could pounce, crushing your skull in their brutal jaws. But I felt certain the felivet was teasing me. Mocking me.

I didn't answer. I couldn't think of an answer.

"Prove to me that you are a dairne," the felivet said.

"I am," I replied simply.

"They say dairnes are infallible when it comes to separating truth from fiction."

"So I've heard."

"Let us test the notion, shall we?"

I sighed.

"My name is Elios Str'ank, but my friends call me Gambler. Or. Or, my name is Hadrak the Third, Lonko of the Dread Forest."

The felivet waited.

I said, "But . . . both are true."

The felivet let out a slow hiss. "Well done, dairne. I've been trying to convince these so-called scholars of this for weeks."

"Why don't they believe you?"

"The same reason they don't want to believe you exist, dairne. There are many scholars, but few seekers after truth. Humans believe the things that make them feel safe. They care little for difficult facts."

"My name is Byx."

"Call me Gambler."

"I've never met a felivet before," I admitted.

"But you fear us?"

"Of course. You eat dairnes."

"We eat many things. Deer, cotchets, antelope, mira-bears, some types of serpent—only the tender ones, of course—wobbyks, badgers. And, occasionally," he added with a dramatic pause, "humans."

"And dairnes!"

"Nonsense," he replied. "We are not humans. We felivets keep our promises. In two hundred years, no felivet has knowingly killed a dairne. We've needed your kind. It's true that in the old days, before the Coimari Treaty, we did hunt dairnes. But as we came to deal with humans and natites, your usefulness was apparent. Humans are such very good liars, you see, and natites are no better."

"And the others?" I asked.

"Terramants will not lie. Raptidons will keep silent and conceal truth, but they're too proud to lie. As we developed dealings of a nonfatal variety with humans and natites, we needed dairnes to act as truth tellers."

"But we were taught to fear felivets."

Gambler laughed, which in felivets sounds a bit like a cough. "Who rules the forests, Byx the dairne? Do you not wonder that you have never seen one of us except perhaps briefly, at a distance? For many years we kept your kind safe from humans. But . . ." He sighed. "But our numbers dwindle, too. We are a quarter of what we once were. Humans hunt us, though they deny it. They train huge mastiffs that track us in packs. They poison our waters, sickening us, so we cannot bear kits. All the while, the Murdano pretends ignorance."

I let this shocking news sink in. The idea that felivets might be endangered, just like dairnes, was hard to fathom. "But why would humans want to destroy dairnes and felivets?" I asked.

"You obviously don't know humans," Gambler said sadly. "They are not great hunters, like us felivets. They don't walk alone in the night, facing prey and predator alike. They issue forth in armies to make cowardly battle of the many against the few."

Yes, I thought. I had seen the Murdano's army. I had seen its handiwork. Armed humans against unarmed dairnes.

"It's humans who hate your kind," Gambler said. "They hate that you make it impossible for them to lie. And they hate us, the felivets, because we raise our voices against them in their mad wars for conquest. They have purged the world of dairnes, but we won't be far behind. And then the raptidons will be brought down, and the terramants will find men with spears and arrows waiting for them at the mouths of their tunnels. In the end, humans will attempt to destroy even the natites, although there, they may have great difficulty. Still," Gambler said with a heavy sigh, "never underestimate the human when it comes to duplicity and slaughter."

We both fell silent. I shivered, not from cold but from fear.

Could it really be that dairnes weren't the only species under attack? It meant this might be a far bigger, far darker battle than I'd dreamed.

I forced myself to speak. "How can you be sure of all this, Gambler?" I whispered. "Maybe you're wrong."

"Felivets range wide and far, dairne. We see all. We are not wrong." He hesitated. "I wish we were."

I could hear the jailer pacing back and forth, his slow, heavy steps accompanied by the rhythmic jangle of keys.

I could hear the whispered scurry of rats through straw.

I could hear the muffled sobs of some fellow inmate.

But above all else, I could hear the echoes of Gambler's words to me: Never underestimate the human when it comes to duplicity and slaughter.

29.
Luca Returns

I dreamed that night of an eerie green light. I awoke with a start to see that it was no dream. Before me floated a glowing cloud, just outside the bars of my cell.

It was not sunlight. It was not a torch. I rose and moved closer, fascinated and disturbed.

I could just make out a human form beneath the light. I squinted, trying to discern features.

"Silence, dairne," a voice said.

It was Luca.

He emerged from what could only be a theurgic light and showed me a key. He was clearly nervous, eyes darting left and right as he slid the key into the lock. The door swung open with a groan.

"My theurgy isn't strong," he said, voice hushed. "I breathed in the jailer's ear and put him to sleep. But a loud noise might rouse him."

I crept to the door as quietly as I could. "Where are you taking me?"

"To Khara. She convinced me this is best."

Again I felt not a lie, but a withheld truth.

"Thank you," I whispered. I followed him a few steps into the gloomy passageway. But then I stopped. "There's another we should free."

"What?"

"In that cell. A felivet who—who knows useful things."

"You made a friend in jail and now you want me to break him out?"

"Yes. Please."

"A felivet," Luca said. "A ruthless predator."

I hesitated. How sure was I? "Yes."

Luca shook his head in disbelief. "Are you insane?"

"Possibly," I admitted. "But . . ." I recalled decisions I'd made that had seemed right but later turned out to be foolish. There were more than a few.

Yet some instinct, or maybe just a sense of gratitude for the company Gambler had given me, told me this was the right thing to do.

I went to the door of Gambler's cell, stepping out of the miasma of light. "Gambler!" I called softly.

The felivet's reaction was startling. In less time than it would have taken me to cough, Gambler's pale blue eyes snapped open and he lunged with easy grace, landing at the cell door, teeth bared, claws extended. He was a lanix, huge and sleek, his coat pure black except for a series of delicate white stripes on his face. His long, muscular tail reminded me far too much of a serpent.

"What is this, then?" he asked.

"I'm escaping," I said. "Would you like to come?"

"Escaping?" He tilted his great head and peered into the light. "Ah, there is sorcery here."

"Yes," I said. "I need you to tell me something."

"Oh?"

"If I free you, will you attack me? Or any of my companions? One . . . or two, perhaps, are humans. One is a wobbyk."

"If I'm freed, they will be safe. From me, at any rate."

"You believe him?" Luca asked skeptically.

"I do," I replied. Quickly I added, "And there might be a horse, Gambler."

"Free me," he said, "and I will be your servant, and you my master."

I looked hopefully at Luca, who made an exasperated noise. "Well, they can only execute me once."

Seconds later, we were out of the dungeon and moving as swiftly and quietly as we could: Luca, no longer wreathed in light, Gambler, and I.

I trusted that Gambler had spoken truly. My instincts

had told me as much. But a lifetime of terrifying tales about the huge cats would not allow me to relax. In seconds, Gambler could kill Luca and me with ease.

Luca didn't take us back the way we'd come, but instead led us down a narrow stairway, through an echoing unlit space, down another stairway, and into an airless corridor.

He pushed open a door, and there stood Khara and Tobble.

Tobble screamed. "Felivet!"

Khara's hand went to her sword.

"No, no!" I cried. "He's a friend."

"Felivets have no friends," Khara said harshly. "They're barely trusted on this isle. And never trusted beyond it."

"True," Gambler said, and for a moment I wondered if I'd made a fatal mistake. "We are solitary creatures, unlike you humans. We make our own way." He offered up a half grin, baring his glistening teeth. "We hunt alone," he added with pride.

Tobble moved bravely to my side. "This is one dairne you won't be hunting," he said in a trembling voice.

"Thank you, Tobble," I said, placing my hand on his shoulder. I'd missed him more than I'd wanted to admit. "But I trust Gambler."

"We have a code of honor, wobbyk, whatever you may think of us. I have given my word to serve Byx."

"Wonderful," Khara said with a groan. "Now we have to hide a felivet?"

"What's the plan?" I asked. "Is there a way to get off the isle?"

"Not yet," Luca said. "But after the eumony, thousands of people will be crowding the ferries and private boats. We stand a better chance in all that confusion."

"So this . . . this travesty funeral is going ahead?" I asked.

Luca nodded, looking at Khara. "It cannot be stopped. If the scholars admit they were wrong and dairnes aren't yet extinct, they'll lose all influence with Araktik, and with it, most likely, the protection of the Murdano. Araktik is the Murdano's most trusted adviser."

We fled, moving quietly, silently, even Tobble. The sky was just beginning to lighten. Luca knew the way and walked ahead, with Gambler just behind him. Two humans, a vicious predator, a comical wobbyk, and a not-yet-extinct dairne on all fours, one whose very existence was a threat to great powers.

"Luca has a place," Khara whispered.

When we encountered a constabulary patrol, we ducked into an alley. Luca muttered theurgic words. They wouldn't stop the constables from seeing us, he explained, but would ensure they weren't concerned. The men passed us by with their swords sheathed.

"I turned fifteen a few months ago," Luca said with a

shrug. "I'm just beginning to learn basic theurgy."

"Worked well enough just now," Khara said with an admiring glance.

"Are all the constables human?" Tobble asked.

"No. Any species can work for the constabulary," Luca said. "Though most are human or raptidon."

"You'll never catch a felivet wearing anyone's livery," Gambler said proudly.

We came to the edge of a vast open space, a square surrounded on all sides by buildings three and four stories high. "The Plaza of Truth," Luca said.

We crept around the plaza's perimeter, and Luca led us into one of the buildings. It had scaffolding rising up over its face, and once inside we saw that it was being completely rebuilt. It was empty: no furniture, no light, no scent of food, but also no recent scent of humans.

We climbed a stairway to the top floor, then came upon a ladder that led to a trapdoor in the ceiling.

The ladder was easy enough for the humans, difficult but manageable for me, and entirely impossible for Tobble and Gambler. Khara let Tobble scramble onto her back, but Gambler weighed more than the four of us together. Fortunately, felivets are rather . . . capable.

"Leave the trapdoor open and step aside," Gambler instructed.

He squatted low, bunched his muscles, wiggled a little to get himself set, and leapt ten feet straight in the air, up and through the narrow trapdoor, landing on the floor beside us with the usual nonchalance of his species.

"You're just showing off," Tobble said. Instantly, he covered his mouth in horror, realizing he'd just teased one of the most feared creatures in the world.

"Nonsense," Gambler said, his voice so smooth he was practically purring. "If I'd wanted to show off, I'd have done a somersault in midair."

I made a note to myself—despite his oath of allegiance—never to annoy this particular kitty.

The space we now occupied was dusty and gloomy, filled with stuffed chairs and tables, mirrors, chests, and wooden crates.

"They moved everything up here while they're working below," Luca said, dusting a cobweb off his trousers.

"Won't the workers discover us when they come to work?" Khara asked.

"The eumony's a holiday. No one will be working," Luca said. "We'll actually have a view of the ceremony." He pointed to a row of dormer windows overlooking the Plaza of Truth.

"Won't you be in terrible trouble for this?" I asked Luca.

"Mmm," he said, nodding. "Ferrucci would turn me over to the constables and I'd be thrown into the dungeon. Or killed outright."

"Why are you risking that?" Tobble asked.

Khara spoke before he could answer. "Because unlike Ferrucci, that treacherous old fraud, Luca is a true scholar."

She was speaking the truth, at least as much as she knew of it. But something nagged at me, a feeling that there was more to know about Luca. I'd had so little exposure to lying, especially to human lying. It was hard to know what to listen for.

"We take an oath," Luca said. "To pursue truth, and only truth. And what's happening now"—he gestured toward the plaza where the eumony would soon take place—"is the obliteration of truth."

This, too, was true. And still, something made me ill at ease.

"Gambler believes this eumony is just the first of many," I said. "The felivets have seen their numbers dwindle because of the Murdano."

"The dairnes are merely the first of the great governing species to fall victim," Gambler said, nodding. "The felivets will be next, and after that—"

"Do you think so little of humans?" Luca interrupted.

"I don't think too little," said Gambler. "I know too much."

Khara, Tobble, and I exchanged worried looks. I wanted to press on, to ask a thousand more questions, but I was suddenly overwhelmed by a wave of exhaustion. I found a pair of pillowy blue chairs, and Tobble and I each settled into one. Instantly, we both fell sound asleep.

When I woke, it was to the sounds of a huge crowd outside, boisterously "mourning" my own nonexistence.

30.
The Eumony Begins

"Before we begin this solemn ceremony," a raptidon voice cried, "I must make a few announcements."

I stood at a window, watching the spectacle unfold below me. For a pup who'd grown up in the distant reaches of the world with nothing but a handful of fellow dairnes, the sight of what had to be twenty thousand creatures crowded together was overwhelming.

A large platform stood at one end in the shadow of the massive central library. The library was a pillared beast of a building with friezes and bas-reliefs showing the long line of Chief Scholars—humans, felivets, raptidons, natites, terramants, and dairnes. The Chief Scholar, Luca had explained, was granted a twenty-year term of office, with the position rotating through the governing species. There had been no dairne Chief Scholar in over two hundred years, however, due to my species's dwindling numbers.

Khara and Tobble joined me. Luca had gone in search of food. Gambler, stretched out on the floor, yawned, showing his teeth in a grimace.

"Each species should occupy its own designated area," the raptidon continued, "with the exception of servants, of course." A shaggy, ancient bird with talons gripping an ornately carved stand, he spoke with the accent typical of his folk. Raptidons have their own language and dialects, but when speaking the Common Tongue, they have trouble with the sounds of *w*, *b*, *d*, *f* and *m*, all of which they tend to drop or turn into vowels.

I could understand the speaker, but only if I concentrated. "Food carts will make their way within each section" became "ood carts ill ake their ay ithin eash shection."

The Chief Scholar, a natite, was already onstage, seated in a sort of throne that was half submerged in a constructed pool. Two other natites floated within the tank as well.

The natite audience was arrayed along the banks of a C-shaped canal. The blue-green water entered the plaza at the southeast corner, curved through, and exited by the northeast corner. Within the space delineated by that canal, felivets paced or lounged on cobblestones. There were hundreds, if not thousands, of the cats, in all their dizzying variations. I saw coats of beige with red patches, pure midnight blue, black, dusty orange, and tan with blue spots. A few had pure white fur ribboned with black, like bare trees in snow.

"Please take care with bodily fluids and do not foul the water," the speaker continued. "Raptidons in flight are urged not to relieve themselves over non-raptidon sections."

In spite of the grim setting, I laughed.

Like the natites' canal on the east, a semicircle was carved out of the west portion of the plaza, though this space was formed by what appeared to be a dirt canal. No paving was visible, just bare earth pierced by a dozen or so terramant tunnels. The massive insects sat throbbing on the dirt or poking antennaed heads out of holes.

"Not many bugs," Tobble said. "Good."

"You're not fond of terramants?" I teased, trying to keep the mood light.

The raptidons were located in the space corresponding to the felivet section. They perched in large numbers on wooden Ts arrayed like a stunted forest, though at any given moment half the birds were in flight, hovering above their section, or floating higher up without regard for seating protocol.

In the center of the plaza was the human section, an hourglass shape between natites and felivets on the right, terramants and raptidons on the left. The humans were packed in tightly, and were far more numerous than the other four species.

"Today's events will unfold as follows," declared the speaker. "There will be a brief statement from the Chief Scholar, followed by a recounting of dairne history, followed by the appearance of the Seer to the Murdano, the great Araktik Vel Druand. After that we will unveil the Statue of the Dairnes, whom we mourn today. And then we feast!"

The crowd seemed pleased about the last part, not so enthusiastic about the speeches or the statue. But I, for one, was actually anxious to hear a recitation of dairne history. And I was curious to see the statue, which was in front of the stage and covered with a tarp.

"Please remember that this is a solemn occasion," the speaker said sternly. He spread his wings, swooped over the crowd of humans, and banked to his right, disappearing among his fellow raptidons.

Luca came back, carrying a heavy sack slung over his back. He plopped it down with a groan.

"I hope this will do, Gambler." Luca drew out a package stained with leaking blood. He unwrapped it, revealing a cotchet about Tobble's size.

"My thanks," said Gambler. "That will do nicely."

Luca heaved the body toward Gambler, who caught it with his teeth in midair.

For the rest of us, Luca had procured a loaf of bread, a hunk of cheese, two sausages, and a bottle of cider. We fell to, and I missed much of the Chief Scholar's speech, which rambled on as I chewed and swallowed. But as soon as I was done eating, I returned to the window. The natite Chief Scholar was just finishing.

". . . and therefore, having taken careful account of all the facts, we had to conclude, sadly, that the dairne species is extinct, gone forever from our world."

31.
Araktik

Gone forever.

The two words seem to squeeze my heart. I closed my eyes, and when I opened them, I realized that Tobble, Khara, Luca, and Gambler were all watching me with a mixture of pity, worry, and, in the case of the felivet, detached interest.

I straightened my shoulders and turned my attention back to the stage. An old man, feeble and bent, was ascending the steps, assisted by two helpers.

"It's Ferrucci," Luca said.

"That old fraud is going to tell the history of my people?" I demanded.

Luca shrugged. "He's considered the greatest scholar of dairne history."

"Greatest disappointment is more like it," Khara said under her breath.

Ferrucci's voice was weak, and I could make out only frustrating snatches.

". . . then, in the Time of Troubles, Charles Mordan, the Tribune of Hursk . . . warring kingdoms . . . to talk peace with Met'an Nur, the felivet Hunter Supreme . . . both sides bring a dairne to ensure . . . and that meeting began . . . led to . . . the first human-felivet treaty."

Upon hearing the name "Met'an Nur," the felivets below let loose with a brief but terrifying roar. The humans managed halfhearted applause, the terramants politely burred their flightless wings, and the natites slapped the surface of the water. The raptidons, for their part, made no response.

". . . the Third War of Rivermouth . . . natite queen. . ." I heard the name of the natite queen, but the sounds—whistles and clicks, along with an indecipherable string of consonants—were impossible for my dairne mouth to repeat.

"I have heard of war, but I don't know exactly what it means," Tobble said. I was not the person to enlighten him, as I knew little more than he did. Dalyntor had barely mentioned the word in our lessons.

"A war," Khara said grimly, "is when large numbers of fighters from one tribe or city or species attack and attempt to kill those of another tribe or city or species."

It was true as far as it went, but—as was often the case with Khara—I sensed other things withheld. Her reaction to the word "war" was personal and painful.

"In any case, there are no wars now," Gambler said with unmistakable sarcasm.

Khara glanced back at him but said nothing.

Ferrucci continued down a list of wars, negotiations, and treaties, pointing out the role that dairnes had played in each. "Indeed," he said, pausing to wheeze, "it could be said . . . vitally . . . necessary to . . . without which war might . . . history was made."

"He's reaching the conclusion," Luca said.

"How do you know?" Khara asked.

Luca laughed. "I wrote most of the speech. Ferrucci dictated a bit, and I filled in the rest."

"I can't believe I thought Ferrucci would save Byx," Khara said. "I was sure he was a good man."

"Good men don't always stay that way," Luca said simply, touching Khara's shoulder for a moment. Impatiently, she brushed away a tear with the back of her hand.

Hearing those words, seeing that tear, I suddenly knew with absolute certainty that Khara had never meant me to come to any harm. She'd genuinely thought Ferrucci would be my salvation. Certainly she'd expected to be paid, but not for my pelt. For my living self.

". . . and thus, with deep sadness . . . the end of a species . . . great and . . . now nevermore."

At last the speech was done. The raptidons set up a loud

squawking, apparently believing that only the end required any sort of response. A murmur of anticipation went through the humans below, and the natites kicked themselves higher in the water to get a better view.

A line of soldiers marched onto the stage. Each wore the Murdano's red-and-silver livery with an additional sigil, a painted symbol of a blue eye over a rune *S*.

From the back of the plaza came another procession of soldiers, marching straight through the human crowd. At the end was a palanquin carried by twelve muscular men. When they reached the front, they gave a mighty upward heave, extending their arms until the door of the palanquin was level with the platform.

With impressive synchronization, the soldiers already on the stage formed into two lines, while their officer stepped smartly forward, opened the palanquin's door, and stepped back.

"Here she comes," said Luca.

I don't know what I was expecting to see. I had no notion of what a Seer might look like. Vaguely, I'd imagined someone like Ferrucci, ancient and bowed, with an expression of smug superiority.

Humans, I now knew, came in various colors and shapes and sizes, though nothing approaching the breathtaking variety of felivets or raptidons. This was one of the light tan humans, a female with jet-black hair hanging down to her midback. She wore an ankle-length gown in shades of red, embroidered with silver stars.

Her bare arms were covered in tattoos, blue and red and green. Luca explained that they were magical runes and seals, the visible manifestations of powerful theurgic charms. "It's said that she cannot be killed," he told us.

"I could always try," Gambler said. He loped over and, by resting his forepaws on the windowsill, took in the view. "The Seer is no friend to felivets."

Luca shot him a look. "Araktik is friend to no one."

"I'm not that familiar with humans," I said, "but isn't she quite young?"

"Barely nineteen," Luca confirmed. "Not much older than Khara and me."

Araktik stood facing the crowd, absorbing the cheers and squawks and water slaps. The terramants burred their wings and dipped antennae. The felivets remained silent.

"I feel that I am home," Araktik began in a strong alto voice. "For many years I lived here on the isle. I learned much from great scholars of all species."

"She cheated her way through exams," Luca said, smirking.

"So she's not so smart," Tobble said.

"Don't ever imagine that she's not intelligent. Intelligent, cunning, ruthless, and dangerous." Then, in a different tone, Luca added, "And a bully."

"You know Araktik?" Khara asked.

Luca nodded. "When I was six and she was ten, we were in the same dormitory. She once made me eat soap."

"That must have tasted worse than wobbyk," Gambler said.

"Hey!" Tobble protested. "I've had enough of that. I'll have you know that we're delicious!"

"Be glad my belly is full of cotchet," Gambler said, "or I'd test your claim."

"Wait—did I say delicious?" Tobble asked. "I meant poisonous."

Gambler started to respond, but he suddenly froze. Tobble and I gasped.

"You hear that?" Gambler asked.

I nodded. So did Tobble.

"What?" both humans asked at once.

"Someone is coming," Gambler said. "More than one someone."

32.
Trapped

"You two must hide," Luca said to Gambler and me. "We can explain our presence to the constabulary, but we can't explain a felivet, let alone a dairne. Even if you play dog, they'll see the truth if they examine you closely."

I heard at least six sets of human feet pounding up the stairs. Had we been seen? Or was this just a routine security patrol?

Frantically I searched the room. Chairs, tables, mirrors, chests. Yes, a chest! Gambler considered the rafters overhead. He focused on a large crossbeam at least a dozen feet above us. He squatted, wriggled his hindquarters, and seemed to levitate straight up, landing on the beam as if he leapt like this every day of his life. And, I realized, he probably did.

I opened a dusty chest half full of decaying clothing. I rolled in and pulled the lid down just as the humans burst in.

"Here then," a crude voice boomed. "What is this all about, eh?"

"We're just watching the eumony." It was Luca.

"Don't you know this building is shut down? Who do you think you are, anyways?"

"We were just seeking some privacy." Khara's voice now. "Luca and I, well, our parents don't approve, but we . . . enjoy each other's company."

Khara's words were so obviously false, I could not believe they would convince the constables.

"Young love, eh?" A different voice, more cultured.

"Well, I wouldn't say love," Luca said, sounding embarrassed.

"That's not what you said an hour ago!" Khara protested.

The chest muffled sounds, but still I heard Araktik's voice from the stage.

"Thanks to the generosity of our great and magnificent Murdano, we are come together to mourn . . ."

"Love or not love, you have to get out," the first human said.

"Yes, I'm afraid you must," the second agreed. "Or we'll be forced to arrest you and spoil this important day."

"But we only want to—" Khara protested.

"Ah ah ah," came the second voice, sounding firmer now, though still amused.

"Then I suppose we must join our friend Vallino," Khara said, pitching her voice loud enough so that we would hear.

"And take that fuzzball with you," the first man said.

I heard Tobble mutter, "Fuzzball!"

Three sets of footsteps left the room. But the constables didn't follow them out. "Let's look around and see if there's anything . . . um . . . useful," the smoother voice said.

"Useful, eh?" The other laughed. "And profitable, too?"

I heard the sounds of things being shoved and overturned. Holding my breath, I thanked fortune for poor human hearing. A felivet would have had no trouble hearing my frenzied heart.

Steps paused just outside my hiding place. The lid flew open, and I found myself staring up into a bearded face.

"Ho!" the constable yelled.

"Grrroooowwwr!"

Gambler roared, a sound that shook the walls. The man staggered back, drawing his sword. The huge felivet landed soundlessly on the floor.

All six constables drew weapons and formed a semi-circle. They were scared, clearly, but not panicked. These were men accustomed to dealing with various species, and as powerful as Gambler was, I didn't believe he could fight six swordsmen.

"Run!" Gambler shouted.

I made for the trapdoor, but there stood two more constables, swords at the ready. As I skidded to a stop, I heard more feet rushing up the stairs. Gambler's roar had carried far, and reinforcements were rushing to the scene.

Outside, the Seer droned on, although with the blood pounding in my ears I couldn't make out a word.

I spun and raced back through the room.

I was cornered. Cut off.

And this time they would make sure I was dead.

With an earsplitting roar, Gambler swiped at a careless constable, leaving bloody tracks down his sword arm.

Everywhere I looked, I saw men with swords.

Every exit was blocked.

Escape was impossible.

Unless.

I ran like a beast on fire, straight for a window.

33.
Pursued

I leapt and sailed through.

As soon as I spread my glissaires, I caught a warm updraft.

I was high above the crowd, but that wouldn't last long. My gibbering mind calculated glide paths. I had very little choice.

On the one hand, I could veer left and land amid the terramants.

On the other hand, I could try a sharp right that would kill my speed and leave me splashing in the natite canal.

On the one foot . . . Oh, who was I fooling? There was no good answer.

Time froze.

I hung in the air.

I saw faces on the stage raising eyes to me.

I saw hands begin to point.

Then, with a roar of wind in my ears, I felt the full speed

of my glide. I was hurtling like a falcon in a stoop, right toward the stage.

Right toward the Seer.

Araktik looked at me with icy blue eyes. I saw her eyebrows rise, her eyes widen.

I saw the moment she realized what I was: a dairne zooming above the funeral for her own species.

It dawned on me that I was not alone in the air. Raptidons, some below me, some above me, twisted their heads to catch a glimpse of the clumsy animal intruding on their sphere.

My jerky movements caused me to spin, reducing my view to brief flashes of creatures, stage, and sky.

Any hope was gone that I could catch just enough air to sail harmlessly over Araktik's head.

A soldier on the stage made a mad dive for Araktik, knocking her aside just as I swept over the stage. I missed her by inches, so close she must have felt the wind from my passing.

I landed hard, rolling as we are taught to do, and came up running.

It wasn't a bad landing, all things considered.

For a split second, the crowd seemed to be gasping in unison. But when someone screamed "Dairne!" a great roar of shock and amazement went up.

Running on all fours, I leapt from the side of the stage. I

landed in terramant dirt, yelped in horror, skidded between the legs of one of the bugs, jumped onto and then off a squat terramant, feet scrabbling on the chitin shell, and barreled heedlessly beneath the T-stands of the raptidons, setting them all into confused, panicked flight.

I tripped in raptidon excrement and, as I came up, chanced to look back at my hiding place. There I saw Gambler. He'd left through the same window I had, but he was climbing up onto the roof, digging his claws into wooden beams and plaster as constables stabbed up at him with their swords.

I had no time to see more. I was out of the plaza in a narrow street, hands and feet sliding in muck, food vendors and souvenir stalls surrounding me. Behind me, I heard the shouts of pursuing constables and soldiers.

I had just enough presence of mind to remind myself that I had to make for Vallino's stable, and do it without leading my pursuers there.

Easier said than done.

I skidded into a sharp turn that took me beneath a fruit vendor's stall, hit the vendor's leg, and yelled, "Sorry!" over my shoulder. I squeezed behind the close-packed stalls, making it harder for the constables and soldiers to keep pace.

And then: luck!

An open door.

I was through it in a heartbeat. Slamming the door behind

me, I set the bolt. I needed to find another route. The streets belonged to humans.

Ahead of me was a set of worn stairs. A little human boy sat at the bottom, sucking on his thumb and holding a stuffed toy raptidon.

"Pardon me!" I said, bounding past him, panting so hard that each breath was like scalding steam on my throat.

Up and up, to the top floor. I ran to a window facing away from the street. Without a pause I leapt, spread my glissaires, and landed on a rooftop a hundred feet away.

Let the humans try to follow me now, I thought.

But my triumph was short-lived. As Luca had told us, not all constables are human.

A swift raptidon screeched at me as it sailed in, its yellow talons raked forward. Its wingspan was wider than my body was long. A ribbon of blue and red, the colors of the isle's constable force, trailed from one leg.

Above him, I saw two more liveried raptidons vectoring toward me.

I had landed on a rooftop patio. I pushed my way past a startled old man and raced down a set of stairs. I brushed by a grandmotherly type peeling carrots and headed into a narrow alleyway.

Unfortunately, it was a dead end. And at the mouth of the alley, led by screeching raptidons, stood two constables, grinning in anticipation of the moment when they could run their swords through me.

I was trapped.

I saw no door. Nothing I could climb. No escape.

"Come peaceful or come dead," one of the men said as they stalked toward me.

There was nothing to say. Nothing to do.

"Peaceful," I muttered, panting furiously, "it is, then," just as a dark shape fell from the sky, landing as if it weighed less than a feather.

Gambler.

The huge cat turned to the men and said, "Two humans against me? I don't like your odds."

Evidently they agreed. Both took nervous steps backward.

"Byx, get on my back!"

I was in no position to argue. My legs were shaking, my heart hammering. I could barely breathe.

I used the last of my strength to grab hold of Gambler's fur. He bunched his muscles and soared straight up, an impossible leap that took him just short of the eaves of the building above us. He shot out a claw, snagged a rain gutter, sank the claws of his other front paw into tile shingles, and by sheer brute power pulled us up onto the roof.

A reckless raptidon constable came at him, talons at the ready. In one move, Gambler knocked him out of the sky and sent him in a tangled, bloody heap down to the alley below.

Gambler twisted his head to check on me. I gave a small nod and we were off. We ran and jumped and practically flew. Across roofs, down through windows, into alleys, and back up to the rooftops.

I'd thought I had a pretty fair idea of what felivets could do. I'd thought I had a reasonable appreciation of their power.

I knew nothing.

Gambler moved like a raging river through a steep canyon. He was sheer, sinewy power combined with fluid grace.

Compared to Gambler, I was less than a wobbyk. I was a clumsy, stumbling warthog.

Terrified and exhausted as I was, I watched the magnificent way he moved through the world—his absolute certainty that every move would be the right move—and felt the same emotion I'd had the first time I saw the ocean: pure awe.

34.
The Not-So-Simple Truth

We met back at the stable, where, to our immense relief, Luca, Khara, and Tobble were waiting with Vallino.

Vallino took one look at Gambler and reared up on his hind legs with a furious snort.

"Horses," Gambler said with a sneer, "are nothing more than wagons with tails."

"He got us this far," Khara said, stroking Vallino's flank to calm him.

"Thank you, Gambler," I said as I climbed down off his back, landing in the soft straw. "You saved my life."

"But that's my job!" Tobble cried, dashing over to embrace me.

"Believe me, I'm delighted to have two lifesavers in my company," I said quickly, patting Tobble's head.

"Were you followed?" Luca asked.

Gambler nodded. "By every constable on the isle, it

seemed," he said. He licked a paw with casual grace. "We must not linger here."

"I've arranged a smugglers' boat with Eldon's help," Khara said. "We just need to make it to the waterfront."

Our route to the water wasn't nearly as difficult as we'd feared. Luca knew all the back alleys, and the throngs of merrymakers filling the main streets meant it was easy for us to go unnoticed.

As we made our way, we were surprised to see hastily printed handbills posted on every corner by the constabulary, claiming that the "flying dairne" was a hoax perpetrated by enemies of the Murdano. Luca was at the top of the list, described as a "conniving traitor and mediocre scholar." Khara was labeled a "renegade poacher and Murdano-hating terrorist." Gambler was named, too. He was "an example of a treacherous felivet" who had lent his "vicious nature to the aid of this conspiracy."

I was not listed. They couldn't exactly describe me as a dairne. Not if I was extinct.

Tobble wasn't included either, which caused some hurt feelings. "They never even noticed me," he complained. "It's like we wobbyks don't even count!"

When we reached the shoreline, we found natites busily loading boats, checking to make sure that everyone had paid the water tax and had permission to use the sea. But the crush of boats soon overwhelmed them, and we slid through unchallenged. Fortunately for us, Eldon's brother-in-law was a smuggler.

The battered boat, named *Devil's Smile*, was large but old, the floor slick with green algae. Once we were safely out to sea, I sidled up beside Khara. She was in the stern, looking back at the isle. She looked weary. But then, we all did.

"You look anxious," I said.

"I suppose I am. It's just that we're in the middle of some very serious things. The reputations of the scholars, the loyalty of the isle to the Murdano, the eumony, all of it. And Gambler's theory that the Murdano wants to exterminate more great governing species . . ." Khara sighed and shrugged. "It's way over my head."

"Because you're just a simple poacher girl," I said, half tease, half reproach.

Khara started to say something and stopped herself. I knew what she was thinking as clearly as if she'd spoken. She'd been about to tell me an untrue story about herself. But she'd realized I would know she was lying.

"Khara," I said, "I saw your sword when you cut up those serpents. That was not the sword of a simple poacher."

"You heard me say that I expected a reward for you," she said gruffly. "You didn't sense a lie then, did you?"

"No," I admitted. "You did expect a reward. But that was only a small part of the truth."

Khara sent me a challenging look. "And what is it you think is the whole truth, Byx?"

"I am starting to think you are much more important than you pretend to be."

I knew the question had to be asked. Politeness was a luxury I couldn't afford. I needed truth.

"Tell me about your family, Khara."

"Yes, tell us."

It was Luca's voice. I turned to see him striding toward us, with Tobble at his heels.

Khara crossed her arms over her chest. "All right, then." She exhaled slowly. "You deserve to know. My full name is Kharassande Donati."

The name meant nothing to me, but it clearly meant something to Luca.

"Donati?" he repeated, eyes wide. "As in the Donatis?"

Khara gave a slight nod.

"And this name is important to humans?" Tobble asked.

"Long ago, when the first Murdano came to power, three clans rose up against him: the Corplis, the Rantizzos, and the Donatis," Luca said. "The war lasted ten years."

"Yes, and we lost," Khara added. "At the most important battle of the war, the Corplis turned traitor, and the Rantizzos and Donatis were defeated—"

"Although," Luca interrupted, "historians say their defeat

was inevitable, regardless."

Khara looked at him sharply. "Not the historians I've read. In any case, my great-grandfather was Baron of Riverhome, Keeper of the Arms of Kainor the Magnificent. He was captured and given the treatment reserved for traitors."

"Which was?" Tobble asked.

"He was roasted over a slow fire for days, screaming in agony, before they finally cut off his head. My great-grandmother was thrown into a dungeon, where she caught the wheezing disease and died. Our soldiers were killed or enslaved. And our estate, Watersmeet, was turned over to the Murdano's Seer. The grandfather of Araktik took control, then his daughter, and now Araktik."

I blinked in disbelief. "The Seer lives in your home?"

"She murdered her own parents and now owns Watersmeet, though she has renamed it Sorcerer's Spike. As for me, I grew up in very different circumstances. My father barely escaped the constant purges. He changed his name and hid deep in the forests. He fed us by poaching the Murdano's private stocks." Khara allowed herself a momentary smile. "That's where I learned my tracking skills. It's also how I came to know Ferrucci. We would bring him strange and unusual creatures for his study. My mother collected herbs and potions and made a meager living for us as a healer. We had nothing of the old days left to us. Or . . . almost nothing."

I watched as Khara's hand dropped to the hilt of her sword, and I put the pieces into place: "the Arms of Kainor the Magnificent" meant the armor, the shield, and above all, the sword of Nedarra's greatest hero.

I was only an ignorant young dairne, little versed in history, blissfully unaware of the wars and strife of humans and other species. But even I knew of Kainor the Magnificent, the man who'd defeated the Svorsk invasion. At least, I'd heard the name and knew it was held in reverence.

This girl who passed as a boy, this poacher, now carried the most famous sword in history.

Just as I could sense Khara's moods, she seemed to be sensing mine in the weight of my silence. And then, looking straight at me, she told a lie. "It is a very nice sword, too good for me. But of course nothing like any of the Arms of Kainor."

A lie. A deliberate lie. A lie she told knowing that I would know it was a lie.

The lie, I realized, was for Luca.

"It doesn't look like much," Luca said.

"It's camouflaged by powerful spells," Khara said. "Until it's drawn in anger."

"Does Ferrucci know you are a Donati?" Luca asked.

"No. He only knew my father as a poacher who brought him rare animals."

Luca nodded slowly. "I wonder whatever became of the

Arms of Kainor. The Murdano would give anything to get his hands on the Light of Nedarra, I'm sure."

"Which is . . . ?" I asked

"The famous sword," Luca said.

Khara laughed. "I'd be happy to sell it to him, if I knew. The story my father tells is that Kainor's sword, shield, armor, and battle mace were all stolen when our home was sacked." She shrugged and Luca seemed to accept her words, despite what to me was unmistakable dishonesty.

If Khara was lying, it could only mean that she knew where the Arms of Kainor were. And she knew even better where the Light of Nedarra was.

In fact, her hand was resting on its hilt.

The sudden rush of the crew alerted us that we were nearing land. What would happen, I wondered, once we disembarked?

"Where are we going?" Tobble asked, speaking my question aloud.

We all looked at Khara.

She shook her head and instead turned her gaze on me.

"We are going," she said firmly, "where Byx wishes to go."

35.
The Choice

We did not land at the same port from which we'd departed. This was, in fact, no port at all, just a rickety pier in a reed marsh. The only thing visible in the misty twilight was a small shack, presumably used by the smugglers for their illegal trade.

The five of us—six, if you counted Vallino—could barely see three feet beyond our noses. What I smelled was not encouraging, though: mud, oozing gases, decayed plant life, and more than a hint of equally decayed animal life.

"So," said Khara, who had changed back into her poacher's clothes, "where to, Byx?"

I gazed at the ground, as if I could find an answer waiting there. The weight of the decision was too much to bear. I was just a pup. I wasn't ready for so much responsibility.

I wasn't ready to lead anyone. Not even myself.

"I don't know where to go," I admitted.

"Sure you do." It was Tobble.

"I do?"

"To the place on your drawing."

"What drawing?" Khara asked.

"I . . . it's nothing," I said, embarrassed. "A map I drew based on a myth. A silly tale. I was just a pup when I made it."

Luca gave a short laugh. "'Just a pup'? What are you now? Elderly?"

"It doesn't matter, anyway. Back on the isle, I tossed the drawing away."

Tobble held up a paw. He reached into his leather pouch, dug around, and finally revealed my crumpled map. "Ta-da!"

"That's twice you've rescued that old thing, Tobble."

"Rescuing is my job," he said proudly.

I took it from him. "It's just a pup's scribbling."

"May I see it?" Khara asked. Gently she took the map from me, flattening it as best she could. "What is this place?" she asked, peering at the smudged lines.

"A mythical land called Dairneholme. My teacher said there was a river and a deep, deep valley, hidden away from the world on a magical sentient island that floated from place to place." I looked down, suddenly embarrassed. "Like I said: a silly tale."

"A sentient island?" Khara said. "There are two such."

"What?" I asked. "There really is such a thing?"

"They're called rooklets, islands created in long-ago times. They're not rock and earth, but ancient living beasts of enormous size. The rooklets move slowly over the ocean, attracting debris—anything that floats. Over many thousands of years the creature practically disappears beneath layer upon layer of dirt, floating trees, and seeds borne on the wind."

Khara held the map close, trying to make out its features in the waning light. "One island is called Rhomboo. The other is Tarok. But if there truly is a valley and a river running through the island, Dairneholme can only be on Tarok. Rhomboo is much smaller."

"Tarok," Gambler muttered. "There's a name to conjure with."

"Why?" Tobble asked.

"It's believed to be a carnivorous island," Luca said.

I gulped. "Carnivorous?"

"The island itself is thought to . . . well, to eat humans and felivets," Luca said. "The raptidons stay well clear of it, and of course there are no terramants. The only beings who know its location are the natites."

We all fell silent. The word "carnivorous" had that effect, it seemed.

Cautiously, we picked our way through the marsh. The mist parted slightly and we glimpsed a road not far off.

When we reached it, Gambler said, "We must go either

one way or the other. That way"—he flicked his tail, indicating north—"takes us near to the Murdano's capital city, Saguria. It also takes us to the port of Zebara. If we are to find this sentient island, that's the way."

When I said nothing, he went on. "If we go south, we head back to places we've known. I can return to my own territory. Khara can rejoin the poachers. Luca can perhaps ingratiate himself again on the isle, or find his own people. And Tobble can go back to his folk."

"Saguria, at least, is a civilized place. There's not much to speak of in the southlands," Luca said. "Other than a lot of squirrels and cochets."

"Still, the farther north we go, the more we'll encounter the Murdano's soldiers," Gambler said. "The border between Nedarra and Dreyland is very tense. Many believe the Murdano intends to invade Dreyland when he has sufficient forces, so Zebara will be an armed camp. We have me and we'll have your blade, Khara, but the odds would be very long against us. And if by some miracle we find this mythical island, and if dairnes are there, then what?"

"There's more to consider," I said. "What about the felivets' belief that the end of the dairnes is just the beginning? That more species will follow, if the Murdano has his way?"

"You base this on what?" Luca asked Gambler. "Your superior feline instincts?"

"We base it on the fact that felivets are students of history," said Gambler evenly. "If you want to know the future, study the past. And the past tells us that there's one thing you can be certain of with humans: they always want more."

"More?" Tobble repeated.

"More territory. More power. More glory. It has always been so. And it will always be."

The group fell silent.

To everyone's surprise, it was Tobble who finally broke the quiet. "Look," he said, "I'm only a small wobbyk. I know very little. But I choose to believe Gambler. At the very least, we have to consider the possibility that the Murdano means to wipe out the felivets next. And after that, perhaps, the raptidons."

He paused, as if carefully working out his next thoughts. "If the natites survive, it may be only as servants to the Murdano. This is wrong. This is not the world we want, is it?"

"No," Khara said. "And yet we must consider the facts, Tobble. They say the Murdano has five thousand knights and a hundred thousand men under arms: archers, spearsmen, ax wielders. He has Araktik and her theurgy. He has the scholars and their science."

"But he does not have the felivets," Gambler said. "And maybe the raptidons will see the truth and join us."

Khara shook her head. "Maybe. But I've always heard

from poachers that raptidons hate you felivets. Do you really think they'd join with your kind?"

"I cannot say for sure," Gambler admitted.

"There is only one way to fight lies," Tobble said firmly. "With truth."

He looked at me. And so did Gambler.

"It's a simple choice," Khara said. "South to what we have known, to live our lives as well as we can in the shadow of the Murdano's growing power. Or north toward danger and only a fool's hope."

"I, for one, say north," said Luca. He shrugged. "There's nothing in the south for me."

"Byx?" Khara said.

I gazed at them, waiting for me to tell them what to do.

Me.

The runt, the youngest and by-far-and-away smallest of my seven siblings.

Too young to be clever. Too small to be helpful.

Me.

"What do I know?" I said at last. "I'm just a pup. I can't force all of you to go on such a pointless quest."

I took the map from Khara's hands and stared at it. "I should just accept that I'm the endling," I said. "The eumony may have been premature, but when I die . . . well, then it will be time."

No one spoke. Mud crickets made gentle music. The mist, softened to pink by the setting sun, hung over us like the question that only I could answer.

I fought back tears. "This hope of mine is ridiculous. And I'm a fool."

"True enough," said Tobble. "You were a fool to rescue me."

"You were a fool to trust me," said Gambler.

"You were a fool to believe me," said Khara.

I sighed. How had it come to this?

"Well," I said at last, "It seems we agree that I am a fool."

"So, my fool of a dairne," Khara said. "Which way?"

We turned north.

PART FOUR
ALLIES AND ENEMIES

36.
Swordplay

Our journey would prove to be rough and wearying, and yet, to my surprise, I woke at sunrise looking forward to each day.

I knew the odds against me were long indeed. I knew that death could be waiting around the next hill. But every day brought new things for me to learn. Fresh scents, strange vistas, surprising species. For a curious sort like me, it was impossible not to relish the possibilities.

I felt the way I had when I'd walked into Ferrucci's office and seen the walls lined with books. How much I didn't know! How much there was to learn!

Luca was kind enough to give me a small leather-bound blank journal, not much bigger than my hand, a goose-quill pen, and a thin vial of ink. "Suspect you'll make more use of it than I," he said.

"But you're a scholar," I protested, although I was anxious to accept his gift. "Won't you need it to take notes?"

"I am taking notes," Luca said, and he tapped an index finger to his temple. "Foremost among them, I'm observing you. For years I've read about dairnes in books, and now, here you are before me, Byx: a real, live specimen."

His knowing smile gave me pause. But I happily took the book, pen, and vial and tucked them into my pouch. Whenever it came time to rest, I wrote down my impressions of the day or drew pictures. When the ink ran out, Tobble and I gathered berries, which I crushed into a pale but adequate substitute.

At Khara's suggestion, we followed the road by night and slept in remote areas during the day. This was perfect for Gambler, as felivets are nocturnal hunters, and I, too, was used to it. It was much harder for Khara, Luca, and Tobble, but they did their best to adapt.

On good days, we found sheltered places where we could make a fire. Once Khara managed to snare a juicy weldfox. Unfortunately, we had to eat it raw, because we were too near a long line of soldiers passing through. Another time, Gambler brought us a scrawny, slightly mauled cotchet we were able to cook.

Even then it was barely edible.

At one point we were unable to travel at night. Khara, who'd scouted ahead, had glimpsed a roadblock set up by the Murdano's men. To bypass it, we walked far inland—something we could only do with light. This alone consumed two days.

Another time, Khara returned to camp silent, grim, and shaking after she'd been out scouting routes. In her trembling hands, she carried something wrapped up in the cloak of a Murdano officer. She handed the bundle to Luca, and he opened it to reveal a short sword, a long knife, and a pair of sandals—Luca's city-boy footwear was falling apart.

Khara didn't answer questions about what had happened. And we didn't press her. The bloodstains on her shirt told us all we needed to know.

The next day we kept to the woods, where we found a pleasantly sweet stream meandering through a stand of mara saplings. The gentle breeze set their pink, clover-shaped leaves whispering. Gambler found a patch of sun and instantly closed his eyes. We settled nearby on the grass, welcoming the chance to relax, but Khara had other ideas.

"Luca. Byx. Come with me," she said in the no-nonsense tone we knew well.

We obeyed. We'd all come to obey Khara, even Gambler, who often hunted or scouted with her. It wasn't that they'd become close—friendship isn't part of the felivet culture— but they shared a mutual respect.

Gambler opened one eye and yawned. "Good luck," he said with a smirk.

"Why do we need luck?" I asked, but Gambler was already back to sleep, or at least pretending to be.

"What about me?" Tobble asked, trailing behind us.

"By all means, join us, Tobble," Khara said, though it was clear to me that she hadn't intended for him to come.

Khara led us to a level spot where the ground was covered in leaves. She passed the soldier's sword to Luca, who held it the way you might hold a poisonous snake.

"Byx?" Khara said. "Take this."

"This" was the long knife she had . . . found, along with a leather scabbard and belt. I attached the belt around my waist and took the knife. It felt strange and awkward in my hand. It was, after all, designed for a human grip much wider than mine.

"I am going to teach you both how to use those things." Khara's gaze was resolute, but her voice suggested she had doubts about her plan.

Luca and I exchanged panicked looks, then gulped identical gulps and nodded identical nods. My hand was sweaty on the knife's hilt before Khara had even finished her sentence.

"Luca. You first, you're taller," she said, and I relaxed a little. "The basic move is the downward cut. You hold your sword like this."

Khara demonstrated with her hands but did not unsheathe her sword. Still, I couldn't help staring at it with a mixture of fear and fascination. Rusted and bent though it seemed, I was looking at the sword of Kainor, the Light of Nedarra.

"Put both hands on the hilt," Khara continued. "Like so.

You face your opponent with your left foot forward, balancing your weight."

When Khara saw Luca's awkward pose, she suppressed a sigh. She stood behind him and moved his hips and elbows until she approved of his stance.

"Position your sword vertically," Khara instructed. "Oh, come now, Luca, you're a very bright boy or you wouldn't have been at the Academy. Vertical. You know the word, right?"

He did.

"Left hand in the lower position on the hilt. Hold the hilt close to your chest. Good. Now push your arms forward and angle the tip toward the enemy. This makes it harder for him to sweep his sword toward you. Step forward with your back leg and slightly to the side."

Luca mostly managed to follow her instructions.

"Now," Khara said, "bring the sword down on the enemy's neck."

Luca glanced at her uncertainly, blinked, and sliced his sword downward.

Khara made Luca do this ten times. Then she said, "Good. Now try it on me."

Luca shook his head. "But I don't want to hurt you!"

Khara laughed, and as always, I was struck by how much I loved the musical sound. She drew her sword, which—I assumed because it was not drawn in anger—concealed its true nature. "Try."

Luca tried, and she effortlessly blocked his blade. "Try harder."

This time Luca struck faster. And again, faster. Soon, sweating and frustrated, he struck by surprise, slashing at Khara's neck.

She knocked his sword aside like an annoying insect.

"You rest up, scholar," Khara teased. "Your turn, Byx."

I nearly swallowed my tongue. "I'm ready," I said, trying to sound eager.

Khara pursed her lips, considering me. "You're too short for the moves I taught Luca, and that may be an advantage. The Murdano's men are trained to fight humans with swords, felivets with spears, terramants with axes, and raptidons with arrows. They are not trained to fight dairnes. They'll have no experience facing a creature whose head is where a man's chest would be."

I nodded as if I understood. I didn't.

"You'll need a different approach." Khara circled me. "Yes, I think we have to use your height to our advantage. Start by taking the same pose as Luca. Hips square, left leg forward, knife—well, let's call it a sword—vertical. The scholar can explain that word if you'd like."

"Very funny," Luca muttered.

"Now you're going to hold your sword vertically and leap forward, aiming for the ground just beyond the enemy's legs while keeping the sword stiff and vertical."

"What?" I asked.

"Luca," said Khara. "Stand up in the fighting pose."

He did. Khara bent down until she was more or less my height. "See, a soldier is prepared to counter attacks. He knows how to parry the usual sword strokes. But he's not trained for this."

With that she dived between Luca's legs, landed hard on the ground, and slid beneath him, her blade angled just so. The blade slid along the inner seam of Luca's trousers.

"Ah!" Luca cried, checking himself for cuts.

"Stop being a baby! I didn't cut you." Khara jumped to her feet. "Although I could have."

Luca gave her a sour look. Tobble giggled behind his paw.

I practiced the move, but not with Luca. Ten times Khara ordered me to leap and hold my blade high, and ten times I landed on my chest and elbows. Then came the alternate approach, a leap and a midair twist that landed me on my shoulder and hip. That move was less painful and would have drawn my "sword" along the inside of a foe's thigh.

"There's a great deal of blood if you cut the right artery," Khara said in a calm voice more suited for discussing the weather.

She kept us at it for hours, and Luca and I were both exhausted by the time she called a halt.

"I need a weapon, too," Tobble said firmly.

"Your best weapon, Tobble," said Khara, "is the very fact

that no one expects you to put up a fight."

"Tobble is braver than all of us put together," I said.

Luca laughed, but Khara's glare shut him down. "That little wobbyk fought an onslaught of serpents to defend Byx. I doubt you'd be up to that task, scholar."

"You don't want to see an angry wobbyk," Tobble warned.

Luca rolled his eyes. "I stand forewarned," he said, polishing the hilt of his sword with his tunic. "In any case. Am I ready to face down a soldier, Khara?"

Khara's lips fought a smile. "Attack me," she said. "Use everything you've got."

Luca did. Thirty seconds later, after much furious swinging and stabbing, he let his sword drop to the ground. "What point is there if you can beat me so easily?" he demanded.

"Soldiers are trained from the age of sixteen, when they're first enlisted as cadets," Khara said. "I was trained from age three. We Donatis may be in disgrace. We may be impoverished. But my father made sure I knew how to fight."

Without another word, Khara spun gracefully and with breathtaking speed attacked a nearby sapling. In less time than it would take me to blink twice, she had lopped off two branches and hacked the tree in half.

It fell, scattering a family of mice.

Luca and I gaped in disbelief.

"Now listen to me," she said, her voice intense.

"Understand something. Your enemy is not helpless just because you've drawn blood. Your enemy is not helpless until he stops breathing. If you find yourself in a fight, that is your goal: not to frighten, not to wound. But to kill."

The scabbard belt around my waist felt very tight. The dagger in my hand felt very heavy. But weightier still was the fear that I might someday have to put to use what Khara had taught me.

37.
In the Land of the Raptidons

We came to a vast, open plain called "the Infina." As far as the eye could see, the land stretched in low, rolling hills criss-crossed by streams that, Khara explained, disappeared in summer and returned with the autumn rains. Here and there small clumps of trees punctuated the green-and-gold tapestry.

The raptidons flew here, high overhead, forever on the lookout for prey. Half a dozen were within sight, circling as they rode the upwelling air. Every stand of trees contained a rookery.

"We have to stay off the road," Khara said. "But we'll be in the open. Never forget that some of the raptidons may have arrangements with the Murdano's army."

"You mean they spy?" Tobble asked.

"Not most," Khara said. "They're proud folk, the raptidons. Most won't sink to spying, but a few will."

"They're impressive scholars," Luca observed. "On the

isle they teach about what they call physicalism, the science of world forces. They are deeply knowledgeable about wind and rain, angles and curves, the effect of the ground's natural attraction to objects. And they know their stars as well as the wisest human scholar."

"In any case," Khara said, "we will attempt to avoid dealing with the raptidons. They have no claim on the land, only on their own rookeries and nests."

Since we were off the road and in unknown territory, we decided to travel by day, despite our fatigue. The sun was bright, and only a few fleecy clouds floated overhead, their shadows racing across the grass. Recent rain had filled the little streams so we could wash and drink and brew tea.

That night, while we set up camp, Khara rode Vallino ahead to scout. She came back with a pair of pheasants and a wild yekat. Tobble and I plucked the feathers and gave the yekat to Gambler, as it had fewer bones. We dressed the pheasants and roasted them over a small fire.

Khara brought news as well. "I spotted a troop of garilans heading south."

"Garilans?" I asked.

"Ah, real food. At last!" Gambler said. Perhaps unconsciously, he extended his needle-sharp claws in anticipation.

"Being from the south, you may know them as dervi, Byx," Luca said, licking his fingers. "They're huge beasts that run on six legs, have long necks, and—"

"Yes!" I interrupted. "Dervi! They come south in the spring, along with other species."

Khara put another branch on the fire. "Do you know about the northern migration that happens each fall, Byx? In Nedarran it's called the 'Viagatto.'"

"Maia told me about it. And Myxo, our pathfinder, spoke of it often."

I felt my chest tighten. Merely saying those names aloud—Maia, Myxo—brought back all the pain of their loss. Tobble put his paw on my arm and gave me an encouraging nod.

"The last day I saw Maia," I said softly, "we saw four butterbats. That was not even a month ago. She said they were heading north. They were so—" My voice caught.

"So beautiful?" Tobble finished for me.

I nodded, and tears fell against my will. The fire spit and crackled, and a stardove let out a mournful call from a nearby tree.

I felt guilty letting my pain show. These were my fellow travelers, taking risks for me, and it was my job to be strong. I wasn't the leader—clearly that was Khara's role. But we'd all been through hardships.

"I'm sorry," I said, looking at each in turn. Khara, her gaze steady and thoughtful. Tobble, the picture of concern. Gambler, his tail flicking, eyes slitted, unreadable. And Luca, watching my tears fall with the odd fascination of an academic.

"You don't need to be sorry, Byx," Khara said. "We know you've gone through a lot."

"We all have," I said, chin raised, voice firmer. "So. Tell me more about the garilans."

"By the time they reach the south, they begin to break up into smaller herds and bands," Khara said. "But during the Viagatto, you can see tens of thousands of them, all moving as one. Most animals head south as it gets colder. But a few species—garilans, tirralopes, butterbats, giant warblers—go north. No one is certain why."

"You think they'll come this way?" Gambler asked, unable to hide the glittery excitement in his predator's eyes.

"I suspect they'll follow the Telarno River north," Khara said. "It's about, oh, half a day's walk to our west."

The next morning we started out early. Gambler walked far to our left, closest to where he hoped the garilans would pass. I felt sorry for him. He was doing many things that weren't natural for a felivet, starting with the fact that he was traveling with others. Felivets assemble to debate and discuss, and they mate and have young. But most don't form a family.

Add to that the fact that Gambler was traveling with creatures he was perfectly capable of killing and eating. I didn't wish for the death of any dervi (or garilans), but I did hope Gambler could find a satisfying meal. At very least, it might allow Tobble to relax a bit. He was still skittish around the big cat.

It was noon when three of us—Gambler, Vallino, and I—smelled something on the breeze.

I stopped, breathed in, and found familiar clues in the faint tendrils of scent-bearing air.

Vallino pranced nervously and tossed his head.

"Humans," Gambler said.

"Yes," I agreed.

"And horses," Gambler said.

"You may be smelling farmers or other travelers," Luca suggested.

Khara swung herself up onto Vallino's back, shaded her eyes, and looked south. "I see a dust cloud. A league away." She shook her head. "I can't tell what they are."

We kept moving, but Gambler and I kept exchanging worried looks. Human and horse, leather and dogs. Maybe it was a hunting party. But maybe it was not.

"Would your poacher friends still be looking for you after all this time?" I asked Khara.

She shook her head and laughed. "Poachers don't have the attention span for a long trip unless there's a sizable reward at the end. They're criminals, not soldiers."

The word "soldiers" hung in the air.

Khara led us toward a stand of trees thick with raptidons, poised on nearly every branch like giant fruit. She stopped us at a respectful distance. Facing the rookery, she unbuckled her sword belt and placed it on the ground.

"Come with me, Byx," she said.

"But . . . but you said they can be spies. Do we want them to see me?"

It was Gambler who explained. "As your nose is superior to a human's, so the eyes of the raptidons are superior to the eyes of all other creatures. Do you see that raptidon perched on the highest branch? He not only knows you're a dairne. He knows the color of your eyes. He sees the bread crumb on your lip."

I blinked and brushed the crumb away.

"Are you coming?" I asked Gambler. I had great faith in Khara's sword, but I'd also ridden on Gambler's back and knew his speed and power.

"We don't get along, felivets and raptidons. They steal our kills." Gambler chewed a nail. "And in retaliation we occasionally eat one of their kind."

I grinned. "You forget. I'm a dairne."

A felivet's smile is all in the eyes. "Are you suggesting that I've told an untruth?"

"The words 'retaliation' and 'occasionally' sort of leapt out at me."

Gambler let loose his loud, hoarse laugh. "I may have

shaded the truth a bit. It's possible that I've eaten one or two raptidons, maybe three."

I gave him a look.

"Or it maybe closer to twenty or thirty."

"Let's get this over with," Khara said, squaring her shoulders. "Come on, Byx."

I dropped my own sword—to my mind, that sounded more reassuring than "knife" or "dagger"—and fell into step beside her. We walked forward, hands held out at our sides, palms forward, to show we were unarmed.

"Be careful, Byx!" Tobble called.

We'd gone only a few paces when Khara stopped. She turned, hands on hips, and said, "Tobble, we don't have all day."

"Me?" Tobble leapt to his feet and dashed toward us.

Khara winked at me. I'd never seen a human wink before, and my first thought was that she had something in her eye, until I remembered my lessons from Dalyntor. Dairnes don't wink, as it often implies a shared secret or even a lie.

Still, I realized what Khara was telling me: She was asking Tobble to join us for his sake, not for ours. It was a kind gesture, even if it didn't make much practical sense, and I was grateful.

We walked slowly, the three of us, trying not to seem threatening. What had from a distance appeared to be just a stand of a dozen or so trees turned out to be far more elaborate.

T-perches were planted in the earth, and the trees contained numerous platforms. As we neared, a raptidon guard with red tail feathers swooped down to land on a perch.

"You approach a raptidon rookery," the guard announced. "Why do you come?"

"You see that we are unarmed," Khara said.

"I see many things. I see a girl human pretending to be a boy human. I see a felivet and a wobbyk and a horse. And I see one who does not exist anymore." His last sentence was uttered with what I interpreted as a smirk. Raptidons do not have lips. They speak using only their tongues and throats. So the smirk was all about intonation, not facial expression. Raptidons are known to have a high opinion of themselves, and little respect for "ground worms," as they sometimes call flightless species.

"The eyes of your people are legendary," Khara said in a placating voice. "No one has greater respect for the raptidons than I. You are rulers of the sky. I approach with humble questions, not threats."

The raptidon debated her request, head tilted to one side. "You may enter," he said at last.

And so we did.

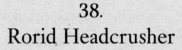

38.
Rorid Headcrusher

We crossed the perimeter and stepped beneath the trees. Birds were everywhere, in the branches above us, gliding by in the air, even strutting on the ground. Nests of all shapes and sizes dotted platforms and hung suspended from branches. Some were plain and workmanlike, made of mud and reeds. Others were more elaborate, woven with a tapestry of silver and gold vines.

Here and there, food lay in neat piles: dead mice and voles, salamanders and frogs, tiny, broken songbirds. Two kestrels snacked on a disemboweled weasel, not much smaller than Tobble.

We faced a cleared space amid the trees. In the middle stood a T-perch, ornately carved and taller than all the others. I felt a shadow as a great raptidon swooped down to land with disdainful ease on the perch.

The guard said, "You have the honor of addressing Rorid Headcrusher."

"Rorid Headcrusher" was not a name to inspire much confidence in a small dairne, let alone a wobbyk. Rorid spread his gray and tawny wings in a display meant to impress us, and impress us he did. It was easily thirty feet from tip-feather to tip-feather. His yellow talons, which ended in filigreed silver tips, were as thick as Khara's ankles. His beak was hooked and sharp, as cruel looking a weapon as I had ever seen.

He was terrifying, and no part of him was more terrifying than his pale yellow eyes, each encircled with a black ring. They cut right through us, those eyes.

"My lord, Rorid Headcrusher," Khara said. She knelt on one knee, and Tobble and I followed suit.

Rorid was not one for casual conversation. In a squawking accent he asked, "Have you brought me tribute?"

"We are but poor travelers," Khara said. "We have nothing that would interest a great lord of the sky."

"You have a wobbyk," Rorid said flatly.

"He's a friend," Khara said. "It's not the habit of my people to sacrifice their friends. Not even for one so mighty as you, my lord."

Rorid emitted a sound like a crow. I think it was a laugh. "Ah, yes, humans never turn against their friends."

"Let me amend that. I do not betray my friends."

Maybe Rorid appreciated her courage. Maybe he was already bored. Maybe he was planning on summoning his folk to tear us all apart. I was desperately hoping Khara could read a raptidon's expression. I certainly couldn't. However, if he lied, I would be able to sense it—I hoped.

"You seek information," Rorid said. It was not a question.

"Yes, lord. We have noticed a band of humans on horses. But our eyes are not the eyes of the raptidons."

"Information," Rorid said. "If you want information, you must give information. Tell us something we do not know."

"Your sources are better than mine," Khara said. "But I can tell you that—"

Rorid fluttered a wing, cutting her off. "Dairne. Do you undertake to perform the ancient duty of your people?"

It took me a few seconds of blank and panicky staring to realize he was asking me whether I would vouch for the truth of what was being said.

"Yes, sir. I mean, my lord, um . . . Headcrusher."

He jerked his beak at Khara.

"I can tell you that we have come from the isle," Khara said. "From the eumony, the premature funeral of the dairnes."

"Ah. Scholars."

"Not I," Khara said. "But the other human with us was an apprentice to scholars."

"And you are a hunter."

"Sometimes, yes."

"A killer of raptidons?"

"Never by design," Khara said evasively. Then: "I have killed one. I was aiming my arrow at a squirrel but it flew wide of the mark. It was a mistake."

Rorid took this in. "A mistake indeed, but at least you admit it. So, hunter, what news of the isle?"

"Well, you know about the eumony. And you see that I have a dairne with me. We meant to reveal the truth—"

I held up a hand. If Headcrusher was to believe us, I needed to perform my duty fairly.

Khara saw it, looked annoyed then accepting, took a deep breath, and said, "I captured this dairne while hunting in the south. I meant to sell her to a scholar of my acquaintance, a man I trusted would welcome such a discovery."

Rorid laughed his bird laugh, long and hard. Had he been capable of tears, I think he might have wept from laughter.

His penetrating gaze fell on me again. "Let me tell you what happened. This scholar betrayed you."

"Yes." I nodded.

"Do you know why dairnes were so prized in ancient times?" Rorid asked.

"I've been told it was because we could separate truth from lies."

"It's because no other species could trust humans unless dairnes were there to speak truth. Humans are liars," he said, venom in his voice. "Their word is meaningless. Their promises last only until the echoes of their lies have died out."

Turning back to Khara, he said, "So you flee the isle."

"We flee Araktik," Khara said.

"Indeed? Why?"

Khara thought for a moment. "Well, to begin with, Araktik the Seer was very nearly harmed while performing the eumony."

"Oh? Harmed? By whom? By you, female-human-pretending-to-be-male?"

Khara didn't answer immediately, and I wondered if she thought she might endanger me if she told the full story. "I can explain," I said.

I recounted the whole tale. When I got to the part about swooping down in a barely controlled glide right at Araktik, Rorid started laughing again. He called out the names of other birds, and they joined him on lower perches. "Tell it again, dairne," he commanded.

I started over. There are few more disturbing sounds than a dozen laughing raptidons, all glaring at you like they're considering where exactly to sink their talons.

Rorid stopped laughing, and instantly so did all his fellows.

"That was not perhaps information," he said, "but it was a wonderfully humorous story. Many do not know that we raptidons have an excellent sense of humor."

I was not about to argue.

"Then, may I ask . . . ," Khara began.

Rorid turned his gaze on a young golden eagle, who nodded obediently. "Twenty-four in number," he reported. "All on strong horses. Six horses for spares, twelve mules to carry supplies. Six dogs. All the humans wear the livery of the Seer. All boast the blue eye sigil on their shields. And all are armed with sword and crossbow." He paused. "At their head is a Knight of the Fire."

Khara gasped. I had to restrain myself from asking why.

"I thank you," Khara mumbled, then added, "My lord."

"I see from the sword you relinquished that you are well armed yourself, young hunter." He paused, taking in our wary reaction. "I was old when every living human was young, and what are legends to you are memories to me. Do not imagine that the spells and charms around your sword hide its true nature from me. Rorid Headcrusher is not easily tricked."

For long minutes Rorid stayed silent, and his fellows waited in respectful stillness. More than once Khara glanced nervously over her shoulder, clearly anxious to move on.

At last he announced his decision. "The affairs of humans are not usually our concern. But we see much and know much. We have seen the slow decline of many species. Some were our prey. Some were, like us, governing species."

He nodded at me. "One thing is certain: the world grows emptier with each day. The causes are many—disease, famine, outright slaughter. But behind each cause there is a single perpetrator: the human who styles himself Murdano and his murderous young Seer. These humans do not understand the balance in life. They do not understand that their will to dominate and control, to use and abuse, is destructive to all." He paused. "It will end in a eumony for the human species."

Tobble and I glanced at Khara. She stood still, perhaps as uncertain as I was, though she revealed nothing.

"We raptidons know our friends, and we know our enemies," Rorid continued. "He who fights the enemies of the raptidons is a friend to the raptidons. The Seer has sent her foul beasts after us more than once, all the while professing innocence. We see what has been done to the dairnes. We see what they are doing to the felivets. We are not fools. If two dozen of Araktik's guards and a full-fledged Knight of the Fire are after you, it seems I must consider you our friends."

"Thank you, my lord," Khara said humbly.

"Go," Rorid said. "Go and be quick."

We did. And we were.

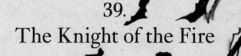

39.
The Knight of the Fire

Frantically, we grabbed our weapons and fled.

Gambler was the fastest among us, but he tired easily. Luca ran doggedly, but life in a library had not prepared him to run long distances. I was not as fast as Gambler, but dairnes have stamina. Tobble, the slowest of our party, rode atop Vallino.

But it was Khara who led. She seemed tireless. Relentless.

Overhead a raptidon wheeled lazily, perhaps merely curious, perhaps sent by Rorid to report back on what he must have assumed would be our slaughter.

I ran beside Luca. Panting, my heart beating steadily, I asked, "What is so fearsome about a Knight of the Fire?"

He was red in the face, sweat bleeding through his tunic. "They are the greatest . . . of warriors . . . sword, spear, doesn't matter . . . but it's the fire . . ."

He waved me off, unable to talk and run.

"Take a break," Khara called, and we fell in heaps on the long grass. Khara swung up onto Vallino's back to get a better view. I watched her face as she concentrated.

"They're definitely after us," she reported. "And they're gaining."

"Can we hide?" Tobble asked. He reached forward to stroke Vallino's damp neck.

Khara waved her hand around, encompassing the great, open emptiness. "Not likely."

"We can surrender and beg for mercy," Luca said, still gasping for breath.

"Mercy? From a Knight of the Fire?" Gambler shook his head. "They're not mere soldiers, Luca. A soldier may show mercy—not often, but sometimes. A Knight of the Fire?" He laughed.

"Let's go," Khara urged, and after less than three minutes of rest, we were running again, stumbling now and then as our limbs grew heavy.

Ahead I heard the low grumble of thunder, although the sky was clear. With a start, I realized Khara's desperate plan.

She was taking us toward the Viagatto. Toward the end-less herd of garilans and other animals heading north.

Glancing back, even I could see that the Seer's men were gaining on us, and gaining fast. I could make out individual faces beneath helmet bills. I could faintly see the blue eye sigil on their shields. And I could see him. The knight.

He rode a massive black horse, its head protected by silver armor. The knight himself wore full plate armor that glimmered in the sun. With his visor down, I saw no face, just a moving mountain of steel.

"Why 'Knight of the Fire'?" I asked. Even though I knew I shouldn't waste precious breath on a question, I needed to know what we were up against. "Why"—I stumbled on my own feet, but caught myself in time—"why are they called that?"

It was Gambler who replied in a low, worried voice. "Pray to your gods, dairne, that you do not find out the answer."

We topped a low rise and I almost stopped dead.

Nothing could have prepared me for the magnificent spectacle unfolding before us.

A great mass of animals moved like a slow, relentless river stretching to the horizon. Tens of thousands, I guessed. Maybe even hundreds of thousands of the animals, grazing and moving, grazing and moving.

Most were garilans, oddly beautiful in such numbers. Six-legged but graceful, they had deep crimson bodies and thick golden tails. Their necks, also golden, were ridiculously long and arched, their horns creamy spirals as long as their tails.

Beyond them, I saw tirralopes and blue-striped xia deer, along with a handful of other species I'd never encountered before. They moved as one, undulating like a swarm of midges, and although their pace was leisurely, the noise of hooves on earth was deafening.

As awestruck as I was by this moving mass of life, I realized at once that they were too far away to be of any help. Behind us the knight had spurred his warhorse, pulling away from his soldiers.

"We won't make it," I said, my voice trembling like the ground beneath me.

Khara gave a curt nod. "I'll slow him down," she said, nodding toward the knight. She helped Tobble off Vallino and was about to mount the horse when Gambler spoke.

"He'll kill you," he said. "This is not a job for a hunter on horseback. It's a job for stealth and surprise."

Khara hesitated, her hand on Vallino's mane. She knew Gambler was right, but she seemed to feel it was her duty to take on the terrifying steel-clad warrior.

"Keep running," Gambler said.

Khara took in the scene, considered, nodded. "You heard him. Move!"

We set off at a run as Gambler crept, almost on his belly, into the tall grass. He was lost to sight within seconds, but still I kept glancing back until the towering knight reached the spot where we'd left the great cat.

I stopped. I watched as Gambler exploded from the grass. He flew through the air, paws outstretched, and slammed full force into the knight.

The knight toppled from his horse but was up in a heartbeat, reaching for his sword.

Gambler leapt on the knight before he could draw and knocked him on his back with a metallic clang. After that, there was little Gambler could do: it was tooth and claw against steel.

Gambler bounded away, racing to catch up with us. As the felivet moved toward us, I saw something I would never have imagined was possible.

The knight stood. He reached for his spear and leveled it.

"Gambler!" Tobble screamed, although his voice was swallowed up in the noise of the herd.

We watched in horror, waiting to see the spear cut through the air.

But what we saw instead was even more terrifying.

From the end of the spear came a jet of flame. A miasma of fire.

A torrent of death.

40.
Stampede

The flame, which seemed almost liquid, quickly caught the grass. Fire and smoke billowed, obscuring the knight.

The blaze moved with unnatural speed, not driven by the breeze, not burning randomly, but moving as if with a will, faster and faster, faster even than Gambler.

Gambler saw the pursuing fire and dodged a sharp left.

The fire followed him.

He cut sharply back, and still the fire tracked him.

Pursued him. As if it were alive, sentient, planning.

"Theurgy," I whispered. "Sorcery."

"The living fire!" Luca cried in horror, practically weeping with fear.

Gambler ran, but no longer toward us. He bolted straight toward the garilan herd, as the fire raced to cut him off.

Suddenly he stopped short. A line of flame had rushed ahead of him. Two lines of fire now converged.

Gambler was surrounded.

I could just make out his figure through the smoke, head darting this way and that, searching for escape that did not exist.

To my shock, I didn't plan my next move. No "on the one hand, on the other foot."

I simply acted.

I jumped atop Vallino, stood up facing the knight, and yelled, "Here I am! Over here!"

The steel visor rotated toward me. The knight was less than two hundred yards away. The thundering herd was twice that distance ahead. Gambler was wreathed in smoke and flame, perhaps three hundred yards north—close, but not close enough, to the garilans.

"Go, Vallino!" Khara yelled, and the horse leapt, knocking me flat on his broad back. I dug my fingers into his mane and held on for dear life.

Vallino's speed changed the possibilities. I might—might—just make it to the herd with his help.

But even as Vallino galloped at full speed, the knight pointed his spear toward me. Instantly the living flame sped in two distinct lines to cut me off.

There was no stopping.

It was a race between Vallino and the fire, with my life as the prize.

Vallino flew, his mouth foaming, his powerful muscles

propelling him at speeds not even Gambler could match.

Vallino. The fire. Vallino. The fire.

Suddenly the flames were before us, a searing, smoking blockade, and I felt Vallino's muscles tense beneath me.

He was going to veer. To recoil.

But no: he leapt!

We soared through a veil of smoke, above a fire that had barely caught hold, and landed hard on the other side.

The garilan herd—the refuge we sought—had smelled the fire. Even as we approached, they were veering away, panicked and stampeding. Vallino could only keep pace as we tore away to the west, the whole mighty flow of beasts turning with us, a diverted river.

The knight stayed focused on me, galloping through an opening in the flame, turning to match course with the terrified herd.

I stayed low, hugging Vallino's sweating back, gripping handfuls of mane, hoping to stay atop the horse, my only chance.

I caught fragmented glances behind me. The soldiers were taking aim at Khara, Luca, and Tobble. The fire was still after me, racing along the ground behind the hooves of the knight's war charger.

I'd never tried to speak to Vallino—I'd always assumed that even the cleverest of horses understands just a few words—but I found myself saying, "Vallino, I'm going to slide off. Keep running!"

We'd reached the outer edge of the herd as the garilans ran stolidly on. I judged my moment as well as I could and half leapt, half fell from Vallino's back. Frantically I grabbed at the back of the nearest garilan. There was nothing like a mane to hold on to, so I clutched handfuls of its bloodred fur.

The animal felt me—how could it not?—and reared up, almost throwing me off. After a moment, it seemed to decide that fire was the greater threat, and it continued its mad gallop with the rest of the herd.

I wondered if the knight had seen my move. Hugging the garilan close, I kept low, hoping that thick smoke and sheer speed would hide me.

I needed more control. Foolish as it was, I dared to reach forward, clinging to the garilan's neck, and grabbed the end of its long left ear. I pulled it to the left, hoping it might serve as a primitive rein.

To my utter amazement, the beast veered left, jostling through its brothers and sisters.

When I checked again I saw the knight sweep by, never looking my way. He was still intently pursuing Vallino, along with the sentient fire.

I couldn't see Khara or Luca or poor little Tobble. But I understood that I couldn't help them.

I was the target. Where I went, the knight and his soldiers would follow.

Far off now, Vallino slowed, worn out. He turned sideways, his profile revealing that he no longer had a rider.

The knight reined instantly. His fight was not with a horse.

He stood in his stirrups, scanning the horizon. Looking for me. I had drawn him off Gambler, but I knew I could do nothing to stop the soldiers who would soon surround and kill Khara, Tobble, and Luca.

I wanted desperately to help them, but I could do nothing, nothing but wave at the knight from my position deep within the herd. He lowered his spear. To my shock, the fire seemed to be sucked back into the tip, like a robin eating a worm.

The knight's fire wouldn't help him now. If he used it, the herd would flee with renewed energy. And he must have known that his warhorse would never move quickly between the garilans.

I closed my eyes, trying not to imagine the slaughter of my friends.

My friends, who would die because of me.

Once again, others would perish, and I would escape.

My parents and siblings.

My pack.

And now my new family.

That's what they were, I realized with a sharp pang. Khara, Tobble, and Gambler had become my new family.

And now they were lost to me forever.

41.
Xial Renarriss

I don't know how long I rode on the garilan's back. I don't know how far we traveled. I was lost in living nightmares, besieged by guilt.

Alone.

Alone as day ended and the herd, now calm and back on track, moved ever farther north.

I cried. I cried for my mother and father, my siblings, my pack. I cried for brave Khara and loyal Tobble. I cried for Gambler, my improbable felivet friend.

I did not cry for Luca, but I regretted his death. I had never warmed to him—he was enigmatic and distant. But he, too, had been lost because of me.

Sometime that evening I slipped from the garilan's back and landed in the eternal grass. Sleep turned my sadness and regret to dark dreams of faces torn apart by steel.

I dreamed about my drawing, my silly, childish map with its sentient island and its imaginary colony of dairnes.

I dreamed of Dalyntor, reciting that ancient poem:

Sing, poet, of the Ancients who dared forth—
Brave dairnes, o'er mountains treacherous and cruel,
Who crossed the frigid waters of the north
To Dairneholme, living isle and floating jewel.

I dreamed that a great bird swept low over me as I slept, circling once before flying off.

When the sun woke me, I was on my back, lying on a stony ridge that divided the garilan into two streams.

I was certain that I hadn't landed on rock. I had landed on soft grass.

Had I dreamed that, too?

It hit me then, a rush of sensation, of smells familiar and welcome, of human and . . . and felivet?

I jerked up to find Tobble holding a waterskin to my lips. "Tobble?" I yelped in joy.

Tobble grinned. "Drink first. Answers later."

I drank greedily.

Breathed deeply.

Embraced Tobble.

And that was when I saw Khara, Luca, Gambler, and

Vallino all gathered on the island of rock in a sea of garilans.

"How . . . what . . . how . . . ?"

I may have repeated that several times. I may also have wiped away more than a few tears.

My friends. My new family.

They had escaped. But not unscathed.

Patches of Gambler's fur were scorched, leaving dark skin glistening with dried blood. Khara wore a thick bandage on her left arm and another above her knee. Tobble's right ear was torn and bloodied.

"How?" I demanded. "Not that I am anything less than ecstatic to find you alive."

"Crows!" Tobble said. "The soldiers caught up to us, and Khara . . . well, I wish you could have seen it!"

"Crows?" I repeated.

"Just as I was sure Khara was done for," Tobble continued, the words pouring out of him, "fighting three soldiers at once, down came the crows."

"Crows. As in black birds?" I asked.

"Crows," Khara confirmed. "The soldiers were not expecting an attack from the air. Crows can't kill a man, but they can blind him. They can rip his ears and lips and throat."

"Rorid?" I asked, puzzled.

Luca, looking disturbed, said, "The raptidons have no direct control over crows. However . . ." He shrugged.

"As humans use dogs, so raptidons use crows," Gambler said. "They're intelligent birds, the crows. Useful and deniable."

I shook my head. "Deniable?"

"It seems Rorid is a wily old bird," said Gambler. "He didn't want to directly commit himself or his followers to help us, but crows? He can claim he had nothing to do with that."

I pointed to Gambler's wounds. They were terrible.

"You must be in pain," I said.

"Yes," he acknowledged. "But we are good at handling pain."

"I cannot tell you how happy I am to see you all alive." I had to pause to choke back more tears. "But at the same time, it makes my heart heavy. You might have died, and why? For what's almost certainly a lost cause."

"If you're the endling dairne, then the cause is lost," Khara said. "But if you aren't, if we can expose the Murdano and Araktik as liars who've tried to bring the dairnes to extinction, if we can bring dairnes back as truth tellers . . .well, it's probably still a lost cause"—she smiled—"but at least there will be hope."

Her words were meant to be encouraging. But all I felt was their weight on me, a know-nothing pup of questionable judgment.

"In any case," said Khara, "it's all the cause we have."

She stood slowly, wincing at the pain. But as she straightened, her weariness seemed to vanish. "So," she said, "what shall it be? Do we continue, or do we not?"

Tobble was the first to speak, and the loudest. Luca voted last. The vote was unanimous. Still, I couldn't help worrying that my friends might come to more pain because of me.

At Khara's direction, we settled in for a few hours of rest. I volunteered to keep watch. I sat near the group with a blanket draped around my shoulders. It smelled, just a bit, of horse, but that was fine with me. I felt nothing but gratitude toward Vallino after our wild ride.

Under the twinkling canopy of night, I watched everyone sleep. Khara, making her soft toad sounds. Luca, tossing and turning. Gambler, tail flicking. Vallino, standing upright, head drooped. And Tobble, dear Tobble, lying next to me, his round belly rising and falling.

My new family, bathed in a sheen of silver starlight. Wounded, exhausted, but not necessarily defeated.

I thought about how my parents used to check on us while we slept—or pretended to sleep. How protected I'd felt! How certain that my family would always be a part of my life!

I reached into my pouch. Carefully I removed my crumpled map, the flat stone Tobble had retrieved near the mirabear hive, and the little leather-bound journal Luca had given me.

The moon was bright enough for me to just make out my scribblings:

> Heard a marsh wolf cub howling for its mother.
> Charred vole meat for breakfast. Tobble had willow leaves.
> I feel sorry for dogs. They must have so much they want to say, and no way to say it.
> Sometimes I think of Dalyntor's lessons and wish I'd asked more questions.
> So afraid today. Afraid every day, it seems.
> Am I truly the endling? Why me?

"Am I in there?"

It was Tobble, watching me with one eye open.

"Of course you are." I turned to another page and read: "'Tobble is so little and yet so brave. I wish I could be more like him.'"

Tobble smiled with satisfaction. "That stone, Byx," he said. "What does the writing on it say?"

I picked up the smooth black stone, running a finger over the tiny letters, so carefully carved.

"Xial renarriss," I said. "It's Old Dairnish. No one speaks—spoke—it, except for Dalyntor and a few others. My parents knew a bit, too."

A breeze eddied the grass. Tobble pulled his blanket

tighter. "What does it mean?"

"It was the motto of our pack. It means 'In truth lies strength.'" I squinted at the letters. "I'm not sure who this belonged to. Myxo, maybe. Our pathfinder."

"You're the pathfinder now, Byx."

I shook my head. "Not me. Not yet. Not ever, probably. I'll never be ready for that."

"I disagree," said Tobble. "But I understand how you feel. It's like the wobbyk stibillary."

"The tail-braiding ceremony?"

He nodded. "Maybe someday it will happen when I've earned it. Not yet, though."

Tobble closed his eyes. I watched him fall asleep the way my parents had watched me so many times, and for the first time in a long while, I felt a strange kind of peace settle over me.

42.
Saguria

The weather grew worse day by day.

Autumn in the south, where I am from, is a time of fantastically tinted leaves, occasional drizzle, cool days, and chilly nights. How I'd loved those nights, my whole sleeping family woven together for warmth, with our tangled tails and our dream-twitching paws! Each night we created a refuge on the ground as reassuring as the nests our ancestors had once twined in the treetops.

Autumn in the north was far different. Each day we encountered more rain. And rain is not encouraging, especially when you're not sure you're doing the right thing.

Mud sucked at my feet until my legs ached. Vallino's hooves were clumps of muck and leaves that Khara had to scrape off every hour. Gambler managed to stay clean, but only by virtue of spending hours at night grooming his fur.

Tobble, who insisted on walking, sometimes sank up to his waist in goo.

But it was Luca who worried me. Thus far, he'd been sullen and reserved. He'd also been deferential to Khara, who had no hesitation about chiding him when he moved too slowly or failed to carry his fair share.

Now, day by day, Luca seemed both friendlier and more argumentative. I wondered if he was one of those types who actually enjoy bad weather. Or maybe he was just shy, and had finally grown more relaxed around us. Every now and then I caught him looking at me in ways that made me uncomfortable, but each time I met his gaze, he would simply smile.

"Today we will reach Saguria," Khara said on our eighth day of mud. We were walking side by side as she urged Vallino along.

"The Murdano's city," I said.

"Yes."

"Saguria the Great," "Saguria the Impregnable," the capital of humankind in Nedarra.

Saguria, capital city of the Murdano.

It was said to be home to a hundred thousand humans, plus many thousands of natites who clustered at the water's edge. Districts had been set aside for felivets and raptidons as well, while terramants had dug a network of tunnels beneath the city. Still, there was no question who was in charge. Saguria belonged to the Murdano.

"Khara?"

"What, Byx?"

"What are the chances that we will make it through?"

She didn't answer. She did, however, glance down at her sword, as if for reassurance.

"Can't we go around the city?" I asked.

"Not without going hundreds of leagues out of our way," she said. "And do you honestly believe we can manage a hundred-league detour?"

I glanced at our miserable, underfed, wet, cold crew and said, "Perhaps not. But how can we possibly pass through? Isn't it packed with soldiers?"

"The upper city, certainly. But the lower city is a sort of sprawling mess of random streets, home to all manner of vice and corruption. Or so I'm told. I've never been there."

The land had transformed from gently rolling hills to stony rises. The road, far off to our right, passed through the rocky areas by way of tunnels and bridges. For our part, we moved the hard way, up and down, feeling our way forward, occasionally finding our path blocked so that we had to double back.

The only good news was that we'd seen no sign of the Knight of the Fire, nor of the soldiers who'd been attacked by the crows. Maybe we had lost them. Maybe they had given up.

As the afternoon passed into evening, Khara led us up a tall hill, hoping to spy out the route ahead.

From this height I got my first glimpse of the Perricci Mountains, a long line of stony peaks topped with snow all the year round. They ran like an endless wall, and I understood why Khara had decided to risk passing through Saguria.

But it was the city ahead that took my breath away. I had not known that humans could build anything so imposing and impressive.

"There it is," Khara said. "Saguria."

The city sat astride a narrow strip of relatively flat land, hemmed in by the sea to the east and the mountains to the west. As if in response to some great theurgic spell, the clouds parted briefly and a shaft of golden light shone down.

"They say the walls are seven leagues around," I said.

Khara didn't answer. I saw her hand move, as if sketching out a path forward. "We need to find a place to camp for the night. Tomorrow we can join the road just half a league from the south gate."

I was barely listening, so focused was I on the city itself. I gazed in amazement at a wedge-shaped rock outcropping that rose hundreds of feet in the center of the city, like a stone pier or even a promontory. At the far end this mass of stone seemed almost to grow from the northern walls, but the walls were man-made and this . . . this was far beyond anyone's ability to create. It rose steeply from the northern walls, sheer cliffs on both sides, then widened out to shape a plateau, upon which sat the palace. From that plateau the stone promontory had been deliberately shaped, the stone carved into a central ramp that, when it reached ground level, merged seamlessly into a broad avenue. On both sides of that long ramp, and in carved-out flat spaces, were shops and great mansions painted in russet, ocher, and pale pink.

At the top of this impressive act of nature was the palace itself, a sprawling mess of different architectural styles that testified to centuries of building, each new generation adding a tower or a dome or a crenellated defensive wall.

I was awestruck. It was impossibly old and, despite the clashes of style, incredibly grand. The isle had left me astonished, but this was many times larger, and it spoke of great wealth and terrible power.

"How could the human who controls that care about dairnes?" I asked.

"He doesn't care about dairnes," Khara said. "He cares about power."

"Is that all humans care about?" I asked. "Power?"

Khara patted me on the back. "Not all humans, Byx. Just most of them."

She thought she was reassuring me. Instead she'd made me think. The possibility that a lust for power explained many humans was interesting. Interesting, and just possibly useful.

43.
The Pale Guard

It rained very hard in the night, so hard that the poor shelter we'd found by pressing ourselves into a shallow cave was almost useless. The next morning we set off wet to the bone, hungry, and cold. We crossed a rain-swollen ditch and joined the road. We were a curious sight, even with Khara passing as a boy and me back to playing dog. There was no avoiding the fact that we were humans traveling with a felivet and a wobbyk. Oddly, I was the least suspect of the group. On all fours I could play my part quite convincingly, and no one ever questions the presence of a dog.

We moved at a snail's pace, as the night's drenching had washed out parts of the road. One of the bridges over a churning stream was barely hanging on. Guards ensured that everyone crossed in single file but paid no closer attention to us. Increasingly weary and frustrated, we trudged on between collections of shacks that hoped someday to be villages, through drab villages hoping someday to become towns, and into a town with the remarkably functional name of Outpost.

Outpost was the last habitation outside Saguria's outer wall. It was a busy, bustling place of warehouses and stables, with heavily laden wagons moving to and fro. All the food and supplies Saguria relied upon were assembled and organized in Outpost. It was both servant and wholesaler to Saguria.

"Should we press on?" Lucas asked Khara. He was as weary as any of us but seemed in more of a hurry.

Khara shook her head. "At best we would reach the city walls at sunset, and at night the streets will be heavily patrolled. Better to move through with the usual daytime throng."

Using almost the last of Khara's coins, we were able to find a dry barn with fresh straw. We spent the night there with Vallino. A nearby pub sold us simple food, which we consumed like wild beasts. The barn smelled, as barns do, but it felt luxurious compared to many of the places we had passed a night.

Unfortunately, a barn full of horses is no place for a felivet. Horses will not happily tolerate the smell of a predator. Vallino had grown used to Gambler, but the huge cat terrified the other horses. In the end, Gambler decided to sleep in the woodshed behind the pub.

At least we were all dry for the first time in ages.

"Have you ever been to Saguria?" I asked Luca as we settled in.

"Yes," he said. Then, when I let the silence build, he added, "My family does business in the city. We own an estate a few leagues west."

"Don't you want to visit your family since we're near?" I asked.

"No," Luca said curtly.

It was the first false thing he'd said. It was easy to catch, at least to my ears, like hearing a cat bark. But it was hard to interpret. In fairness, I could understand why a boy who'd fled his sinecure on the isle to help an unknown dairne escape might not be welcomed by his family.

"Do you know anyone in Saguria?" I asked.

Luca's eyes narrowed. "Why do you ask?"

"I thought perhaps you might know people who could help us," I said innocently.

Luca stared directly at me. "I know of no one in Saguria who would help us."

It was carefully worded—not a denial that he knew someone in Saguria, merely a statement that he knew no one who would help us. But he walked off, and I could press no further.

The morning was gloomy but dry and we set out early.

As soon as we'd left Outpost, I saw the walls of Saguria looming. They were built of dark basalt, gray and grim, and stood ten times a man's height. Off to the right I saw the distant, whitecapped sea.

The south gate was a tall arch between two massive, circular towers. The crenellated towers and the nearby wall were lined with soldiers. I could make out their helmets and the tips of their spears above me.

Half a dozen soldiers stood guard at the gate, checking wagons for contraband, demanding to know why travelers wanted to enter the city, and, according to Luca, taking bribes.

"I have no more coin," Khara said.

"I'll speak to them," Luca volunteered. "I have this." He pulled up a delicate chain that hung from his neck and showed us a silver talisman, a cunningly wrought silver fish.

"Isn't that precious to you?" Gambler asked. "Humans place a high value on objects. Especially gold or silver." He didn't disguise the mild contempt in his tone.

Luca shrugged. "I value my life more highly."

As we approached the gate, Luca moved ahead. We watched him draw an officer aside to speak. I strained my ears but heard nothing, though I did see Luca lift the silver talisman from his neck and hold it out to the guard. What the guard did with it I couldn't tell, for he was blocked by Luca's body.

In any case, it worked. They waved us through the gate and into town. I should have relaxed. But the guards seemed to avoid looking at us too carefully. And once we'd passed, I glanced back and saw their eyes following us.

As we entered the city, I immediately understood why it was called, among other names, "Saguria the Impregnable." The intimidating basalt wall was only the outermost defense. Just fifty feet inside rose an inner wall, this one made of crusty pink coral. On closer inspection, I realized that the chaotic surface was in fact festooned with protruding daggers of coral, each shaped like a raptidon's beak, the sharp points turned down to impede anyone trying to lay a ladder against the wall.

At the top of this wall were gargoyles, mouths open. I assumed they acted as drains, but Luca claimed they were ports for pouring boiling water and liquid fire down on invaders.

We had to walk a quarter of a league counterclockwise down a grassy green band to come to the next gate. Here the guards only searched us for weapons like crossbows. They cared nothing for our swords and smirked at Khara's rusty-looking blade.

Luca's sword excited slightly more interest, since it looked like the sort of weapon carried by soldiers, and indeed it was. But evidently the guards thought Luca too pale and weak to be much of a threat and laughed at him when he identified himself as a scholar.

Inside the coral wall was the town proper. It had none of the free-and-easy feel of the isle. Here men and women kept their eyes down and avoided making eye contact with strangers. Mothers clutched their children's hands. Careful nods replaced joyful greetings.

We saw shops, but they were gloomy and utilitarian. Every building seemed to be the same weary shade of brown. Saguria was a serious place, its people burdened and furtive. At least it was here in the lower town. Between buildings I caught glimpses of the massive promontory, of the great shining mansions, many painted in bright colors, some glittering from golden adornments.

The palace itself was visible, at least to a degree, from just about anywhere in the city. It felt domineering, intimidating, and I realized that the effect was deliberate. Our lords and masters were up there, above us, in the mansions and especially in the palace. They wanted all who passed to be reminded that it was they who held all our fates in their hands.

I had come to understand humans better, and I could sense the emotion that ran through the lower town: it was fear. Soon I understood why when we saw the crowd ahead of us parting, rushing to hug the walls.

Coming toward us down the street were three men

wearing light armor beneath tunics of snow white. Their coat of arms was terrifying: a great sword stabbing downward, surrounded by three smaller swords, each dripping blood, against a stylized black mountain. On the right side was a white bird against a field of green.

The men in white swaggered down the street, faces red and eyes suspicious. Each carried a short stick carved with runes and topped with a red gem of impressive size.

"The Pale Guard," Khara whispered. "Up against the wall! And don't look at them."

We all moved instantly, even Gambler. But as a mere dog, I was able to stand aside and watch the Pale Guard stalk past.

"Watch your dog," one of them snarled at Khara. He kicked me in my ribs with enough force to knock me over.

I stifled my instant reaction and substituted a reasonable facsimile of a canine yelp of pain, tucking my tail like a good dog.

"They have the power of life and death," Khara explained when the guards were safely past. "All they have to do is touch a person with their staves to send them to be tortured, and often killed."

"Let's get out of this miserable place," Tobble said, patting my head.

I couldn't have agreed more. But just at that moment, I realized something had changed.

I checked to make sure it was safe to speak. I was, after all, still a dog.

Even before the words were out of my mouth, I knew Khara was thinking the same thing.

"Where is Luca?" I asked.

44.
Attacked

Khara scanned the crowd. When she looked at me, I saw stark fear in her eyes.

"Move," she said. "Now!"

We set off at a trot, weaving and pushing our way through the press of bodies. But without Luca, we had no clear notion of the city's layout. It wasn't long before we ended up near the port. The pink coral inner defensive wall continued straight out into the water at that point, forming a protected harbor. I realized with a shock that the coral hadn't been taken from the sea. It had been grown in place.

"The natites must have—" I started, but Khara silenced me with a jerk of her hand. Ahead of us were more members of the Pale Guard.

After veering down an alleyway to escape them, we were soon hopelessly lost in a maze of crooked streets. We pushed on into a tangle of houses and shops, down alleys so tight that sunlight never touched the cobblestones. I stopped short upon seeing a bleached and tattered handbill nailed to a door. It advertised the eumony on the isle of Ursina, a *Solemn Ceremony to Mourn the Passing of a Governing Species*.

No mention of dairnes, just "a Governing Species." I wondered darkly if the handbills would be reused for the end of the felivets.

We turned a sharp corner and found ourselves face-to-face with a creature no bigger than me: an arratoi, a foul thing with spiky fur that seethed with fleas. It was a sort of rat, but much larger, with curved teeth and a prehensile tail that whipped back and forth like a parody of a happy dog.

The arratoi stared at us with red, rectangular-pupiled eyes that reminded me of a goat.

I heard Khara curse under her breath. Then she said a single word. "Gambler."

We were thirty feet from the arratoi, but Gambler covered the distance in a single heartbeat. He pounced, claws outstretched. The arratoi was quick and leapt aside with a screech. But Gambler wasn't easily fooled. He caught the vermin with one paw, sank claws into flesh, and whipped the creature off its feet.

After a frenzy of movement and a stifled cry from the arratoi, Gambler ended the creature's life with a bite that crushed its skull. But as the arratoi breathed its last, a second one poked its snout around the corner, saw the bloody spectacle, and ran away squealing in a voice to raise the dead.

"Was that necessary?" Tobble protested.

"They spy for the Murdano," Gambler said, spitting the arratoi's blood from his mouth.

"We have to find our way out of here and reach the north gate or we're finished," Khara said.

We ran, fear lending us renewed energy. Gradually the buildings began to spread out, the streets widening. Now and then I caught glimpses of pink coral, which I fervently hoped was the north wall.

"But aren't we going to look for Luca?" Tobble asked breathlessly.

"No," Khara answered. "He's looking for us."

"Yes," Gambler said. His voice was grim. "And from the looks of it, he's found us."

Two members of the Pale Guard stood directly ahead.

A third stepped out of an alleyway behind us.

"Ignore their sticks," Khara said. "Beware their swords."

"I have the one behind us," Gambler said.

"Halt and surrender yourselves!" one of the men in white yelled in a booming, authoritative voice.

I think they expected us to obey. They definitely did not expect Gambler to turn and attack the pursuing guardsman.

Nor did they expect a young boy to draw a blade that suddenly glowed bright.

Khara went straight at them. I drew my "sword" as well, intending at least to die fighting. I was the endling, or so it seemed. I had to make a good account of my species here at the end of our hopeless trek.

Khara ran toward a guardsman and very nearly managed to stab her sword right through the Murdano's insignia. But he was quick and well-trained. He spun away as he drew his own sword, and what was meant to be a killing blow merely tore his white tunic and glanced off the chainmail beneath.

In the act of spinning he sliced horizontally at Khara. She only managed to avoid him by falling onto her rear and scuttling away, pushing herself with her heels.

I readied my pitifully small sword, my hand shaking, my throat tight.

But I didn't know what to do. One man was busy with Khara, the other with Gambler.

I heard snarls and cries of pain, both human and felivet. I smelled fresh blood.

The remaining guardsman did not advance on me. Instead he drew something from a deep pocket in his tunic. To my shock, I realized it was a net, no different from something a fisherman might use.

Nearby, Khara, still on her back, kicked at her assailant's leg and knocked him off balance, but he recovered instantly.

The other guardsman calmly walked directly toward me, the net spread between his two hands.

He meant to take me alive.

I stuck my sword out and said, "I will stop you!"

"Will you?" The man laughed. "I've never had to fight a talking dog before."

He was definitely not terrified. He kept coming.

From behind me I heard a feline screech of pain.

Ahead, the guardsman brought his weapon down in a powerful blow. Khara raised her sword to defend herself, but the force of his strike knocked it clattering on the cobbles.

Over soon, some part of my mind observed.

It would all be over soon.

45.
Beware the Angry Wobbyk

The guardsman twirled the net once, twice over his head, and I leapt.

I leapt forward as Khara had taught me, aiming to slide between the guard's legs and slice upward. But I am not Khara, and my bold attack drew no blood.

Still, the guard must have felt the side of my sword slide along his inner thigh, for he cursed and began clutching at his tunic, pulling it back to see whether he'd been cut.

Outraged, he threw the net and it fell over me. I tried cutting it with my sword, but I couldn't gain any leverage.

As I twisted and fought to free myself, and Gambler battled desperately, I saw Khara stagger from a savage blow from the hilt of a guardsman's sword against the side of her head. Her eyes rolled up.

It was three guardsmen now against Gambler. Not even he would survive that.

I sobbed, flailing helplessly in the net.

And then something happened.

Reinforcement. In the form of Tobble.

It was as if he'd been struck by a bolt of lightning and absorbed all its power.

His fur stood on end.

His little claws came out.

His tiny teeth were bared.

He was gibbering something in a language I had never heard.

"Etz shi falk wan!" he cried.

Tobble hurled himself with mad fury on the guardsman who had struck Khara, dug his claws into the man's ears, and began ripping at his nose.

The guardsman could do nothing with his sword. Frantically he tried to rid himself of Tobble, but the wobbyk had the man's nose in his teeth. Blood flew everywhere.

The guard who'd netted me rushed to rescue his companion. But Tobble detached himself from his first target and, with a shrill scream that should have come from some much more impressive creature, he threw himself on the second man's neck from behind. He reached around the guard's head and grabbed the sides of his mouth, spreading his lips in a gruesome smile. Then he began gnawing at the man's neck like a lunatic badger.

Finally, I found my way out of the net. I shouted at the

top of my lungs: "For the dairnes!"

And then I did what I had never wished to do, never imagined myself doing.

I plunged my sword at Tobble's first victim. I speared his rear end and he howled with pain.

Staggering, my mind nearly gone, I swung around and slashed at another guardsman behind the knee, where he wore no armor.

Both men bellowed as I headed toward Gambler's opponent, blood pounding in my ears, my breath coming in gasps. Tobble got there first and began chewing the man's ear with remarkable ferocity.

Gambler, given the momentary distraction, was up in a flash. He leapt and closed his powerful jaws around the guard's neck as the man, the cat, the wobbyk, and I all tumbled to the ground.

I pushed free and saw Khara rising to her feet, the side of her head red with blood, fury in her eyes. Fury, which turned to amazement as she saw one of the dreaded Pale Guard soldiers on his knees clutching his rear end, a second one crawling away on his elbows dragging a crippled leg, and a third guardsman frozen beneath the paws of a fearsome-looking Gambler.

"What the . . . ," she began.

Then she saw Tobble, his fur matted with blood, heaving giant breaths.

"Vallino," Khara said. "I'm sorry to burden you, but we need speed!"

She grabbed her sword and swung astride the horse. She grabbed me, then Tobble, and placed us before her, reaching around to hold the reins.

"I told you," Tobble said, panting heavily. "We wobbyks are slow to anger, but we are not helpless!"

"Friend wobbyk," Khara said, "I am completely convinced." She glanced over her shoulder. "Gambler?"

"Coming," he called, glancing at the terrified guardsman still pinned beneath his paws.

Khara said a word to Vallino and we abandoned any pretense of secrecy. We dashed through the streets, trailing the blood of our enemies.

"There she is!" a familiar voice cried as we rounded a bend.

Ahead of us a dozen soldiers ran to block our path. Khara spun Vallino around, his hooves striking sparks from the cobblestones, but a second string of guards was right behind us.

From the first rank of soldiers stepped Luca.

"Take her," he said in a confident, commanding voice. "And don't forget her"—he gave us a cold grin—"dog."

46.
The Murdano

It's not easy to shackle a dairne. Our wrists are not built for it. It will only work if you squeeze the manacles on very tightly.

That was what the Murdano's soldiers did. Supervised by Luca.

To me, to Khara, and to Tobble.

They did worse to Gambler. They wrapped thick rope all the way down his body, binding his legs to his torso. Then they loaded him onto a cart.

That was how we were pushed, shoved, and dragged down marble and mirror corridors until we were finally deposited at the base of the Murdano's throne.

I tripped and tried to right myself. Luca shoved me down on my face. "Kneel before the Murdano, dog!" he said.

Terrified as I was, I had a hard time taking it all in. The room was enormous, and had been made to seem even more enormous with massive mirrors. Gold was everywhere: on candle chandeliers, in wall sconces holding still more candles, in the grout between marble squares, in the frames of paintings portraying stiff, scowling, unnatural-looking humans.

Six steps led up to a platform on which sat a massive throne. Ornate carvings on the throne featured humans, felivets, raptidons, natites, and terramants—and, in a position of surprising prominence, a very dignified dairne.

"What is this interruption?" a voice demanded. It was a sneering, petulant voice, and it belonged to an older human male. He stood to the left side of the throne and wore a long, draping gown of darkest blue.

On the other side of the throne was another male. He was broad and beefy, with strong arms crossed over his barrel chest. He wore a magnificent version of the soldiers' livery, covered with medals and ribbons. His black boots were tall and polished to rival the mirrors.

Luca spoke. "I have brought a rare gift. A gift of inestimable value."

"And who are you?" the man on the left, who seemed to be an adviser of some kind, asked.

"I am Luca, a student from the the isle of Ursina. But my full name"—he paused to send a look of pure hatred toward Khara—"is Luca Corpli, second son of Fredoro Corpli."

I heard a sharp intake of breath from Khara. She sent him an icy stare. "Treachery runs deep in your family."

Luca swung a backhand and hit the side of her face with a sharp report that seemed to echo off the walls.

Khara did not react.

The adviser started to speak, but the Murdano cut him off with a wave. "Why should I value this gaggle of nondescript creatures?"

The Murdano seemed young by human standards. He wore a carefully trimmed beard that matched his gleaming ebony hair. Unlike the medal-bedecked soldier to his right and the fabulously attired adviser to his left, the Murdano favored simpler clothing, leggings and a tunic. They were of the finest materials, but still humble compared to the others.

"Your Majesty," Luca said with a bow and a sweep of his hand, "I bring you the world's only surviving dairne. The endling of her species."

The dozen or more courtiers standing nearby murmured excitedly.

The Murdano said, "Clear the chamber, all but my chamberlain and my general-in-chief." He leaned forward and directed a hot gaze at the withdrawing courtiers. "And I warn you that if word of this escapes this room, the guilty person will rot in my dungeons until disease takes him."

The murmuring stopped and the courtiers quickly departed.

"A dairne, eh?" the Murdano said, eyeing me. "It is said that a dairne can tell if a statement is true or false." He stroked his beard. "I will put you to the test."

I nodded. I was quite sure I didn't need to grant my permission.

"This morning for breakfast I ate a cold pheasant breast and dates with yogurt. Is that true or false?"

"True." My voice sounded puny in the great room. "I mean, true, Your Majesty."

"Yesterday I attended a wrestling match."

"No, Your Majesty. You did not."

"Lucky guess," muttered the beefy man with medals.

"Perhaps, General." The Murdano smiled. It was not a nice smile. "Three days ago I was shown an ancient scroll."

"Yes, Your Majesty," I said.

"And the day before that I watched a sword-fighting class."

"Yes, Your Majesty."

"It was held in the central auditorium."

"No, Your Majesty."

"The ballroom?"

"No, Your Majesty."

"In my private chambers?"

"Yes, Your Majesty."

"And as I watched I was joined by my daughter, Princess Coral."

"Yes, Your Majesty."

"She enjoyed the demonstration."

"No, Your Majesty."

The Murdano aimed a sideways glance at his general. "In fact, the princess excused herself after just a few minutes, claiming to be upset by the . . . exertions."

The general grimaced. "I still don't believe her."

"Sir, that is not true," I said. "You do believe me."

"Why would my general lie?" the Murdano demanded.

"I don't know, Your Majesty," I said. "I only know whether a statement is true or—actually, Your Majesty, what I know is whether the person speaking believes what they've said or not. I do not know whether a thing happened, or anyone's motives. Only whether they believe they speak truth or falsehood."

The Murdano's eyes were alive with the possibilities. "General Origal, do you love your Murdano?"

The general blinked. "I love Your Majesty with all my soldier's heart!"

The Murdano cocked an eyebrow at me.

I realized how right Khara had been about the danger I could pose to other people. Including this general. Reluctantly I said, "No, you do not, General."

"Indeed," the Murdano said mockingly. "Well then, General, let me ask this. Are you a loyal servant?"

"Absolutely!"

"True," I said.

The Murdano nodded. "I care nothing for love, but loyalty is something I value highly, just as I despise disloyalty."

"The general is loyal, Your Majesty."

The Murdano sat back, all the while keeping his gaze on me. Finally he said, "Lord Chamberlain. Prepare a room for our guests in the remotest tower. Treat them well. This creature will prove useful. Araktik returns tomorrow, and I shall speak with her about this expensive eumony she staged. She'll need to explain herself in the presence of this proof that the dairnes are not quite extinct."

Luca spoke up. "And me, Your Majesty?"

"You and your family will be well rewarded for this service," the Murdano said indifferently. Then to me he added, "The general will select his best men to guard you. Men who understand that if they speak of this, I will have their tongues torn from their mouths."

The general nodded obediently. "I will send the Pale Guard."

"Yes," the Murdano said. "And understand this, dairne: if you attempt escape, I will do far worse than remove the tongues of your companions."

47.
Imprisoned Again

The Murdano was true to his word.

Guards marched us down endless corridors. Each hall was cleared in advance by soldiers of the Pale Guard. No one saw us pass, unless it was through a keyhole.

We climbed steep circular stairs, at last arriving at a stout wooden door hinged and strengthened with heavy brass.

Inside we found a round room with four narrow windows at the compass points. It was not a marble-and-gold palace, but it was roomy and came equipped with four beds, rugs on the stone floor, and even a faded tapestry on one wall.

Since no servant could be trusted, members of the Pale Guard brought us platters of food: fruit and nuts, cheese and cured meats. They even procured an anteleer leg for Gambler and fresh herbs and grasses for Tobble.

"My horse?" Khara asked.

"It is a fine horse," the head guard said gruffly. "We value fine horses."

"And my sword?"

"You'll have no further need of that old piece of rust."

Khara blinked but otherwise remained stone-faced.

They shut the door on us, and I heard the sounds of bars sliding and locks turned.

Khara went to one window and whistled. "Well, at least we have a view."

Tobble ran to another window and leapt onto the sill. "We're leagues up!"

I crowded behind Khara and almost stopped breathing. We were in the tallest tower of the sprawling palace complex, high atop the great stone spur, far above the town below. "We're almost in the clouds," I said.

"You did well, Byx," Khara said.

"No," I said bitterly. "If I'd done well, I would have seen Luca for what he was."

She put a hand on my shoulder. "This isn't the first time my family has been betrayed by the Corplis. And in any case, it was I who trusted Luca and led us here."

"Somehow," I murmured, "I convinced myself Luca was a scholar in search of the truth."

"Oh, he's in search of something, all right," Khara said. "Gold for his family's coffers. And power."

We ate well, but in glum silence.

That night I slept in an unfamiliar but warm, dry, and comfortable human bed, and I woke to low murmuring. I sat up and saw Gambler standing before the south-facing window. His white-striped face gleamed in the moonlight.

I listened and realized that he was singing softly in a language I did not know or understand.

> *"Vir ghaz wast farl*
> *Vir ghaz wast marl*
> *Enweel ma koorish*
> *Jinn ma santwee . . ."*

He stopped and turned to me. "I am sorry if I woke you."

"No, I'm sorry if I caused you to stop. I don't understand the words, but the melody is beautiful."

Gambler nodded. "It's the death song. A felivet who knows he is about to die sings his love to the moon and stars, our guides."

His words hit like a punch to the stomach. "Are you so sure it's hopeless?"

Gambler sighed. "I believe you will be kept alive so long as you serve the Murdano. It has obviously occurred to him that while many dairnes are a threat, the man who has the only dairne possesses great power. He will allow us to live, but only as prisoners. My kind does not like cages, and I have already endured many days in the dungeon of the isle."

"So . . ." I looked around the spare room. Khara and Tobble still slept. "You don't intend to—"

"To end my own life?" Gambler laughed sadly. "No. We believe that a felivet who dies well in battle ascends to a great forest above the clouds. There we hunt endless prey and gather sometimes with others of our kind to tell of our great deeds in life."

He seemed to accept this fate. Perhaps even to welcome it.

"When I have a chance to do it without endangering you, I will take the opportunity to attack the guards. They are prepared. Well armed and well trained. I will attack and, with fortune's help, send at least one to his human afterlife, whatever that is. They will kill me, and I will rise to meet so many of my kind who have died bravely and gone on before me."

"But Gambler—"

"Yes, Byx?"

"But . . . but I would miss you. You're my friend."

Felivet faces are not very expressive, but his eyes were moist. "I am honored by your words."

"Just—just do me one favor. Hold off at least for a while."

Gambler said nothing. Perhaps he knew the truth: that I had no real plan and saw no real hope.

"Will you do that?" I pressed. "For me?"

Gambler lowered his head and was silent for a long time. "Three days," he said. "I will endure this cage for three days."

In the morning, I found Khara arranging her blankets and looking preoccupied. Tobble was helping her with the blankets—if "helping" meant "enthusiastically making things worse."

"Gambler is upset," I said.

Tobble looked over his shoulder at the felivet. "Maybe I can cheer him up," he said. He smiled at me. "I never thought I'd say this, but I've kind of gotten used to that big old kitty. He's not so bad, for a dangerous predator."

I watched Tobble waddle off. "Gambler says the Murdano has realized that while dairnes may be a threat, one dairne, singular, under the Murdano's control, would be a power to be reckoned with."

Khara nodded. "He's right, of course. I'm bothered, though, by what Luca did not say to the Murdano. He knows, but didn't say, that I am a Donati. He has glimpsed my unsheathed sword and must at least suspect its true nature. Yet he said nothing."

We sat on the edge of Khara's bed. "I noticed that as well," I said.

"My guess is that Luca hopes to steal the sword and take it to his father," Khara said. "Fredoro Corpli is an ambitious warlord. He would love to head north and lead a war against Dreyland, should the Murdano decide to go forward with it. If Corpli wielded the Light of Nedarra, men would flock to him."

"Simply because of a sword?"

"Because of that sword," Khara replied. "Corpli would very quickly become the second leading power in Nedarra, just behind the Murdano himself. And of course Luca would triumph over his older brother, who's heir to the Corpli lands and fortune."

"Some family," I muttered.

"Yes." Khara sighed. "There's a reason felivets don't trust humans. We have complex motives, endless greed and ambition, and uncertain loyalties."

Our morning meal arrived, and we ate in silence. We had nothing to do but wait. Gambler dozed off in a patch of sunlight, while Tobble sat nearby, occasionally even stroking the cat's silky head.

I watched dust motes twirl. I listened to mourning doves coo outside our window. I let my mind wander.

And then it hit me.

A glimmer of hope. And the beginning of a plan.

Humans lie. And I knew their lies.

No human, felivet, raptidon, wobbyk, natite, or terramant could lie in the presence of a dairne.

No one could lie in the presence of a dairne.

Except, of course, a dairne.

48

Araktik Arrives

It was two days before I was summoned again to the Murdano. I resisted, saying that I was too shy and needed Khara
to stand with me.

The Pale Guard soldiers must have had instructions
not to mistreat or upset me, because they allowed Khara to
join me. Not only that, they turned a blind eye to a certain
wobbyk.

It was a long walk down interminable stairways and
mazelike corridors before we stepped out once again to face
the Murdano.

"Ah, my little endling and her . . . escort," the Murdano
said. "Stand at the back of the room. And remain silent until
I call upon you."

We bowed appropriately and went to the back of the
chamber behind a row of soldiers at attention, where no
one would notice us unless they were looking closely. A few

minutes later, when a handful of the Murdano's advisers entered, I nudged Khara and directed her gaze to the group.

Luca was there. We had hoped he would be.

When Araktik the Seer entered, she didn't even look our way. All her attention was focused on the Murdano. She was dressed much as she had been at the eumony, and she swept in with supreme confidence. It seemed clear that Araktik believed she had nothing to fear, which meant she felt certain that her Knight of the Fire had finished us off.

This was good news. But only a start. The plan I had worked up with Khara, Gambler, and Tobble—who could be surprisingly devious when he managed to focus—was risky and tenuous. My throat was tight, and several times I felt my knees start to buckle.

Life and death were on the line. Not just my life, or the lives of my companions, either. The lives of any species that got in the way of the Murdano's ambitions hung in the balance as well.

"My lord," Araktik said, executing a grand bow.

"My great and loyal Seer," the Murdano said. "It's good to have you with us again. Tell me: How did the eumony go?"

"Very well," Araktik lied. "There were some small disturbances, comical in nature, but otherwise everything went according to my plans."

"Comical? Please share. You know how I love to laugh."

The Murdano was lying. He did not love to laugh.

Araktik was no fool. She knew something was amiss. I could smell the subtle scents of a human body preparing for trouble.

Still, she was an accomplished actor. "Well, Your Majesty, the ceremony was disrupted slightly when a pranksterish child released a kite meant to resemble a dairne. The wind seized the kite and it very nearly flew into me!"

She laughed. The Murdano laughed as well.

"That is indeed amusing," the Murdano said. "Did you catch the culprit and scold him severely?"

"Yes, Your Majesty. I advised the parents to whip the child."

"Of course. Very wise and appropriate."

Araktik bowed in acknowledgment, and I sensed her relaxing. She thought her lie had been believed.

"So," the Murdano said with a deep sigh, "it's true that dairnes are gone from the world. A pity."

"Yes," Araktik agreed solemnly. "It is a sad reality."

"Mmm," the Murdano said. "Now that I come to think of it, it was your own mother, my father's Seer, who suggested that the dairne population should be exterminated."

"A wise policy."

I grimaced. They were talking about wide-scale slaughter in a casual way. The destruction of my species.

"Still," the Murdano said, "it's a pity. Having many of the

creatures was, well, inconvenient. But if there had been a way to keep just a few alive as servants . . ."

"They all had to be destroyed," Araktik said harshly. "Your Majesty."

"Yes, so you say," the Murdano said. "And so I believed."

Araktik stiffened.

"But lately I've begun to wonder if it might not be useful to have at least one dairne."

The Seer paused. She cleared her throat. "For what purpose, Your Majesty?"

The Murdano was silent for a long time. His mouth formed a cruel smile. His eyes bored into Araktik.

"I have a surprise for you, great Seer." The Murdano raised his voice and said, "Step forth!"

With that, the file of soldiers parted and a hand propelled me forward. Khara and Tobble followed close behind.

Araktik's glare was so intense, it should have set me afire.

"As you see, Araktik, the eumony, which I allowed on your assurance that dairnes are truly extinct, was a bit premature."

Araktik's mouth moved, but no sound came out.

Humans emit a particular smell when they are afraid. Araktik stank of fear.

"Tell us, endling of the dairne species," said the Murdano, "does my Seer speak truth?"

49.
The Truth

We dairnes also emit a scent of fear, and I'm sure I smelled of pure terror. But I summoned all my fragile confidence and said, "No, Your Majesty, she does not."

"Oh? How so?" He was playing with Araktik now. "Surely my Seer, my most trusted adviser, would not dare to mislead me?"

"I do not lie!" Araktik said, struggling to maintain calm.

"Were you present at the eumony, endling?"

"Yes."

"And did you witness this dairne-shaped kite?"

I shook my head. "No."

"Indeed? What do you claim happened?"

"Your Majesty, I was that kite. My place of concealment had been discovered by the isle's own constabulary. Fearing for my life, I leapt and glided—"

"Glided?"

"Yes, Your Majesty." I spread my arms wide and extended my glissaires. "We dairnes can glide for short distances. But we're not birds, and we have little ability to control our direction in flight. Though I did not intend it, I nearly ran into the . . . into . . . her."

"Your Majesty," Araktik said, "I—I believed it was a kite."

"Endling?"

"That was false."

"This creature lies!" Araktik shouted.

"I have questions for you, Araktik," the Murdano said. His voice was low and sinister, the playfulness gone. "Answer truthfully. Your life depends on it."

Araktik was trembling. I didn't know if the other humans could see it, but I could.

"Have you pressed for the extermination of this dairne in order to avoid being caught in a lie?"

Araktik looked sick. "No, Your Majesty."

"Endling?"

"Lie, Your Majesty."

Araktik started to sputter in protest, but he silenced her with a wave.

And then came the question.

"Tell me, Seer, are you aware of any other dairnes?"

I gasped out loud. Khara and Tobble turned to me, eyes wide.

I desperately wanted to hear the Seer's answer. And

desperately feared what it would be.

The Seer shook her head, refusing to speak.

"Do not play with me!" the Murdano roared. "Yes or no, Seer: Do you know of any other dairnes, or is this truly an endling?"

"There are"—she paused—"rumors."

"Which you concealed from me, your lord and master!"

"I didn't ... I ... Rumors are merely ..." She shot a poisonous, panicked look at me. "These are only rumors!"

"True," I said, my heart bounding in my chest.

"Ah, but you believe these rumors, do you not, Araktik?"

At that, the Seer hung her head. She knew she was defeated. "Yes, Your Majesty, I do."

The Murdano looked at me. I nodded.

Rumors. Mere rumors, I told myself. And yet Araktik believed them to be true.

More dairnes.

Hope.

"You were desperate to kill this endling to avoid being exposed," the Murdano snapped. "Was it your plan to find the few of her kind who still lived? To use them as truth tellers, perhaps? But only for yourself?"

Araktik raised her face to him then, no longer terrified, but resigned. She squared her shoulders. "I am your Seer. It would be useful to have such creatures to serve me. Dairnes are dangerous if everyone has them. They are useful when only one person has their power available."

The Murdano nodded. "I do not need the endling to tell me that you now speak truth. You conspired to use me to reduce their number until only you had that power."

Araktik didn't bother answering.

"And you would have used your power to further manipulate me, to fool me, to increase your own influence. You could have concealed your dairne behind a screen and known the truth or falsity of everyone who spoke to you—including my own servants, my allies. My enemies."

"What I did was for the good of Nedarra," the Seer said defiantly. "This war you're considering, this obsession with the conquest of Dreyland, is madness! War is impossible without the consent of the natites and the raptidons. They control the sea and the air and could just as easily help Dreyland!"

The Murdano rose to his feet. Rage glowed from him.

"You dare to question my will?"

He descended the steps from his throne and stood within arm's reach of Araktik. "My father's father vowed to bring Dreyland to heel, to bring all the world under the banner of our family. He failed. My father vowed the same but failed. I will not fail!"

Araktik wilted in the face of his fury.

The Murdano ranted for five uninterrupted minutes about the perfidy of Dreyland, how they had financed pirates and coastal raiders, how they had preyed upon Nedarrans, how they had humiliated the Murdano and more. It was a mix of truth and lies, things the Murdano believed and things he did not.

But the Murdano did not ask me to tell the truth or falseness of his statements. And I had no reason to open my mouth.

At last the Murdano fell silent. He returned to his throne, seeming tired and sullen.

"Take her," he said without looking at Araktik. "She is hereby charged with and convicted of treason."

"Your Majesty," Araktik began. "I am no traitor. I only wished to—"

The Murdano waved a hand. "The penalty for treason is death," he said without emotion. "The slow death. Take her. And make it a very slow death."

50.
In Which I Demonstrate a New Skill

I suppose I should have felt some pleasure that the Seer who had tried to have me killed was about to die. But the words "slow death" made me sick to my stomach.

She screamed as she was dragged away. She screamed that she was loyal, that she'd only meant to serve ... and then began to shout curses and insults, telling the Murdano he was a stupid child who should be shoveling horse manure in a stable, not ruling Nedarra.

When at last she was gone, a heavy silence descended. Still, the Seer's words echoed in my brain: *There are ... rumors*.

Rumors that she'd believed.

More dairnes. More dairnes. More dairnes.

I told myself to focus. We were still in danger. Hope, even just the possibility of hope, had to wait.

The silence stretched on and at last Khara took charge.

"If I may speak, Your Majesty?"

He nodded.

"Your Majesty, Luca"—she pointed to Luca, who narrowed his eyes—"told you some of the truth, but not all. He knows but did not tell you that I am of the family Donati."

That got the Murdano's attention. "A Donati?"

"Yes, Your Majesty. My father, having no use for a daughter when he had two sons, sent me out into the world to pass as a boy and search for opportunities to reverse our disgrace. When I came upon this creature"—she indicated me—"I knew that I'd found a rare opportunity. From that moment I have endured great pains, rigors, and risks to bring this dairne before Your Majesty."

"Is this true?" the Murdano asked, turning to me.

I swallowed past the lump in my throat. I'd been practicing for this moment.

"Yes," I lied.

Khara had no brothers. Nor had she labored to bring me to the Murdano.

The Murdano turned to Luca. "You have seriously harmed your family's prospects with this . . . oversight."

"Your Majesty, allow me to—"

"Take him away," the Murdano interrupted, with a jerk of his chin.

Whimpering and muttering, Luca was led away by two soldiers.

Khara glanced Luca's way, expressionless, then continued. "The Seer tried to stop me. She even sent a Knight of the Fire after me, and I only survived by virtue of the courage and ferocity of the felivet in our company."

The Murdano cocked an eyebrow. "You fought a Knight of the Fire and survived?" he asked incredulously.

"The scars are still clear on the felivet's body," she said.

"And what would you have from me, Kharassande of the Donatis?"

"Only the opportunity to deliver any other surviving dairnes into your hands," Khara said, hardening her voice. "To find them, seize them, and deliver them as servants of Your Majesty. If I succeed, I mean to beg your forgiveness for my family so that we may once again be in your favor, and prove our loyalty by forming a small part of your army of conquest."

The Murdano didn't even ask me if this was true. Without meaning to, he had completely accepted that I would speak up in the presence of a lie.

The Murdano tilted his head. "If Araktik could not locate these rumored dairnes, how would you?"

Khara turned to me and said, "Show His Majesty!"

"It's my own private—" I protested.

Khara slapped me hard across the face.

Truly hard. Hard enough to look real.

It certainly felt real.

"Show His Majesty, dairne!"

Slowly, reluctantly, I drew my childish drawing from my pouch. A soldier jumped to take it from me, bowed, and handed it to the Murdano. He unfolded it and frowned.

"What is this?"

"A foolish drawing I made as a child," I said. But then, as if reluctantly compelled to speak truth, I added, "It was based on a tale we tell . . . told."

I brushed at a tear, easily summoned when I thought back on the bodies of everyone I had ever known. "It was a tale we told of a lost colony of dairnes on a sentient island in the north."

"Fables and tales are usually nonsense," the Murdano said thoughtfully. "But often there's a vein of truth in even the most ancient of myths."

Khara said nothing. I said nothing.

It all hinged on this moment.

"It would have to be kept secret," the Murdano mused, thinking aloud. "The whole of Nedarra believes that dairnes are no more." He looked up sharply, focusing on me. "But would your kind submit? And would you, young Donati spawn, lead them into slavery? To serve only me? To keep their very existence secret?"

Khara nodded.

I looked down, as if heartbroken. I shot an angry look at Khara. My voice heavy, I said, "A servant's life is better than no life at all."

"You would serve me?" the Murdano asked.

I nodded slowly. "Dairnes do not lie, Your Majesty. If I swear to serve you, I will. I would have no choice."

This in itself was a lie.

"And do you now swear by your own life, by the lives of all your kind, to serve me and only me?"

Slowly, heavily, as if I were signing my life away, I said, "I do, Your Majesty."

The Murdano sat back, clearly pleased with himself. He turned to the gruff general whose loyalty, if not honesty, I had vouched for.

"Release this Donati, the dairne, and the rest. Give them horses and provisions. And send an escort with them. Hand-picked men. Silent and discreet men." He flashed a sudden smile. "If they find more dairnes, kill all but, oh, let us say five. That should be more than enough. Kill the rest." He tapped a finger to his chin. "Yes, five. Perhaps six. Any more than that, and I risk losing control of them."

With that, we were dismissed.

Within hours we were riding north from Saguria, with Khara and Tobble on Vallino, me on a horse of my own, and three packhorses for food and tents.

Gambler raced around us in graceful arcs, moving just for the sheer joy of it, his feet barely touching the ground.

Khara's sword was returned to her, its true nature still undiscovered. I wondered what punishment the Murdano would inflict on Luca. Would Luca reveal the truth of the sword? Not if he could help it, I realized, not so long as he hoped to gain possession of it for his own family's use.

Riding behind us was a dark shadow in the shape of six members of the Pale Guard.

We were out of Saguria. On a mission to find, betray, and enslave whatever remained of my kind.

Khara, Tobble, and I exchanged a look as we rode, and when we were certain that the Pale Guard soldiers were far enough behind us not to hear, she asked, "Why do you think the Murdano risked letting you go? Why not just send me?"

"Perhaps he realizes that any dairnes who remain—assuming there are some—will welcome seeing one of their own. It's efficient. Without me there, they will be difficult, if not impossible, to find. Besides, he knows the Pale Guard will keep track of me."

Khara nodded. "You know, for a famously honest species,

you dairnes make good liars when you need to be."

"It's a new skill for me," I said. "I'm not proud of it."

"And yet it worked."

I grinned at her. "Yes, it did," I replied. "It did indeed."

PART FIVE
THE BEGINNING ENDS

51.
Something in the Air

It wasn't so long ago that I used to wake from the nightmares of a typical pup: dreams of hungry felivets, evil poachers, or getting lost in the dark recesses of the Forest of Null.

Now it seemed I had more immediate and realistic concerns. There are few things more worrying than a squad of the Pale Guard following you at a distance of a few hundred yards.

We had not exactly figured out what to do about them.

And we strongly suspected that trailing behind them were warriors loyal to Luca's family.

On the other hand, the burdens of traveling had lessened. At night we had excellent tents and plenty of dried food. The rain had passed, and we were even able to collect enough wood to keep a fire going.

Not only that, with the Pale Guard nearby, we weren't

worried at all about bandits or random patrols of soldiers. Still, Khara kept her sword beside her and slept near Gambler. No one sneaks up on a felivet.

Each day's travel brought us farther north to a tumbled land, a world of sparse topsoil, exposed rocks, and deep gullies that blocked our view. We often couldn't see the Pale Guard, but Gambler, Vallino, and I all smelled them.

The road was barely a trail. We passed villages, each poorer and more desperate than the one before. The farther we went from Saguria, the less we saw of soldiers, farmers' carts, or traveling tradesmen.

Sometimes, as much from kindness as need, we would buy supplies from these locals. But even the bare necessities were in short supply. A young hunter sold us a pair of rabbits, but aside from that, we found very little on offer.

On our third night out of Saguria I drew Gambler aside. "Friend felivet," I began, "have you not quite smelled, perhaps, but sensed . . ." I didn't have an ending to the question.

Gambler's eyes widened. "You too?"

I shrugged and shook my head side to side as if I didn't quite believe what I was saying. Which was the truth. "I . . . It's nothing. Just a feeling."

"Like a breeze has moved a branch, and now a twig is scratching ever so gently against the back of your mind?"

I smiled. "Yes, just like that. But I'm sure it's nothing."

"No, Byx. You hope it's nothing, but you are not sure. If you were sure, you would not have mentioned it."

I nodded toward Vallino. He was munching from a bag of oats while Khara and Tobble kept the fire going. But every now and then, Vallino raised his head. His ears swiveled. His nostrils flared.

His ears weren't pointed back down the road to the spot where smoke rose from the Pale Guard's own fire, but rather to the side. It was the same direction from which I felt that "twig" scraping.

"I will make a patrol," Gambler said. "When everyone is asleep."

"May I go with you?"

"You may," Gambler replied. "But you will most likely regret it."

It wasn't long before I found myself riding atop Gambler's back as he ran, then walked, then finally slunk through the night. I had to take care not to rub against any of his still-painful burns.

The breeze was erratic, frustrating our attempts to navigate by scent. Sometimes we stopped and simply breathed, drawing in the aromas of the land: moss and lichen, grass, granite, dying flowers, the droppings of a dozen different species. All that, and something more.

Something neither of us could be sure of.

"You have rescued me twice," Gambler said. "If I were to follow Wobbyk Code, I would have to save your life six times to compensate."

I laughed. "You've already done that, more than once."

"Tobble's not wrong," Gambler said thoughtfully. "Not about the lifesaving code. And he's right about wobbyks being treated as inferior. They are small and look silly, but that is no reason to treat them as disposable."

"That's an ancient unfairness," I said.

"Not to Tobble," Gambler replied.

A sound disturbed the quiet. We both froze.

"A human cry?" Gambler asked.

I nodded. We trotted toward the sound, slowing as we heard a second cry, this one closer and more piercing.

Our eyes began to piece together the story: ahead we saw the glow of fire.

"Wait here," Gambler whispered.

"I think I'd be safer with you."

Gamble crept forward as only a big cat can. Even perched on his back with my excellent hearing, I could scarcely make out the sound of his pads on the ground. He seemed to pass through tall grass without rustling it, even to leap gullies and land with less noise than a pillow dropped to the floor.

The wind changed, and what we smelled was disturbing.

Fire. Smoke. Charred flesh.

My mind told me that perhaps it was just a hunter cooking his prey.

But my heart knew it was something much worse.

52.
The Living Fire

We crept over the next boulder and saw a sullen fire burning the last of what must have been a very small village. Three crude human dwellings were smoldering. One human still lived. He was stretched between four strong saplings, rope running from ankles and wrists, suspended in midair above coals that glowed red in the night.

Standing nearby was a tall man, his back to us, his armor reflecting the firelight.

"The Knight of the Fire?" I whispered.

I felt Gambler's muscles tense.

I drew breath in through my nose and held it, searching for clues. Some faint but knowable tendril caught my attention, a human smell, before evaporating. And was that awful odor wafting through the air the stench of dog?

I definitely recognized the smell of the knight, the same terrifying threat that had attacked us south of Saguria. I wondered if he was still in Araktik's employ. Didn't he know that the Seer had been exposed and disgraced? Was he now on some other master's errand?

As if reading my thoughts, Gambler said, "He pursues us out of revenge."

"Revenge?"

"We escaped him, and a knight who allows such insults to go unanswered does not remain a knight for long."

The suspended human cried out in pain and anger. "You can roast me till I'm cooked through. I don't know where they are!"

The voice was oddly familiar, though it was hard to place, what with all the screaming.

"I believe you," a voice said.

"Then let me go!"

The knight laughed. He walked a short distance away out of the firelight and came back dragging a bare branch. He tossed it onto the fire. The few clinging, dry leaves flared immediately. I knew, with sickening certainty, that the man above the flames would die. Perhaps death would be a relief to him.

The knight began to chant:

"Roast and toast
But do not burn,
Make him scream
And make him yearn

For sweet relief
He'll never earn."

The fire, which had flared instantly, subsided, content to slowly consume its fresh fuel.

The chant was an instruction to the sentient fire. The knight meant death to come slowly to his human prisoner.

I climbed down off Gambler. We looked at each other, silently considering. Wordlessly debating.

We both knew it would be foolish to interfere.

We both knew we nevertheless had to.

I watched Gambler extend his claws, ready to take his chances with the knight. No doubt he was also interested in revenge: this was the knight who had seared patches of fur from Gambler's flanks.

I put a hand on Gambler's shoulder and shook my head.

"We mustn't harm the knight," I said. I kept my voice to a whisper, even though I felt certain the knight was out of earshot.

"What?"

"I think we have a use for him. I have a plan. I think."

For what seemed like forever we listened to the bellowing human. He was not yet seriously burned, fortunately. His clothing was singed but not yet on fire, and his golden hair, though curled and crisped, was still there. Mostly.

While we waited for the knight to go to sleep, I continued

to study the scents wafting my way when the wind cooperated. This person was not unknown to me. But the fire masked his real odor. Perhaps someone I'd encountered on the isle?

At last the knight threw a blanket on the ground and himself on the blanket. I listened intently to the sounds of his breathing. When I was certain he was asleep, I said, "Now."

Gambler crept forward and I moved in his footsteps as soundlessly as I could. My sword was in my hand, but I had no illusions that I could fight the knight. Even Gambler knew the odds were slim that he could defeat someone wielding sentient fire.

At least the knight's great charger was tied up upwind from us. The horse's senses would be far superior to the knight's.

Inch by inch we moved, our few missteps covered by the curses and cries of what I now know to be a human boy of approximately Khara's age.

He was suspended, facedown, his face and hands black with smoke. But as we neared, he turned his head and caught sight of us. His mouth opened, as if to yell, but I held up a hand in what I hoped he would understand as a signal to remain still.

The boy closed his mouth.

I opened mine.

It was Renzo. The boy we'd encountered at the cave.

"I know this boy," I told Gambler.

"He is a friend?"

"No. Not exactly." I scanned the area. "When last I saw him, he had a dog."

"I see no dog," Gambler replied. "Although there's a trace of one in the air."

We moved closer. Renzo grinned, in spite of his predicament. "Hello . . . dog," he whispered. "We meet again."

I put a finger to my lips in answer.

It was a complicated question, how to cut Renzo down, as he would inevitably fall into the fire. I cut a rope holding one leg, but held it taut until Gambler could seize hold of the leg in his jaw.

Next I released one arm, then the other leg, leaving him suspended above the coals, stretched by one arm and the leg Gambler still held.

"Ready?" I whispered.

"No, I'm enjoying the warmth," Renzo muttered.

I hesitated, confused.

"Sorry," he said. "I forget that not every species understands sarcasm."

I cut the last rope. Gambler sprang away as the boy fell. Gambler's speed pulled him free—barely—but the boy hit the ground with a loud *whumpf!*, followed instantly by the sound of the knight rolling over.

"Can you run?" I asked.

"Not without Dog," he replied. He let out an earsplitting whistle and was rewarded with a ridiculously happy bark.

Renzo then demonstrated his impressive running ability by dashing away, leaving Gambler and me to follow.

Behind us the knight roared in fury. A second later, he shrieked, as if in pain.

"Keep moving!" Gambler yelled, speeding away from us, then circling back.

Briefly I worried that he might try to kill the knight, but I felt certain Gambler had understood my plan. He needed to go for the horse, which was tethered to a sparse bush, not the knight.

Gambler brought himself upwind from the charger, which instantly caught the scent of felivet and began prancing in terror. Gambler yanked the bush out of the ground with his teeth, then ran right at the great beast.

The charger, inured to fire and battle but not felivets, did what any sensible horse would do.

It bolted into the night.

Gambler rejoined us and we fled with Renzo. The knight couldn't follow us without his horse, but it was only a matter of time before they reunited.

Then I would see whether the Knight of the Fire would do for us what we could not hope to do for ourselves.

53.
My Desperate Plan

"Khara! Tobble! Get up!"

Khara was on her feet with a speed that even a felivet would admire. Tobble was not, but I grabbed him and practically threw him onto Vallino.

"What is it?" Khara asked, not a trace of sleepiness in her voice.

"The Knight of the Fire. And, um, well, we found someone."

Khara froze in her tracks. She peered into the dark and asked, "Who is this?"

"The knight was torturing him," I explained.

"I don't care if the knight was eating him for breakfast," Khara snapped. Renzo moved closer. His face was covered with soot, his hair singed, his clothes tattered, but Khara instantly recognized him. "You!"

"It's the horse thief!" Tobble cried.

"Delighted to see you again." Renzo bowed.

"Are you insane?" Khara said to me. "You've brought the Knight of the Fire down on us? And for"—she rolled her eyes—"him?"

"The knight was already after you," Renzo said. "Why do you think he was torturing me?"

"And I'm supposed to believe you resisted?" Khara demanded.

"No." Renzo shrugged. "I would have given you up happily, but I didn't know where you were. If you'd like, I could go back and tell him."

For a boy who'd been well on his way to becoming a smoked ham, he did not seem the least abashed or grateful.

"What have you done?" Khara turned her anger on Gambler.

"What I asked him to do," I answered, jumping in. "I couldn't leave Renzo to burn."

"And the knight?" she asked.

"It will take him a while to find his horse," I said. "But then he'll come after us."

"Yes," Khara said, exasperated. "He will!"

"That's my hope," I said.

"There is one bright spot," Renzo said. He gave a small shrug. "That is, if you'd care to hear it."

"You're trying my patience," Khara said through clenched teeth.

"The knight's horse threw a shoe. He was muttering about it while I roasted."

Khara nodded. "That is good news, assuming you're right."

"I'm always right."

"It'll slow him down some. And if we move at top speed and keep our heads low . . ." Khara rubbed her eyes. "Well, at the very least, it'll take a bit longer for him to kill us."

Just then, a filthy bundle of fur and slobber bounded toward us.

"Dog!" Renzo cried. He pulled a bloody piece of fabric from the animal's mouth. "I see you brought a souvenir from the knight. Good work, my friend."

Dog caught sight of me and galloped over, sniffing, snorting, and waggling with embarrassing enthusiasm.

"He likes you," Renzo commented.

"The feeling is not mutual," I said, pushing Dog off before he could deliver a kiss to my face.

I put my hands to my mouth and yelled at the top of my lungs, "Save us! Save us!" Then, more quietly, I turned to the group and added, "Now we should flee."

We fled.

Renzo rode one of the packhorses, Khara and Tobble rode

Vallino, and I had my own horse, Shadewing, with whom I had an uneasy truce: so long as I didn't jerk on the reins or make sudden loud noises, he deigned to carry me. Gambler and Dog raced alongside us.

We flew away at top speed. The morning sun remained just below the horizon, but red and orange light was already seeping into the sky.

Every now and again I yelled, "Help us! Help us!"

I calculated that it would take the Pale Guard at least five minutes to break camp, saddle up, and come racing after us to discover why we were yelling for help.

I also calculated that the knight had by now retrieved his horse.

And I calculated that the odds of my desperate plans working were very dim.

Still, I told myself, my plan to escape the Murdano had worked. Maybe. Just maybe this would work as well.

Or maybe not. Because as the sun rose, I could make out the Pale Guard only half a league behind us, six tall warriors atop some of the fastest and strongest horses in Nedarra.

And I did not see the Knight of the Fire.

"There's a river ahead!" Khara cried. My sense of smell confirmed that she was right.

"Do you see a bridge?" Renzo demanded.

Khara rose in her stirrups and stared ahead. "No."

"Great," Renzo muttered, using the tone I now recognized as "sarcasm"—a style of speech whereby a person could say something that was the opposite of the truth and yet, oddly, not be considered a liar.

"Sorry if this isn't quite the rescue you were hoping for," Khara said to Renzo. She also seemed to be employing "sarcasm."

We moved closer to the river, which shone red in the morning sun. With dread settling in my heart, I realized it was wide and showed no sign of a bridge or ferry. Was it shallow enough to allow the horses to wade across?

I began to plan a story for the Pale Guard. I could tell them that we'd been set upon by a felivet. Or that terramants had suddenly appeared. They might believe that we had panicked.

Then again, they might not.

In any case, our odds did not look good. The horses of the Pale Guard were faster than ours. They were rapidly closing the distance.

Khara let out a curse, and I saw why. The knight was not behind us—he was ahead. Somehow he'd guessed our direction.

He sat astride his own horse between us and the river.

The Pale Guard behind, the Knight of the Fire ahead.

"Should we turn back?" I cried.

To my surprise, Khara was grinning at me. "You never cease to amaze me, Byx. No! No, we don't turn back, you clever dairne, we go straight ahead!"

Khara had realized what I had not. The knight saw us, as did the Pale Guard. And despite its not working quite as I had hoped, they saw each other.

Neither the Murdano's crack troops nor the Knight of the Fire was worried about us. Not at the moment, anyway.

"Help us!" I cried, twisting in my saddle to aim my cries at the Pale Guard. "He's trying to kill us!"

I knew one thing: The Pale Guard had strict orders to keep us alive until we found more dairnes. And the Knight of the Fire looked as if he was going to kill us—a belief made more convincing by the fact that killing us was exactly what he was hoping to do.

"Now," Khara instructed, "act like we just spotted the knight ahead of us. Veer right!"

I let loose a scream. We yanked our reins to the right and put our heads down, as if urging our steeds to greater effort.

The knight spurred his horse and galloped to cut us off.

The Pale Guard was hot on our heels.

And joy of joys, the knight and the guards were going to run into each other before either could reach us.

I glanced over my shoulder and saw the knight aim his lance at the guards. A jet of fire flew in an arc. The Pale

Guard split into two, but the fire swerved in midair to chase one group.

Liquid fire hit the first guard, enveloping him in flame. His horse threw him off and ran in terror. The burning guard hit the ground.

But the Pale Guard wasn't helpless. The two guards nearest the knight unlimbered crossbows and cranked them even as they rode.

It was hard not to admire their skill.

Crossbow bolts flew. One missed. One struck the knight in his right thigh.

The two guards drew swords and went charging at the knight.

The three guards who were still trailing us reined in and headed back toward the battle. As they rode, a second of their number was wreathed in flames.

We were rapidly nearing the river. It was muddy and opaque. There was no way for us to guess its depth.

Khara slowed Vallino. "We can look for a bridge or a ferry, or we can hope it's shallow."

"There's a ford half a league west," Renzo said.

Khara shook her head. "This doesn't look so deep."

"Then go ahead and cross here," Renzo said. "But be prepared to swim."

"Who are you, even?" Khara demanded.

"I'm the person your friends rescued only to get me stuck between the Pale Guard and a Knight of the Fire. Who are you?"

"I'm the person who gave you a horse to ride," Khara snapped. "And if you're wrong about the ford, I'll put my sword through your heart!"

"You could try to put that rusty old thing through me," Renzo said with a sly grin. "But your clothing doesn't fool me. You're a girl."

Khara nudged Vallino, who trotted up close to Renzo's steed. "Let's be clear on something, Renzo: I lead this group. And as for my rusty old sword . . ." She drew it from its sheath, glowing in all its glory. "My sword has tasted blood before, and it likes the flavor!"

"Nice," Renzo conceded. "But the ford is still half a league west of us."

Gambler, Tobble, and I all exchanged a look. Tobble and I were baffled by this pause for argument, but Gambler's eyes were amused and knowing.

Behind us battle raged, and it did not look likely to end quickly.

"West," Khara said grudgingly. "Follow . . . what's-his-name."

54.
The Abandoned Village

What's-his-name was right about the ford, a place where the river widened out and ran swiftly but shallowly.

We crossed safely with only a few stumbles.

"I'm sorry about your village," I said to Renzo when we paused to rest. Khara had taken me aside and asked that I test him for honesty.

"Not my village," Renzo said. "I was just passing through. That crazy knight was busy burning the place down after no one there had any answers for him. I may have said something that annoyed him. Like 'stop killing people.'"

My stomach lurched. "So they died because . . ."

"Yeah, because of you," Renzo said. "And I came close to it myself. Thanks for the rescue, by the way, even if it was your fault I needed rescuing."

"What is your, um, occupation, Renzo?" I asked.

"Me? I'm a thief."

Khara had been pretending not to listen, but that made her turn around. "A thief! Just as I suspected."

"I admitted it the first time we met," he said cheerfully. "Did you think I was joking? I steal from those who have: the rich, the landed, the self-important."

His words were true. For the most part.

"And I suppose you give it all to the poor," Khara said, once again employing "sarcasm."

"Pfff," Renzo said dismissively. "Why would I do that? Oh, don't get me wrong, I'll toss a coin to a beggar from time to time. But I steal to feed myself."

There was not much need for my dairne truth-telling skill. Renzo seemed entirely willing to tell the truth, even when it was less than flattering.

"My turn to ask a question," Renzo said. "How exactly did a human girl pretending to be a boy, a felivet, a wobbyk, and a dairne manage to infuriate both the Pale Guard and a Knight of the Fire? Why are two of the most dangerous groups in humankind after you?"

I gave him a short version. But even the short version took some time, during which I decided that Renzo was a good listener. When he asked questions, they were on point. He was far more knowledgeable about the wider world than I had been.

When I was done with my recitation, he nodded. "So the Seer—and anyone else who wanted to lie to the Murdano—wants dairnes wiped out. But now it's dawned on His Brilliance that a very small number of them, all slaves to him, could be useful. The Seer made a fatal mistake in prematurely declaring you extinct, a mistake she attempted to conceal by sending her Knight of the Fire after you."

I nodded. "Yes. Basically."

"And meanwhile the Murdano is still desperate to start his war with Dreyland. A war that would be easier for him to fight if he could lie, while instantly perceiving the lies of his opponents and doubters."

I shifted uncomfortably in my saddle. The way he put it made it sound as if I could be used as a weapon of war.

"So," Renzo went on breezily, "the Murdano has now consolidated power by eliminating Araktik. He's already reduced the dairnes to—well, just you—and he's been hemming in the felivets, reducing their hunting ranges, killing them off anytime he could come up with an excuse."

"Why do you suppose that is?" Gambler asked, testing him.

"Because you're enormous pains in the rear end, friend felivet," Renzo said. "You don't go along. You don't join in. See, the natites, well, they're practical folks. They sell ocean rights to anyone with cash: merchants, fishermen, pirates. They're not picky, though the saying goes, 'Natites never tell,' so who knows what their true game is? They'll probably let the Murdano launch a navy, assuming he has the wherewithal to bribe them. Which leaves the raptidons and the terramants, who may stand in his way. No one knows what the terramants want. As for raptidons?" Renzo laughed. "The birds just want to be left alone, but the Murdano will have to go after them, too."

"But why, if, as you say, they just want to be left alone?" I asked.

"Because they have power," Renzo said, as if it were obvious. "Imagine if the Murdano does invade Dreyland and the raptidons oppose him. An eagle can fly right over the mountains, land in an enemy camp, and tell them precisely where the Murdano's troops are."

"You're very opinionated for a thief," Khara said.

"Good-looking, too," Renzo said, and Gambler stifled a laugh.

We pushed on, despite the weariness of the horses, until we reached a village. It was a gray, squalid, cheerless place: two dozen buildings, a blacksmith, a leather worker, a stable, a grocer, and an inn.

The inn, we discovered, was completely empty. The proprietor was nowhere to be seen. It looked like a recent departure. There was still ale in the casks and some food in the pantry.

Khara went to spy out the rest of the village, quickly

discovering that the other shops were in much the same state. People had fled. The few who still remained in the village were old or feeble, the sort of people who might not be able to handle a difficult trek.

Khara returned with an old woman who said she used to work at the inn and would prepare a meal for us. What we wanted even more than food were answers.

"Where have all the people gone?" Khara asked the old woman, whose name was Melicent.

"Not long ago, the army took all the young men to be soldiers. Others were forced into labor, though none had committed crimes. Should he decide to invade Dreyland, the Murdano's army will come through the town, and no one wishes to be here when that day comes."

"I suppose they took all their valuables with them?" Renzo asked in a way that mocked his own motives.

"All they could carry," Melicent confirmed.

"Hmmm," Renzo said. "Well, I'll just, um, check to see if that's true." He left, carrying an empty sack.

"Thief," Khara said, pronouncing the word as if it tasted bad.

"Perhaps I should follow young Renzo," Gambler said, eyeing Khara. "We wouldn't want any harm to come to him."

"I don't care what happens to a thief," Khara said.

"No, of course not," Gambler said. But just the same the felivet left to keep a discreet eye on the boy.

"I wonder what happened to the knight and the Pale Guard," Tobble asked. "What do you think, Khara?"

"With luck, they killed each other," she said. "Realistically, we should post a lookout and sleep in shifts. Beyond that, I'm not sure there's much more we can do. The knight may have survived. Or some members of the Pale Guard. Or . . ."

She didn't finish her thought, but I knew what she meant. The Murdano had ordered Luca taken away but had not ordered his death. Surely Luca would set some of the Corpli family troops after us, if he was able.

"I'm not sleepy," Tobble said, suppressing a yawn. "I'll go first."

"So?" Khara asked when Tobble left for lookout duty at the top of a rise. "Is Renzo being truthful?"

"To a fault," I said. "He may be a thief, but so far he's an honest one. And he did take us to the ford."

Khara grunted, unimpressed. "In the morning we'll move on, and he can go where he likes."

"And if he wants to stick with us?"

"Why would he wish to do that?" Khara asked. "We're on a possibly doomed mission to find whatever is left of your species. And after that? We don't even have a plan."

But Renzo returned in the night, his bag now bulging. He dumped out its contents on a table in the inn's pub, and

I gasped to see objects of value: a silver cup, a scattering of gold adornments, and more mundane items like clothing, wooden bowls, and bits of pottery.

"Who would leave silver behind?" I asked, examining the cup.

"People who expected to return," Renzo said. "These are things they hid. Some of the hiding places were quite imaginative."

"Then how did you find them so quickly?"

Renzo winked at me but spoke to Khara. "Shall I show you?"

I nodded, and Khara pretended not to have heard him.

Renzo closed his eyes and stood very still, hands by his side, expression blank, and recited:

"Urgit fa golen
Fa meer distay
Urgit na golen
Ik teer begray."

Suddenly a trail of glittering silver light appeared on the floor. We watched in amazement as it snaked around the tables to the bar, where jugs and bottles were arrayed.

The line of light raced up the wall. It stopped at what looked like a simple piece of paneling, no different from the wood that covered most of the room.

Renzo headed over and studied the panel. From his pocket he drew a short steel tool, flattened on one end and hooked on the other. He dug the flattened edge into the paneling, pried it loose, then pulled it away completely, using the hook end.

There, behind the panel, was a space. And in that space were elaborate drinking chalices, along with little bottles of rare spices and pepper. The hidden wealth of the inn's owner.

"You practice theurgy," Khara said to Renzo.

"It's useful in my line of work," he replied.

"Not—" Khara began, but Tobble barreled into the room at that moment.

"Fire!" he gasped. "To the south!"

"It could be campfires," Khara said.

Tobble shook his head. "No," he said. "This fire moved. It was like someone cracking a whip of flame."

We were gone from the village within five minutes, all hope of a good night's rest gone.

The Knight of the Fire lived.

55.
Northward

Renzo proved useful—even Khara had to admit that. He knew the countryside in ways that we did not.

In time we reached the cold and misty coast, which we continued to follow north.

"I've never heard of islands that move around on their own," Renzo said as we made our way through a stand of trees.

I reluctantly showed him my drawing.

"This is what you people have to go on?" Renzo laughed. "A drawing? A drawing of a legend?"

"You're welcome to go another way," Khara said.

"Oh, but you'd miss me," Renzo replied. "Besides, I've already gone one round with Mr. Flames and Armor. I still stink of smoke." He combed his fingers through his scruffy hair. "Look at the state of my beautiful locks, all frizzled at the ends!"

The coast was not quite as desolate as the road had been, since no one thought the Murdano, should he form an invasion force, would come that way. Still, we found a fishing village that showed signs of having battled a pirates' raiding party. The men all carried homemade weapons, flails, billhooks, and clubs with protruding spikes.

It was true, as the Murdano had said, that these northern lands were ravaged by pirates and bandits. But it was also true that on the rare occasions when soldiers passed this way, they preyed on the people almost as harshly as the raiders.

"What is north of here?" Khara asked a bent old man repairing his fishing nets beside a tumbledown wooden pier.

"North?" He shook his head. "Those are wild lands full of vicious beasts, both human and not. You don't want to go north, young master. There's only death to find there."

Behind us, the Knight of the Fire.

Ahead, bandits and fell beasts.

A treacherous trek ending in almost certain disappointment.

The mood darkened and weighed heavily on me. This was my quest, after all. The others were only there to help and protect me. Me, an endling at the end of the world.

I reminded myself that Araktik had believed the rumors about more dairnes. But putting hope in a rumor, especially one believed by a crazy, evil human, was hardly a reason to trudge onward each day.

The coast grew rockier, with tall cliffs cut by a multitude of rivers and streams that made deep channels into the earth and spilled over the cliffs in glorious waterfalls. We rode along those cliffs, hundreds of feet up, seeing nothing of humankind, or indeed of any of the governing species, except for ospreys and other fish-eating raptidons.

With each hour, each day, the world felt emptier, wilder, farther away from the world we'd known. Eventually we saw no villages, inhabited or abandoned. There were occasional fishing camps each with a shack at the base of a cliff, but these, too, were empty.

The weather was bitter and threatened to grow colder. The wind blew constantly from the sea, and the few trees we saw were gnarled and leafless. We were in a land of bare hills and stark stone, fields of gloomy saw grass and shallow meres. A bleaker landscape I could not imagine.

"Why would any species migrate in this direction?" I asked aloud.

"Most of the animals in the Viagatto head inland, away from the direction we're heading," said Khara. "They stop at a massive wetlands area. A rare lichen grows there that they feed on. At least, that's what scholars say. No one is really sure."

"So they travel half the world to eat some moss," Renzo said. "Brilliant."

"And to breed," Gambler added with the hint of a smile.

"I wonder where the butterbats go," I said, thinking suddenly of Maia, that day at the mirabear cave. It seemed impossibly long ago.

"I don't think anyone knows, Byx," Khara said.

After a steep one-hour climb, we reached a point where we could clearly see the massive, pine-forested mountain chain, the Sovo Ridge, that separated Nedarra from Dreyland.

"What do we know of Dreyland?" I asked Gambler as we surveyed the scene.

"Very little," Gambler admitted. "We know—I should say we believe—that it contains other governing species. And there are many creations of evil theurgy: monsters, golems, creatures of ice that move like men."

Tobble's eyes went wide. "Ice creatures?"

Gambler nodded. "It's said that a wizard rules Dreyland."

"Why does the Murdano wish to make war on them?" Tobble asked.

"Because humans are strange," Gambler replied.

I caught a whiff of smoke at the same time Gambler did. We turned to see that the fishing camp we'd passed just hours before had burst into flames. A pillar of smoke rose into the sky, gray joining gray.

We moved, it seemed, almost constantly. The Knight

of the Fire kept us focused on that goal, though we had not seen him in some while, but in this spare and increasingly unpopulated territory, we found little to eat. The supplies the Murdano had given us had either been consumed or lost in moments of panic. Now and then Khara, Gambler, and Renzo would go off in search of food. Generally they came back with far too little or nothing at all.

Once Dog raced off, snuffling the hard ground, and returned minutes later with a measly ice rat, mangled and drool-covered.

"What a fine specimen you've brought us, Dog," Renzo said. He had a tendency to praise the mangy mutt to excess.

Renzo reached out to accept the bloody mess, but Dog had other ideas. He loped over to me, tail thrashing, and dropped the rat at my feet.

"It's a gift," Renzo said. "He wants to be friends."

I looked at the rat, which was crawling with maggots, and kicked it aside. "I'm not that desperate," I said.

"You could at least thank him," Renzo admonished. "You're practically brothers."

I gave Dog a halfhearted pat on his head. He retrieved the rat and carried it proudly, dangling from his mouth, for several hours.

The horses were ragged. We, too, were ragged, and no matter how disciplined we were, each day we covered less distance than the day before. Each night, after we'd found a hidden place to camp, we saw fire in our wake. I hoped these distant fires were not more innocents being tortured for news of our passing.

As if that weren't enough, more danger lay ahead. The closer we came to the frontier, the more we began to see evidence of troops heading north, no doubt the Murdano's invasion forces. In their wake they left scattered trash, discarded crates, cold remains of campfires, the occasional dead horse left to bloat by the side of the road where it had fallen.

"Are you certain we're headed in the right direction?" Tobble wondered one night as we rested. "And how will we know when we're close?"

I had no answers. None of us did. Our only plan was to keep following the coast northward.

We decided to make camp where we were. No one could move another foot. We built a pitifully small fire in the lee of a bluff where we hoped the glow would not be seen by our relentless pursuer. A brew of herb tea and bitter-tasting roots was our supper, and would be our breakfast as well.

I woke in the night, stomach whining, and climbed to the top of the sheltering bluff. It wasn't too tall, maybe three times Khara's height. I'd hoped to see whether the knight was closer, but thick fog had crawled in from the sea, obscuring the world and softening the moon to a fuzzy orb, like the last days of a dandelion.

Tobble appeared, and I reached down to help him up. "Couldn't sleep, Tobble?"

"My stomach won't let me," he answered.

"Mine, either."

"Byx . . ."

"Yes?"

"Have you thought about what to do when we find the floating island and your lost colony of dairnes?"

I sighed. "Oh, Tobble, you know how unlikely that is, right?"

"But it could happen," Tobble insisted. "The only thing is, well, aren't we leading the knight straight to them?"

It was not a new thought for me. In fact, it had tortured me ever since we'd left Saguria. The knight had eliminated the Pale Guard, but in many ways the Pale Guard had been our protectors. They, at least, had no orders to kill us, though they did have orders to exterminate all but a handful of any dairnes we might conceivably encounter.

The Knight of the Fire seemed to have his own plan. We'd outwitted him and evaded him, and he did not like it. He'd tracked us over many leagues and was perhaps no more than half a league away, in spite of his slow horse and our careful attempts to hide when we needed to rest. He would not be giving up now.

"What choice do we have?" I asked. "If we turn back, the

knight will kill us. If we stay here, we'll either starve or the knight will kill us. If we go forward, we may find nothing, and then we will either starve or the knight will kill us."

"Well, that's a gloomy assessment," Tobble said, trying for a light tone and failing.

"If we go forward and we do find dairnes, they will at least have food. And perhaps even a means to fight."

I stopped myself. It seemed a ridiculous fantasy. Now I wasn't just imagining a colony of dairnes, I was imagining that they could take on and defeat one of the most terrifying humans in existence.

The breeze picked up, tearing rifts in the fog. I peered toward the south, searching for telltale flame. Nothing.

"Look!" Tobble cried, gesturing northeast.

I followed the direction of his gaze and saw two . . . three . . . four fires, far off in the distance.

"Khara!" I called.

She was with us in a few seconds. We pointed, and she looked for a long time before turning to us with an unlikely grin on her face.

"Those are not the knight's fires. Those are tended fires for cooking or drying meat. That, my friends, is Zebara."

56.
Zebara

I had by this time become much more knowledgeable about human dwellings. I had been to the isle of Ursina and to Saguria. I had passed through towns and villages. I had seen the evidence of human ingenuity.

And then I saw Zebara.

In this nearly treeless land, humans had constructed buildings from mud bricks, buildings shaped like a half of a melon, round on the top, with a single low door and a narrow window. Smoke rose from holes cut in the roofs of these primitive huts.

The whole port village seemed haphazardly designed, homes and shops all willy-nilly with nothing but mud between them. A central lodge, still with an arched roof but much longer, sat near the middle of town. It was festooned with antlers from verdelk, wolf pelts, and the bleached bones of great fish.

It was clear that boats were more important
villagers than homes. Dozens of boats crowded the
harbor: fishing craft, swift-rowing smuggler crafts, a.
least one Nedarran pirate ship. Outnumbering these still-
useful boats by ten to one were beached boats, shambling
wrecks with fallen masts, many draped with frayed rope ends
and scraps of ancient sails. Everywhere were crude racks
made to dry nets, and wide fire pits over which strings of fish
smoked.

As usual I assumed my "dog" identity, a ruse that was
harder to pull off with an actual dog in our company. We
were met with open curiosity and little hostility from the
townspeople, a dirty, scowling, dangerous-looking bunch. I
saw many humans with forehead brands of T for thief, S for
smuggler, and P for poacher, and many with ears cut off, and
sometimes hands or legs. A surprising number of Zebarans
wore hooks for hands or pared-down tree stumps for legs.

Branding, Khara explained, was the gentlest punishment
handed out in Nedarra; a second offense would get you gar-
roted. For piracy, the punishment began with mutilation and
got rapidly worse.

Zebara was a dark and frightening place, but in some
ways I welcomed it. If any bunch of humans was desperate
and dangerous enough to give a Knight of the Fire second
thoughts, it was this collection of criminals and renegades.

With some of Renzo's money, we bought some dried fish

and ate it in the open, wolfing it down and following it with gallons of spring water to dilute the cloying salt flavor.

As we sat in the dirt eating, three men came striding up, looking curious and suspicious. Each was armed with several weapons, including knives, clubs, whale harpoons, and wooden stake-driving hammers.

"What business have you here?" The one who spoke had a strong accent that made even the Common Tongue hard to understand. He was missing one eye and had filled the cavity with a piece of fine pottery, a glazed eyeball whose sightless pupil aimed eternally to the right.

"We seek something," Khara said.

"What?"

"We come from the isle of Ursina," she lied easily. "The great scholars there have sent us on a voyage of exploration to find out the truth of a legend."

"What legend is that?" One-Eye asked. His tone was still skeptical, but he had straightened a bit upon hearing that we were from the isle.

"The ancient texts tell of islands that move on their own. Islands that think. Living islands."

The three humans exchanged a look, and my heart leapt. They knew something.

"What would it be worth to have the answer?" One-Eye demanded.

Khara held up her hands in a helpless gesture. "As you see, we have nothing to trade."

"You have horses," the man said.

"They're not our horses to trade," Khara said, sounding regretful. "They are gifts of the Murdano."

The name did not improve One-Eye's mood. He spat on the ground. "The Murdano holds no sway here," he said. "Does he defend us against raiders? No. Does he send a fleet to keep Dreyland pirates from attacking our trade? No. At the very least he could bribe the natites, who could put an end to attacks from the sea. Instead he spends his fortune building an army for a war he's certain to lose."

"Nevertheless," Khara said, "we cannot trade horses we do not own."

"Then I have nothing to tell you." He hooked his thumbs in his rope belt and put on a stubborn face, though he did allow more than one anxious glance at Gambler.

"What about information?" Renzo spoke up. "You have information, I have information."

"What information?" One-Eye asked. "You first."

Renzo nodded, deliberately ignoring a warning look from Khara. "There is a great threat coming your way."

One-Eye laughed scornfully. "That's nothing new. There are always threats."

"Not like this," Renzo said. "Because right now, less than

half a league behind us, is a Knight of the Fire. And he is burning everything in his path."

The mask of indifference disappeared from the three dirty faces. One-Eye drew himself back and made a hand sign meant to ward off evil.

"That?" Renzo said, mocking his gesture. "That will not stop the knight from burning this village to the ground."

"You've brought a Knight of the Fire down on us?" one of the other men cried.

Renzo shook his head. "Don't be ridiculous. We aren't worth his time. No," he said with a sigh, "he's just out for murder, I'm afraid. He very nearly roasted me, and I don't even know these people. I'm not from the isle. I"—he waited for a dramatic beat—"am a thief."

Anticipating a loud rejection upon hearing the word "thief," Khara moved her hand to her sword hilt. But Renzo had estimated his audience correctly. They were mildly impressed by "scholars" but considered a thief to be one of them, someone they could trust.

"Now, I've given you good information," Renzo said. "If you're wise, you'll put your boats to sea and hide your valuables."

One-Eye nodded. "Aye, that we shall do."

"And now your side of the bargain," Renzo said.

"I have seen islands that move," One-Eye said. "Their

location is never certain. They can be quick, and when they move, they can keep at it for days without stop, traveling fifty leagues in a week's time."

Renzo grinned. "But . . ."

"But," One-Eye continued reluctantly, "I was fishing up near Rebit's Sound yesterday. By land it's two, three leagues north, then a short distance down a peninsula to a spot called Landfail. There you should be able to see one of the islands."

I could remain patient no longer. "Have you seen any of my kind?"

One-Eye gaped at me, surprised to hear me speak. He pointed to Dog. "Does that one talk, too?"

"No," I said impatiently. "He's a dog."

"Then what are—" One-Eye shook his head. "Oh, never mind. The answer to your question is no, I've seen no dogs that speak and walk erect." Seeing my despair, he added, "Of course, we don't approach the islands."

"Why do you not approach the islands?" Khara asked.

"The sentient islands are gods to many. Others think they're home to foul beasts and monsters. Still others believe that anyone who sets a foot on the islands will be eaten, consumed by the very trees."

"Wonderful," Renzo muttered.

Khara nodded. "Thank you for your information. We're

moving on. You had best hide until the knight has passed, if you want to live."

"Good luck," Renzo said as we departed. "You'll need it," he added under his breath.

"Not as much as we will," Khara said.

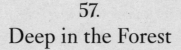

57.
Deep in the Forest

With the few coins Renzo had managed to "collect," we bought more food from the villagers—who were already carrying their belongings toward their boats: baskets, pots, what food they could gather, and the simple tools of their professions—dried codfish and seaweed and a few stunted potatoes. For the horses we could only offer scrapings of moss that they did not relish but could eat.

Two leagues north we stopped, looked back, and saw Zebara burning bright, as whips of fire lashed the buildings and the beached boats. No matter how fast we traveled, it wasn't fast enough.

We turned into a wood made up of tall firs. They stood in tight ranks that blocked any sunlight, which was already in short supply. To make movement harder still, the trees were covered with invasive weeds that spread in black vines along the ground, then wound themselves around tree trunks. Some trees were almost invisible beneath the weed wrapping.

Belligerent tuskers, huge wild pigs, threatened us but withdrew when they caught sight of Gambler. The few birds we saw were skimmers and foam-walkers. We saw only a single raptidon, an aging bird who showed no interest in us.

The peninsula narrowed until we could see water to our north and south. But the one-eyed man had directed us to the end of the peninsula, to a place he'd called Landfail.

"We are on a peninsula with a Knight of the Fire behind us," Renzo said to Khara. "Just how do you propose escaping?"

"I assumed you would have a brilliant plan," Khara replied. "You seem to have no problem pushing your way into conversations and even making deals."

"Not I," Renzo said. "When I am someday caught, it will be a *T* they brand on my forehead, not an *R* for Rebel."

Khara studied the landscape, mentally judging distances as the spit of land grew ever more narrow. She stopped. We all stopped. Then, with obvious reluctance, she motioned Renzo close.

"What theurgy do you know?" she asked.

He shrugged. "Burglar's tricks. I can dazzle with a bright light, I can fill a room with fog, I can coax a recalcitrant lock—but only if I use my picking tools properly. And I can make a noise at a distance, you know, to distract."

"None of that will help us with this." Khara considered. "All right. Here is our line. It's only, what, two hundred feet from the north side to south? Here's where we lay our trap."

"Our what, now?" Renzo asked, head cocked.

"We are going to weave a trap," Khara said, projecting confidence I doubted she felt. "We're going to use these vines, these weeds we keep stumbling over. We'll use them to weave a net."

"He'll burn right through it," Renzo said.

"Mmm," Khara said. "Yes. Now, let's get to it!"

Frantically we hacked at roots and dragged them into place. Tobble supervised the task of weaving long strands of vine into a net stretched between trees across a fifty-foot span. It was exhausting and almost certainly a waste of time, as Renzo kept pointing out. Still, he worked as hard as anyone.

I was skeptical. I doubted. But as we worked, I started to sense Khara's strategy. The net we were weaving with such care was a diversion. Just a few feet past the net, a steep gully cut across the peninsula. It was no more than three or four feet deep and would certainly not stop the knight or his horse—if they saw it.

Khara hacked down branches with her sword, choosing strong, straight limbs and cutting each into six-foot lengths. When she started sharpening the sticks at both ends, I knew what she was planning.

"Byx," Khara said, wiping sweat from her brow. "Climb this tree and see if you can spot the knight."

We are good climbers, we dairnes. But felivets are better, so I wondered why she chose me. I climbed easily—I have no fear of heights—until my head rose above the canopy of trees. It was an eerie sight: leagues of gray-green trees with a blanket of mist upon them.

I searched the horizon for signs of fire or smoke. I strained my ears and breathed deeply, scanning for smells. But the wind cut across us, north to south, and bore me nothing but the scents of salt water and pine sap.

"I don't see anything," I called. "I'm coming down."

"No! Stay," Khara ordered. "And whatever happens, stay up there and stay silent."

I realized with horror what she was doing: keeping the precious dairne, the endling, as safe as she could.

I did not wish to be safe. I wished to fight, and if necessary die, with the others.

"I can't let them die for me," I said aloud.

As I began to descend, I checked around me one last time. I could easily see the end of the peninsula, a five-minute walk away. We were at the edge of the world, it seemed to me. The ocean stretched forever, dotted with whitecaps. I noticed a patch of trees—not gloomy firs, but trees alive with color, blazing reds, vivid yellows, soft greens, like a tiny, forgotten orchard at the edge of the forest.

A wave of loneliness washed over me. The little spot of color reminded me of the only home I'd ever known, the gentler, warmer, more fertile south where my band had always wandered.

A home I would probably never see again.

I'd begun my descent—Khara would have to accept my decision—when I noticed something odd.

The colorful stand of trees was moving.

Not swaying and fretting in the breeze, but moving.

Moving!

I had been ordered to stay up in the trees and stay quiet. Well, Khara had not specified which tree, precisely. I spread my glissaires and glided between the branches, alighting on a nearby fir.

Yes: The patch of color was moving.

I glided to the next tree, and the next, and suddenly I was at the end of the peninsula, the very end, and there before me was not an orchard.

There before me, across no more than a hundred feet of water, was an island.

An island floating past with surprising speed.

Moving like a living thing.

58.
The Final Battle

How I wished I had the eyes of a raptidon.

I stared and strained, leaning as far out as I dared. Was that a nest I saw? Was that a hint of a lean-to?

Just as I opened my mouth to yell down to Khara, I heard the sound of a great beast, a horse, charging through the woods.

The knight was coming at full speed.

I froze, unsure what to do. And in that moment of indecision I saw, out of the corner of my eye, a shape on the island.

It was in the trees.

I watched the distant, indistinct shape move.

I watched its familiar grace.

I watched it spread its glissaires and glide.

Heedless, I ran out to the end of a branch. It bowed and creaked under my weight.

One hundred feet of water. Surely from this height I could glide one hundred feet!

I yearned to do it. Needed to do it.

The island was moving with remarkable speed. If I didn't leap now, I'd miss my chance.

I braced for the glide. I tensed my muscles.

And that was when I heard a wobbyk's cry.

I tore my needy gaze away from the island and looked back to see a jet of flame lancing through the woods.

A simple glide.

A doomed battle.

Something that looked like a dairne. Might be a dairne. What I had come so far and wished for so fervently.

All I had to do was push off and spread my glissaires.

I kicked off. I soared down and down and landed.

I was just short of the gully, now filled with the sharpened sticks Khara had driven into the ground.

I drew my ridiculous sword and waited, heart hammering, breath rasping in my throat.

Through the net I saw him. He was dirtier. His horse looked shaggy and weary. But his lance still spit the sentient fire.

It shot past Tobble and I yelled in fury, "I'm the one you want!"

Gambler dropped from a high branch, his claws out, his

teeth bared, but the horse reared and Gambler missed the knight, clawing red lines down the charger's flank.

Khara, screaming, attacked the knight from her concealed place on his left, opposite his fire lance. But fire wasn't the knight's only weapon. He had drawn his own broadsword. Khara's sword bit first, cutting into the plate armor on his left thigh. The knight, unable to stab her, instead slammed the pommel into her face. Khara fell back, her nose spraying blood.

Gambler was up, with Renzo and Tobble at his side. They leapt from behind the horse, but the charger was ready and surged forward.

"I'm the one you want, Knight of the Fire!" I screamed. "I'm the endling you've come to kill!"

My mind was no longer my own. Some terrible beast of fear and hate was inside me, using me, screaming threats as I brandished my sword.

The knight twisted and lashed the ground behind him with fire. Gambler danced away, but his tail was smoldering.

The knight aimed his fire lance at the net that separated us.

An inferno erupted. Flames seemed to eat, rather than burn, our pitiful net of vines.

But Khara had guessed rightly that this knight was arrogant, used to easy victories, and would charge straight ahead.

The knight and his charger ran at the burning net, and to my amazement, the fire moved aside. He crashed through the crisped and weakened vines.

I heard him cry out in triumph.

But only the fire had moved. The smoke of the fire had not.

The smoke that concealed our trap.

The knight raised his visor and laughed at me, just as he tumbled into the stake-filled gully.

59.
The Thief's Pledge

I hope never again to see anything as awful as the sight of the fearsome Knight of the Fire and his charger, pierced through with sharpened sticks. The knight had died instantly. His horse, impaled by five spears, still lived, whinnying and kicking, but it was clearly doomed.

Khara looked at Gambler, who understood. He leapt down into the pit, carefully avoiding the spears as only a felivet could. Maneuvering behind the huge animal, he sank his ferocious teeth into its spine, instantly ending the horse's pain.

Once the horse was no longer flailing, Renzo slid down into the gully. He removed the knight's helmet, revealing a face that was human after all. Just a man. A dead man.

Renzo stripped off anything of value and tossed it up out of the pit, though an impressive ring on the knight's right hand went directly into Renzo's pocket. He searched the charger's saddlebags, throwing us food, a water bottle, a map, a blanket, a spare horseshoe, and a grinding stone.

Khara, Tobble, and I watched, not quite approving, but not willing to stop him, either. We had need of food. Even food taken from a dead man.

"Did you see anything from the tree?" Khara asked me.

I considered lying. It was a newly discovered concept for me. I could say no, I'd seen nothing. If I told her what I knew, I was dooming us all to continue our quest.

With a simple lie I could, perhaps, set my friends free.

But what was friendship worth if it was built on lies?

Xial renarriss: In truth lies strength.

"I saw an island," I said. I looked at them all, one by one. "Moving."

Tobble squealed. "I'm so excited for you, Byx!"

"Moving in which direction?" Khara asked, ever practical.

"North," I said.

"North of here means Dreyland," Renzo commented, climbing up and wiping his hands on his thighs. "Crossing into it means getting past the Murdano's border guards, then managing not to get killed by the Dreyland border guards. Keep in mind it gets very cold up in those mountains. Very, very cold."

"Scared?" Khara asked derisively. "No problem. You aren't invited, anyway."

"No?" Renzo cocked an eyebrow at her. "Have you

crossed the Sovo Ridge? Do you know the passes? Do you know the beasts that prowl those passes?"

Khara said nothing.

"I thought not," Renzo said. "Well, I have crossed the Sovo. I know at least some of the trails. And I've fought and survived an attack by snowworms."

"Aside from the fact that the knight roasted you and we rescued you, I'm not sure why you'd want to be with us," Khara said. "Why would a thief join an almost certainly doomed expedition with a high likelihood of death and a very low likelihood of plunder?"

"Plunder is not the only way for a thief to profit," Renzo said. "There are other ways. For example, one might sign on to follow a warrior who can promise reward later on."

It was clear that Khara couldn't help but be flattered by Renzo's casual reference to her as a "warrior." But she was not buying his reasoning, and she was definitely not ready to trust him. "I have no reward to offer."

"Hmm," Renzo said, unimpressed. "Do you understand that I have been shadowing you since before the isle?"

Khara gasped.

"But why?" I asked. "And please, don't embarrass yourself by trying to lie."

Renzo shrugged. "Here is the truth, my brave dairne: I saw the sword. The true sword. A thief learns useful theurgy, specific spells. One of the many talents I possess is the power to penetrate spells meant to conceal objects of value. When I first spotted Khara, I knew she carried something very valuable, although I didn't know the history of your sword immediately. There are many enchanted swords hidden by theurgic spells. You may recall that I tried to buy it. When that didn't work, I followed, in hopes of stealing it."

"You tried to buy Byx, too," Tobble said.

"Also very valuable."

"You knew she was a dairne?" Khara asked.

"Of course." Renzo smiled.

Khara drew her sword and pointed it at him. "Any attempt to steal this will end with it in your heart, not your hands."

Renzo seemed unimpressed by her threat, his eyes savoring the glittering, glowing sword. "Dairne, bear witness that I speak the truth."

I nodded.

"I am a thief. And I would happily have stolen any other sword. Any other sword in all the world. But even a despised thief like me has honor. And I am not without learning. I know the legends. I know the epic poems. I know who you are, Kharassande Donati, and I know that the sword you wield is the Light of Nedarra."

Khara lowered her sword slightly.

"Most of all," Renzo continued, "I know the stories of my

own clan. We've always been foes of the Murdano, living on the margins. But my great-grandfather fought in the Long-Ago War, just a humble foot soldier who found himself on the point of death when his attacker's head was neatly removed by the Light of Nedarra."

Khara shot a look at me, and I nodded. It was the truth.

And then Renzo did the last thing I would have expected of the glib thief. He dropped to his knees and bowed his head.

"I am a mere thief, untrustworthy, unreliable, and sadly"—he gave a wry grin—"incapable of behaving myself properly. But I offer my humble services to the living heir of the Donatis, the wielder of the Light of Nedarra. Your servant, if you will have me."

Khara then did the last thing I would have expected from her. She did not laugh or mock. Her face was more serious than I had ever seen it outside of combat. "Do you swear to obey me in all things?" she asked.

"Mmmm," Renzo said, "how about . . . most things?"

Tobble snorted a laugh and quickly slapped his hand over his mouth.

Khara took a deep breath. "Let's try this a different way. Do you promise to do all in your power to guide, protect, and defend Byx, Gambler, and Tobble?"

"I do."

I had no way of knowing whether he would do so, but he

was telling the truth that he meant to do so.

"Will you do the same for me?" Khara asked.

"Even when you don't like how I do it, Kharassande Donati, I will be faithful. I will be true. And there's a, oh . . . better-than-even chance that I will follow your orders."

Khara moved her sword. She placed it on his shoulder, where a mere twitch would send his head rolling on the ground. "I have no power to dub you 'knight,'" she said. "But I accept your pledge and your service." She touched the blade to his other shoulder, then tapped the flat of it on his head.

The tap was a bit harder than strictly necessary. Renzo winced. I might have believed it was an accident, but I had seen Khara wield her sword, and nothing she did with that blade was an accident.

"All right, get up off your knees," Khara said.

Renzo jumped to his feet, grinned, and said, "Let's get moving."

Khara and I exchanged a glance. "There's one more thing to do," she said.

And she smiled at Tobble.

60.
A Certain Ceremony

We all fell quiet, and in that lovely moment, I felt I could almost hear the gentle pounding of our dear wobbyk friend's heart.

"Tobble," Khara said, "we have need of your guidance."

"Mine?" Tobble asked, clearly surprised.

"Yours," Khara confirmed. "It seems that none of us knows how to perform a certain ceremony."

Tobble frowned. "What?"

"I understood the stibillary is a ceremony elevating a wobbyk to adulthood in recognition of, well, of being worthy. We see before us the smallest of our group, who, despite lacking Gambler's teeth, claws, and speed; despite lacking a fabled sword; despite being from a race too long dismissed and treated as lesser, leapt on not one but two soldiers of the Pale Guard, in addition to many other acts of courage and loyalty."

Something was going quite wrong with Tobble. His mouth moved without making sounds. His cheeks quivered. His tails windmilled like some demented spaniel. His chest heaved as if each breath was an effort. Tears spilled from his eyes.

"Does anyone here dispute this wobbyk's steadfastness, honesty, kindness, or courage?" Khara asked. "Or do you find him worthy?"

"Most worthy," Gambler said.

"That's a whole lot of brave in a small package," Renzo said.

Tobble turned to me, and I suddenly found it difficult to speak. I wrapped my arms around him. "More than worthy," I said in a choked voice. "More than brave, more than loyal. You are my brother, Tobble."

There wasn't much to the ceremony. Wobbyks are not great ones for show. Tobble had to recite a poem and sing a song, and for reasons that baffled everyone (including Tobble), we had to locate a centipede for him to eat.

After that, Tobble formally requested that Khara and Renzo and I braid his three tails into one. Gambler observed, felivet claws not being particularly useful for braiding.

When all was done, Tobble was still Tobble. Nonetheless, he did seem to stand a good two inches taller and carry himself with greater dignity. Unfortunately, he kept turning around to marvel at his unified tail and more than once tripped as a result.

We headed back down the peninsula, feeling, if not joyful, at least no longer hopeless.

The island existed. I might have seen a dairne. There was a possibility that I was not an endling.

We knew that Luca had not given up and would come after us.

We knew that by now the Murdano would have realized that he'd been betrayed thanks to my lies, and that he would come after us, too.

We knew that ahead lay terrible, steep mountains, relentless cold, and hideous fell beasts.

But I was beginning to understand that what had started as a simple quest to find others of my kind had changed. I was now part of something larger than my needs, perhaps larger even than the survival of my species. The Murdano was not just the enemy of the dairnes. He was the enemy of all living things who would not bend their knees to him.

Great forces were arrayed against us. Neither Luca nor the Murdano would ever stop hunting us. Their control rested on lies, and they knew that if I found more dairnes and could bring them out of exile, we, the not-quite-extinct, might shake the foundations of their power.

We came clear of the forest and looked up at the awe-inspiring, snowcapped peaks before us. Pain and danger and death were in those mountains. But beyond them might be the one thing that even heroes need in order to go forward: hope.

I glanced north, the direction the moving island had been heading. I couldn't see it anymore, of course. But I knew it was there.

As I turned back, something caught my eye. A glimmer of color high above us.

I looked up to see a butterbat.

Just one. No more.

Lost, perhaps, on its own great journey.

Or perhaps not.

Khara nodded at me. "Last chance to change your mind."

"Well, I've never really seen snow before," I said. "Let's go take a look."

With that, we set off. Renzo, the thief with honor, and his dog, Dog. Gambler, the principled felivet. Tobble, the worthy wobbyk. Vallino, the tireless steed. Khara, the heir of the Donatis, wielder of the Light of Nedarra.

My friends. My companions.

My family.

Acknowledgments

My heartfelt thanks to Tara Weikum, Vice President & Editorial Director, for her brilliant insights, patience, and good humor, along with the many fine folks at Harper-Collins who've helped bring this story to life:

Chris Hernandez, Editor
Sarah Homer, Editorial Assistant
Ro Romanello, Associate Director of Publicity
Ann Dye, Marketing Director
Renée Cafiero, Senior Production Editor
Barb Fitzsimmons, Creative Director
Alison Donalty, Executive Art Director
Jenna Stempell-Lobell, Senior Designer
Kate Jackson, Editor-in-Chief
Suzanne Murphy, President and Publisher
Patty Rosati, Director of School & Library Marketing
Andrea Pappenheimer and the Sales team

READ ON FOR AN EXCERPT
from Katherine Applegate's award-winning novel

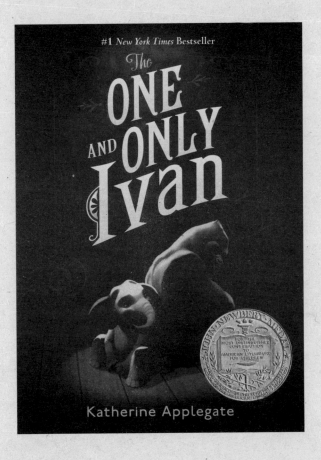

hello

I am Ivan. I am a gorilla.

It's not as easy as it looks.

names

People call me the Freeway Gorilla. The Ape at Exit 8. The One and Only Ivan, Mighty Silverback.

The names are mine, but they're not me. I am Ivan, just Ivan, only Ivan.

Humans waste words. They toss them like banana peels and leave them to rot.

Everyone knows the peels are the best part.

I suppose you think gorillas can't understand you. Of course, you also probably think we can't walk upright.

Try knuckle walking for an hour. You tell me: Which way is more fun?

patience

I've learned to understand human words over the years, but understanding human speech is not the same as understanding humans.

Humans speak too much. They chatter like chimps, crowding the world with their noise even when they have nothing to say.

It took me some time to recognize all those human sounds, to weave words into things. But I was patient.

Patient is a useful way to be when you're an ape.

Gorillas are as patient as stones. Humans, not so much.

how I look

I used to be a wild gorilla, and I still look the part.

I have a gorilla's shy gaze, a gorilla's sly smile. I wear a snowy saddle of fur, the uniform of a silverback. When the sun warms my back, I cast a gorilla's majestic shadow.

In my size humans see a test of themselves. They hear fighting words on the wind, when all I'm thinking is how the late-day sun reminds me of a ripe nectarine.

I'm mightier than any human, four hundred pounds of pure power. My body looks made for battle. My arms, outstretched, span taller than the tallest human.

My family tree spreads wide as well. I am a great ape, and you are a great ape, and so are chimpanzees and orangutans and bonobos, all of us distant and distrustful cousins.

I know this is troubling.

I too find it hard to believe there is a connection across time and space, linking me to a race of ill-mannered clowns.

Chimps. There's no excuse for them.

the exit 8 big top mall and video arcade

I live in a human habitat called the Exit 8 Big Top Mall and Video Arcade. We are conveniently located off I-95, with shows at two, four, and seven, 365 days a year.

Mack says that when he answers the trilling telephone.

Mack works here at the mall. He is the boss.

I work here too. I am the gorilla.

At the Big Top Mall, a creaky-music carousel spins all day, and monkeys and parrots live amid the merchants. In the middle of the mall is a ring with benches where humans can sit on their rumps while they eat soft pretzels. The floor is covered with sawdust made of dead trees.

My domain is at one end of the ring. I live here because I am too much gorilla and not enough human.

Stella's domain is next to mine. Stella is an elephant. She and Bob, who is a dog, are my dearest friends.

At present, I do not have any gorilla friends.

My domain is made of thick glass and rusty metal and rough cement. Stella's domain is made of metal bars. The sun bears' domain is wood; the parrots' is wire mesh.

Three of my walls are glass. One of them is cracked, and a small piece, about the size of my hand, is missing from its bottom corner. I made the hole with a baseball bat Mack gave me for my sixth birthday. After that he took the bat away, but he let me keep the baseball that came with it.

A jungle scene is painted on one of my domain walls. It has a waterfall without water and flowers without scent and trees without roots. I didn't paint it, but I enjoy the way the shapes flow across my wall, even if it isn't much of a jungle.

I am lucky my domain has three windowed walls. I can see the whole mall and a bit of the world beyond: the frantic pinball machines, the pink billows of cotton candy, the vast and treeless parking lot.

Beyond the lot is a freeway where cars stampede without end. A giant sign at its edge beckons them to stop and rest like gazelles at a watering hole.

The sign is faded, the colors bleeding, but I know what it says. Mack read its words aloud one day: "COME TO THE EXIT 8 BIG TOP MALL AND VIDEO ARCADE, HOME OF THE ONE AND ONLY IVAN, MIGHTY SILVERBACK!"

Sadly, I cannot read, although I wish I could. Reading stories would make a fine way to fill my empty hours.

Once, however, I was able to enjoy a book left in my domain by one of my keepers.

It tasted like termite.

The freeway billboard has a drawing of Mack in his clown clothes and Stella on her hind legs and an angry animal with fierce eyes and unkempt hair.

That animal is supposed to be me, but the artist made a mistake. I am never angry.

Come to the Exit 8
Big Top Mall and Video Arcade
Home of The One And Only Ivan
Mighty Silverback!

Anger is precious. A silverback uses anger to maintain order and warn his troop of danger. When my father beat his chest, it was to say, *Beware, listen, I am in charge. I am angry to protect you, because that is what I was born to do.*

Here in my domain, there is no one to protect.

Read the heartwarming sequel from Newbery Medalist
KATHERINE APPLEGATE

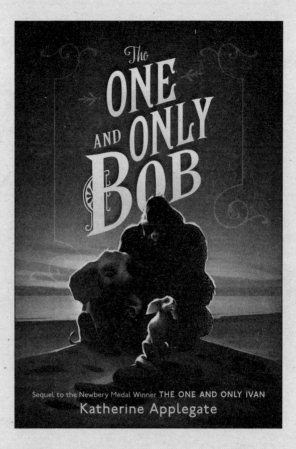

An incredible story about Bob, a courageous dog, and his journey to find his sister with the aid of his two best friends, Ivan and Ruby.

HARPER
An Imprint of HarperCollinsPublishers

www.harpercollinschildrens.com